Anvil Rock
by John Shirley

He stood at the window, looking out at the gray afternoon; the wintry sea stretched out, waiting with vast, cold assurance below his cliffside house.

Grigsby had managed not to go to the locked closet for three weeks. He did drugs, he got drunk, he gambled, he chased women. It kept him away from the closet. He knew full well these things were vices; he knew it wasn't good for him to distract himself that way. But he reasoned that it was better than opening the closet.

Now, standing by the window, his back to the closet—but feeling its pull, which was surely, oh most definitely just in his imagination—he thought about destroying the machine locked within it. But he didn't move; he didn't go to the tool shed for the sledge hammer. He simply stood looking out the window. It was winter in British Columbia, and the sea, constrained by the rocky islands of the Sound, shrugged its chill gray body restlessly, thrashing to white spume against the rocks. Very cold, that water would be. Very cold.

Perhaps…he could go somewhere else. Somewhere earlier. But it always happened that he merged with his earlier self, remembering where he'd come from—remembering the future—but able to make only minor changes in the past. So he'd be drawn as if through a sluice to that Spring day overlooking Anvil Rock, though it took years to get there.

Perhaps he might perfect the machine, to go elsewhere…before his birth. Or to go somewhere after his death. But…

But it called to him now.

Try again. This time you can save her. This time…

Strange phrase, that, 'this time'. In view of…what he'd learned. "'This time,'" Grigsby murmured. "*This* time. This time."

The phone rang. Stopped ringing. Rang again. Stopped ringing. Rang again. Again, again.

It was Sanguelo, of course. He was always very insistent. He would want clarity on the new mine in Santo Miguel. He would want to know if the proper Brazilian authorities had been bribed. Ring. He would want to know if Grigsby were going to supervise the open-pit mine himself. Ring, ring. If the gold assay was indeed confirmed. Ring, ring, ring. If their legal problems had been dealt with…

"Go the hell away!" Grigsby shouted, never turning from the window; his voice rattling the glass.

As if chastened, the phone stopped ringing.

Grigsby snorted. "First time he's…" His voice trailed off. He gazed out the window.

The key in his pocket seemed to press against his hip. The key to the closet.

Grigsby felt the shift inside him that meant he was going to give in. He wasn't going to go to Vancouver to find women, to take drugs, to throw money at a card table; to feel himself slowly burning away, like a slow fuse. No. He was going to do something worse. It was worse because it seemed hopeless. Maddeningly hopeless. Because it meant reliving that day.

He was sorry he'd ever funded Kosinksi's research. *"I can take your consciousness back in time. It remains to be seen if your body can go…"*

Anybody else would have sent him packing, after mad-sounding remarks of that kind. Many had, in fact—Kosinsky had already tried over a hundred possible funders. Grigsby had been a long-shot—he was interested in funding research into mine engineering, not quantum theory, not time travel. But Kosinski was his wife's nephew, and he was sentimental about her memory, so…he'd given him some money to work with. And then, a year later, it had happened and he'd gone desperately to Kosinski and then…

Who knew?

He should have shot the bastard, not paid him. But maybe this time…

He sighed, and turned away from the window, walked across the empty room to the closet, and unlocked it. Inside was…

* * * *

"Hey Dad! Are we going or not!"

Grigsby looked up from his PC to see his daughter, Maria, smiling nervously at him from the doorway. She was an earnest, deeply tanned graduate student—very nearly always, as now, in jeans and work-shirt—with her mother's long wavy black hair and her father's blue eyes; and now she had that "There's something I want to talk to you about" look. She liked to have these talks, always about something she regarded as deeply serious and epochal, in fine restaurants, on the beach, in the back of a cathedral, someplace that seemed to impart drama to the discussion. Today it was a walk along the cliffs near his sprawling house.

It would be her house, one day, he thought. She was his only child and her mother was five years in the grave. If she would just wait for her

Weirdbook

VOL. 2, NO. 12   ISSUE 42

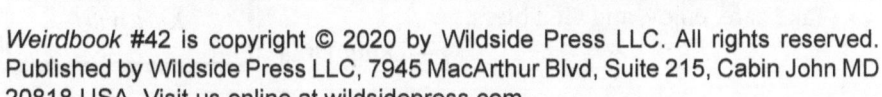

FROM THE
EDITOR'S TOWER

Hello Dear Readers,

It's that time again! If you are reading this, then you rightly know that *Weirdbook #42* has hit the stands.

You might have also noticed that this issue of *Weirdbook* is a little bit different than all of the previous issues. We've done several themed anthologies so far, but this is our very first single author issue. And even though every issue of *Weirdbook* is something *special and unique*, this issue is **SPECIAL! It's 100% JOHN SHIRLEY!!!**

I first read Mr. Shirley's "City Come-Walkin" right after going into the Army back in 1980. I've been a huge fan ever since. His "Eclipse/Song Called Youth" has a very special place in my heart, alongside his short story collection *Heatseeker*.

I was truly flabbergasted last year when Mr. Shirley submitted his short novel *Swords of Atlantis* to *Weirdbook*. I read it and, not surprisingly, it turned out to be a true joy. We exchanged a few emails and decided to do a full John Shirley issue. Which is a true milestone for the magazine. I still have a strong urge to kowtow while chanting, "We are not worthy."

Seriously, Mr. Shirley is the recipient of multiple Bram Stoker and Locus Awards. He has won the International Horror Guild Award twice (along with 6 nominations). He has written two albums for Blue Oyster Cult, the original draft for *The Crow*, and been nominated for an Emmy for his work on the *Teenage Mutant Ninja Turtles* series.

Oh! And he's also scripted for *Star Trek: Deep Space Nine*!

The material presented here includes Heroic Fantasy, Lovecraftian Science Fiction, Dark Fantasy, Song Lyrics, Poetry, and even a little bit of horror.

You are in for quite a ride and—to paraphrase Clive Barker—

Mr. Shirley has such sights to show you!

Take care, enjoy, and God bless.

—Doug Draa

Staff

PUBLISHER & EXECUTIVE EDITOR

John Gregory Betancourt

EDITOR

Doug Draa

CONSULTING EDITOR

W. Paul Ganley

WILDSIDE PRESS SUBSCRIPTION SERVICES

Sam Hogan

PRODUCTION TEAM

Steve Coupe
Sam Cooper
Shawn Garrett
Sam Hogan
Karl Würf

time—let him be himself while she waited—

"Coming, dad?"

"You bet. We taking a lunch?"

"No, I'm going to make lunch for you on the deck, after. It's a beautiful day…"

He looked wistfully at his email. Jose Sanguelo had a very urgent tone—was quite disturbed about the bad publicity, the sudden judicial interference in Grigsby Gold Mines Ltd, when all had been so sweetly copasetic with the Brazilian authorities for so many years. Still, it would keep an hour or so.

He stood and looked for his coat—and then saw that she was holding it out to him, smiling.

* * * *

Yellow crocuses were blooming along the cliff path, waving in the wind amidst new grass. The grass had a fresh greenness, that seemed the very color of innocence. The breakers below were cottony white, in the Spring sunshine, almost the same color as the few wispy clouds in the turquoise sky. A brisk wind whipped their hair, it was true, but there was nearly always a wind here.

"You still seeing that lawyer kid?" he asked her.

His daughter laughed and shook his head. "Oh my God, if he could hear you call him a lawyer kid. He's thirty one."

"Just seems boyish to me, I guess. More like just out of college."

"Because he's an idealist?"

"There's being an idealist and then there's being silly. He always pushes everything too far."

"Well…he doesn't, dad. I mean…I met him when he was working with Amnesty International, in Sao Paulo—they're very established and serious. They're not some flaky organization. The UN respects them."

"Yeah, well, I don't respect the UN either. What was it you wanted to talk to me about? You had that earnest carrying-the-world-on-your-shoulders look."

She scowled. That face-transfiguring scowl she inherited from her mom. From pretty to ridiculous in a split second. "It's pretty serious, dad." She dropped the scowl and stopped at the peak of the cliff, turning to gaze at him, hair whipping around her face. She brushed a few strands from her eyes, squinting in the bright sunlight. "What I carry on my shoulders is my karma—you've paid for everything I have with blood money."

He stared at her. She'd tasked him about his mines before but never so self righteously, so bluntly. "So—would you like to repay me the college funds? Like me to take away the annuity?"

"I won't be taking the annuity anymore, actually. And you may need the money, for your own lawyers. Dad—" Maria made a sound that was something close to a moan. "I had to help Joel when he—he's representing the Santos family."

He felt like he'd been struck by a baseball bat. "Your fiancé is representing the people who're suing me?"

"The Santos brothers have moved to Vancouver. And…" She licked her lips. "I think I'm getting chapped up here. Maybe we should go in the house."

"No! Just stay right there and tell me exactly what you mean by you had to 'help' him!"

"I…copied some of your files. The money transfers to Colonel Vega. Dad, you paid those soldiers to *murder* those people so they'd stop talking about the cyanide from the mine—so they'd keep quiet about your company poisoning the village. What was I going to do? I…look, you're my dad and I love you. I didn't want to just…screw you over, even for a good cause, from a…like, from a distance. I wanted to tell you face to face what I'd done. I think you should own up to it and…pay restitution. I mean, up here, you're not likely to be prosecuted for hiring—"

"I didn't hire anybody to kill anyone *anywhere*!"

Of course it was a lie. But he had learned that lies work best when you're deeply insistent, over and over. And he was never going to cop to having anyone killed—especially not to Maria.

"Dad—I know what you did. You were sloppy about the emails. We have the money trail. You paid to kill those people to keep them quiet. And…it has to end. I mean, Joel told me about it and I…couldn't believe it. I thought of you as tough and conservative and even ruthless but—not without human feelings. I figure you managed to…to forget they were people too, for awhile. I *know* you have human feelings, dad. You were good to me and mom. Mostly. But…"

"So Joel poisoned your mind!" (Why was he saying that, again? This time…he must remember. The closet. The closet. The future. He must… but it was so hard to believe it, so hard to…)

"Dad—should we go over the paperwork? You made me an officer in the company and I…on that authority I gave it to the prosecutor. Now like I said he won't be able to—"

"You gave…you let that boy tell you what to think and you turned your own father in…you…." (No! This time he…but he felt so caught up, so angry, so…) "You treacherous little bitch! I 'm already under investigation for taxes—" All the blue had sucked out of the sky—it seemed white now, with veins of red. The sea seemed to roar in fury—in demand. The wind whined in pity for him—stabbed in the back by his own child…a child he had given everything to!

"I didn't know that you were under—"

"And now you're going to help them destroy me! You already *have*!" (This time, remember—the closet—but the feeling was so strong, so…)

"Dad—it has to stop! It's a matter of conscience! Someone has to—to stop people like you! I'm so ashamed of our family, of the way we live of—"

That was what did it. *Ashamed of our family.*

He lashed out, backhanded her, and she staggered for a moment, teetered, and there was a second when he might have, might have, might have caught her. (Now! Remember! The closet, you—)

But then Maria was falling backwards over the cliff, screaming. Falling, falling. Striking Anvil Rock below…And he was looking over the edge, wanting to throw himself after her, but not having the courage.

Seeing the dark red splash around her head, below, diluting to pink when the wave of high tide washed over her…

Then the machine in the closet detected the 'moment of return' setting and he was caught up in a vortex, screaming, twisting…stopping.

Swaying in the dusty closet. Sobbing in the darkness.

He fumbled for the door, opened it, stepped blinking out into the room, with only moments having passed from the time he'd entered the closet. The winter light came pale through the window of the barren room; the room that had been Maria's bedroom.

He closed the closet door behind him and went to the window.

How many times is that? he asked himself. He thought about it. *How many times have I gone back?*

At least three hundred.

Next time. Next time, the three hundred and first time.

Next time he wouldn't kill her.

✗

Secret Tree
by John Shirley

In a forest nigh to Yorkshire
strange customs yet endure
—some meant to quell uneasy graves.
But the tale I'm called to tell
is of a tree that can't be felled;
of blood that branches as it craves.
There, the Ancient of the Woods
is masked by a tattered hood
so that passersby will not see his gnarl;
and most who come his way
he simply drives away
with a damning curse and a cursing snarl.
But one day came a youth
seeking his ancestral truth—
it was hidden, much like the old man's face.
His mother writhed with shame—
would not speak his father's name—
but said "the Twisted Tree is your birthplace."
So journeyed the youth thither
—the young man's name was Mither—
asking where the Twisted Tree was found.
With shaking heads and shaking fingers
(not wanting him to linger)
folk bade him, "Follow yon weeping sound."
And through the forest he proceeded
till the weeping that he heeded
took him to a twisted willow tree:
a knotted tree which wept
when breezes sighed and swept
through sunless glades to the black stone scree.
He beheld the storied Ancient,
always seated, always patient—
Mither felt a strange and instant bond;
the youth hailed him as he knelt,
and said, "I am a wandering Celt

who seeks in what manner he was spawned."
The Ancient spoke in growls
and in the shriek of angry owls,
and then drew back his foul tattered hood.
And then Mither gasped to see
the Ancient as gnarled as the tree—
Twisted like the tangles of his fate;
Said the ancient, "Each who lives
has somewhere a tree that gives
the shape of his every ugly trait.
And each tormented role
shows in the knotted bole
of a man's secret twisted fate.
I've been waiting for my son
for he is the very one
who'll take my place 'tween these tortured toots.
And when he replaces me
he'll twist like his secret tree—
which grew in pain from his writhing shoots."
The youth then turned to run,
ran till the setting of the sun—
when he fell beneath a youthful spruce;
he recognized the tree,
knew it was his destiny—
his secret tree would never let him loose.

Broken on the Wheel of Time
by John Shirley

The Journal of Glyneth Berling
July 29, 1878
Boston, Massachusetts

Perhaps it is the heat, but Ben seems most particularly quarrelsome. My husband is ever alert to quarrel, but today he seems like a fox quivering to pounce on a hen. I find that I must tiptoe about him, and that is no mere figure of speech—the floorboards creak more in the heat, and he snarls at me if I walk near his workshop. Yet the pantry is close to the workshop, and he expects me to make use of the pantry so to prepare his luncheon. It is as well he forbids "nosy housekeepers"; I would not subject a housekeeper to his choler.

He has only raised his hand to me once, and swore he wouldn't do it again—for I said I would leave him if he struck me again. But if he discovers this journal I expect he'll be tempted to strike me with it; a leather volume in Ben's rough hand would make a painful slap indeed.

* * * *

The Journal of Glyneth Berling
August 1, 1878
Boston, Massachusetts

At last it is Sunday, the day I'm free to take the train to the countryside and be about my observations in the fields and thickets. But as I was packing a lunch, my darling husband bid me stay to home should he "need anything." His work today is most urgent, he said; he cannot be troubled to step out of the workshop to fetch a lemonade.

Ben has not much respect for naturalists, particularly lady naturalists, and fairly jeered, one morning, when he saw me weeping on learning that my correspondent Genevieve Jones had died. She was another Audubon, in a sense; a student and painter of birds, and deserving of anyone's esteem. But when has Ben exhibited respect to any woman?

When he was courting me Ben seemed content to hear me comment at length on the intricate formation of bird's nests, the astonishing industry of ants and bees; he was willing to accompany me as I spoke to ship's officers, at the harbor, asking after the migratory habits of the whale and the dolphin. But within a month of our wedding he fell first into a fit of melancholy, and then became steeped in his arcana. I thought it something I had done, or failed to do. Certainly I have never stinted affection, or denied him marital intimacy. But I encountered his half-brother Harold, who seem concerned to ask me if all was well. I admitted that my husband's dark moods had me blaming myself. But, taking me aside, Harold allowed that Ben had a fixation on death, that he was never able to put aside; he sighed that "Benjamin has always been thus." And indeed in recent years, before the marriage, Ben's fits of angry melancholy have worsened. Had I but known, there would have been no understanding between us!

I thought he had altered since our wedding; but it seems I now see his character undisguised.

I am sometimes sorry that his father left him a stipend, and a bit more; he might be a better man to get out and struggle for a living. This last winter, his fixation on these dank and cryptic volumes has only deepened his faults; his attending to the nattering of alchemists who lost themselves in phantasms before the true coming of Science only accelerated his deterioration: as cracks in a statue widen with the intrusion of ice.

He has forgotten to shave. If a man must have a beard then let him trim it; but Ben will have none of this. His linen is unclean; he will rarely avail himself of the garments I scrub and hang for him. His odor is as sour as his disposition.

Looking back on this journal I become aware of my own sourness— which certainly has not improved my disposition. Surely a wife should have something kinder to say of her husband.

Perhaps I will attempt, once more, to talk to him about this growing distance between us. I could chance it over supper, if I can persuade him to take the meal with me. Too often he bids me leave the food on the table just inside the workshop door. Nor will suffer me to enter further than that table—which is sadly in need of cleaning. He will not allow me to clean it, of course.

* * * *

The Journal of Glyneth Berling
August 3, 1878
Boston, Massachusetts

The worst of the heat has abated, as the sea breeze arrives at last. Ben's bad temper, however, has not abated. He talks to himself in his workshop, sometimes reads aloud in a foreign language, and curses when the experiment goes awry. Then he damns me when I ask if I can help.

Loneliness seems to cry out when my footsteps make the boards creak.

A year, seven months and two weeks of marriage, and I feel like a woman who's married to a sailor long lost at sea. Yet my husband is no more than a dozen steps away.

If only Ben would allow me a pet; but he is quite firmly against it. Animals, he declares, are simply more distractions. He rarely comes to bed and when he arrives, stinking of obscure chemicals, he falls into a troubled sleep; he seems to have nightmares and with a strange regularity, nearly always just after the clock strikes one in the morning.

A little dog to sleep at my feet, to sit on my lap as I read, would be a great comfort to me. But Ben particularly mistrusts dogs. He says they hold a prejudice against him.

Perhaps I might persuade him to let me have a parakeet.

* * * *

The Journal of Glyneth Berling
August 7, 1878
Boston, Massachusetts

A strange change has come over Ben. I should be glorying in it, since the change has wrought a softening of his temperament, but I'm almost frightened by the transformation. I must give a full account.

I was taking my morning porridge in the kitchen, thinking that I had heard him give a plaintive cry at one hour after midnight, and wondering if I should have gone to him then. But in the past whenever I have looked in on him, no matter the provocation, he shouted vile abuse at me, and I was forced to turn away.

This morning I was quite startled to see him appear in the kitchen door, staring at me. He had not changed his clothes in several days; his overalls were blotted by chemicals that seemed a most peculiar shade of blue; here and there were spots of what looked like drips of metal, copper perhaps. He still wore his gloves, equally blotted and in some places burned through by acids; his black hair was unruly, his untended beard, for the most part hiding his lips, showed sharply against his pale skin. His gray eyes had scarlet rims, and in them was a look of shocked disorientation. He seemed a man of fifty rather than the man of thirty-two I knew him to be.

"I am sorry," he croaked at me. "Quite sorry, ma'am, to intrude on you. I found myself here…And I just plain don't know how I got here."

Had he had some kind of blow to the head? He seemed not to know me. "Oh Ben…sit down, rest!" I took him by the arm and drew him to a chair at the kitchen table. I tugged off his gloves, and took one of his hands in mine. "Ben…have you injured yourself?"

"What did you call me? *Ben?*"

"Perhaps you should lay down, my dear. I'll bring you some breakfast and then you can take a nap."

Ben blinked and blinked again, quite dazedly staring around him. "He tricked me. He completely…"

"Who tricked you, Ben?" I asked. Truly he sounded like a raving madman.

Should I be afraid of him? That is—should I be mortally afraid?

He rubbed his eyes, shaking his head as if at a loss to explain. "I'm so tired." He looked around, sniffing. "There's a bad smell…"

"Oh—that's you, dear."

He looked down at himself. "Can I…bathe?"

I almost clapped my hands together. "Certainly you may!" It wasn't until he was in the big iron bathtub, and I was pouring hot water in to keep it warm—the tap water, even in August, being a bit brisk—that he asked, "What year is this?"

I cut short a gasp at the question. Then and there I decided I must get him to a doctor at the earliest possibility.

As I finished pouring the water, watching him from the corners of my eyes, I said, "As you are very well aware, Ben, it is the year 1878."

"That figures," he muttered.

I had never heard him use such an expression. "Does it? Certainly it should. You acted earlier as if you were…as if you didn't know where you were. Or who I was."

He looked up at me, blinking. "You would be Mrs. Berling."

I smiled at him. "I would be indeed, yes."

I shaved him, as he sat in the tub, and clipped his hair—I kept waiting for him to object, but he accepted the barbering with good grace—and then I helped him into a towel, and he dried himself as I went to make his breakfast.

However I found him deeply asleep in the bedroom, a few minutes later, and consumed the eggs myself so that they would not go to waste.

* * * *

The Journal of Glyneth Berling
August 8, 1878
Boston, Massachusetts

I should have followed the doctor's advice, I'm sure, and taken Ben to the brain specialist in Charlestown, but he had seemed to be improving so. Indeed, his company is congenial, his manners improved, and, quite handsome in the light linen suit he only wore once before, he has taken me on a goodly walk down the avenue.

Yet his behavior has been odd. He insists on sleeping on the settee in the drawing room. I feel a certain tenderness from him, for all of that. He now dines with me every evening and holds my hand when we take an after dinner walk. Both the walk and the hand-holding are nearly unprecedented.

He does spend a good deal of time in the workshop, but when I venture to look in on him, he does not send me out as of old. He asked me if I could name certain contraptions on the worktable; devices he himself has built. Of course, I had no knowledge of them.

Yet Ben seems reluctant to talk about the night that he collapsed—that is the expression he used about the event—nor will he say much of the morning he presented himself to me at the breakfast table. He always comes up with a polite stratagem for putting off the discussion.

On a morning walk we saw a small child playing with a little terrier. He astonished me by petting the dog, and when I said I'd always wanted one, he said, "Why not get one, then? Surely there's a shelter, or some such, around here?"

The same morning, as we observed bees in the garden, he said, musing to himself, "I wonder if anyone knows about the waggle dance, at this time, besides the bees themselves."

I looked at him in open puzzlement.

"The waggle dance, Ben, did you say?"

"Yes, it's thought they communicate to one another in the hive, with motions, waggling and back and forth dancing movements, about how to find…" Then he winced and shook his head. "Never mind. Not till 1972." Or so it seemed—perhaps he said 1872. But that would make no sense either.

"I was unaware you had an interest in bees. I supposed you were entirely concerned with electromagnetic waves, galvanic energy and—what did Mr. Edison call it? Aetheric waves…"

He looked as if he was going to once more deny his own identity, but then he compressed his lips and shrugged. "We'll talk about it soon, Glyneth. I'm going to need your help. We'll speak of it after dinner."

Then he changed the subject, and got me talking of bats, and of course it's a favorite subject. I rattled on, especially as—wonder of wonders!—he was carefully attending to my every word.

I must go down and make preparations for dinner.

* * * *

"What I am going to tell you will be difficult to believe," said Ben as we sat on the front porch after dinner.

Regarding my disbelief, as it happened he was not overstating the case.

It was warm and humid out, but dark enough so that mosquitoes were no longer sniping at us. We sat on the wicker chairs, Ben with his hands folded in his lap. This was yet another change in him, as he had always been a restless man, tapping his fingers on the arm of every chair he sat in.

When he didn't go on immediately, I added, "I will do my best to believe!" I gave him my brightest smile, trying to encourage him.

But in fact I was afraid of what he might tell me.

He looked up and down the row of houses, as if to assure himself that no one was close by. "Okay," he said, with a great sigh. "My name is…" He looked at me. "You think I'm Benjamin Berling. But I must tell you, I'm not. My name is in fact Trevor Peaslee. Oh I *know* Benjamin Berling, though I never quite met him face to face. I got to know him fairly well just before I changed bodies with him. Our minds swapped places, you see."

I smiled bravely. But, clearly, this sweeter Ben had quite gone leave of his senses. Once more I wondered if I should be afraid of him. But I found I could not be. He is so consistent in his character, so affable and kindly, I could not bring myself to fear him. There seems no falsehood in him now. This new character resonates as true as a well tuned piano.

His own smile was rueful. "I don't expect you to believe me, not yet, Glyneth. Well, look. Today is August 8, 1878, yes? Where I live, usually, in my time, is in fact Arkham, Massachusetts—but it happens that I was raised in Wallingford, Connecticut, and as a teenager in school I was asked to write about an event in local history. I chose a certain pretty famous tornado, which killed a number of people, and which destroyed quite a bit of property. I picked that event because my own house was built as a result of that tornado. That was part of our family heritage. I looked it all up. The tornado happened…will happen…on August 9, 1878. Tomorrow."

I must have gawped at him.

But he leaned toward me, and went on insistently. "It will happen *tomorrow*, and thirty-four people will die, seventy-three will be injured, and many houses will be flattened. It will be the worst tornado in New England history until 1953."

He said all this calmly and collectedly. It was his casual use of 'until 1953' that prompted my outburst. "Oh really!" I could not help but laugh a little. "You prognosticate not only tomorrow—but the year 1953!"

He gave out an ironic grunt at that. "I could prognosticate more, for you. Two world wars for example. You could not conceive…A man walking on the moon in 1969! But for me it's not prognostication. It's history. I was born in 1976, and came here in 2015, a hundred seventeen years from now so it's all part of the past, to me."

"Ben…" I put a hand on his, and was pleased when he turned his hand to clasp mine. "Tomorrow, we'll see the doctor, and get the name of a specialist. Before we met—did you ever have scarlet fever, Ben? When I think of it there's much of your life I don't know about. It's all quite sketchy."

Ben frowned. "Scarlet fever? Oh, I see! 'Brain fever'! You figure my brain was injured by disease and I'm having a relapse." He sighed, but he only clasped my hand more tenderly. "You're an intelligent, good hearted woman, Glyneth. Instead of making fun of me or running away, you try to diagnose me. You're trying to help. I don't know how that son of a bitch managed to marry a woman like…" He noticed my shocked expression. "Sorry!" He took a deep breath. "Look, I mentioned that tornado for reason. Exactly because it's happening tomorrow. Thirty-four people will die! You can certainly try to warn Wallingford, if you want. I can't bring myself to do it—I'm afraid of what might happen if I changed any stream of time I don't absolutely have to change. And if either of us tries to warn them, what'll they do anyway? They'll only sneer at us."

It occurred to me that this tornado business might be an opportunity to wake Ben from his delusion. "Ben—we shall look to see if this tornado happens. Telegraphs will alert the Boston papers within minutes of such a disaster, I'm sure. But if it doesn't happen…will you then admit that you might have an illness?"

He gave me a long, somber look. "Yes. I will."

He's once more sleeping on the sofa, though I all but implored him to come to bed that he might sleep in comfort.

And I sit up late, writing this account, trying to settle my mind. I have high hopes that tomorrow, he will awaken to his true condition, and we shall set out to find the proper doctor.

* * * *

The Journal of Glyneth Berling
August 9, 1878
Boston, Massachusetts

The morning paper held nothing of a tornado in Connecticut, but most of the paper had been set in type the night before, of course. And so I waited till an evening edition of the Boston Globe might turn up. A catastrophe would spark a special edition, certainly. Once the evening paper came along with no mention of it, I could persuade Ben he must seek help.

After an early supper, Ben and I walked down to the druggist where an evening paper might be had. The shop had already closed, but there was a group of men clustered on the sidewalk waving their cigars and interrupting with questions as one of them read from the evening Boston Globe, relating the awful facts of the tornado that had killed numerous people in Wallingford, Connecticut. The number of the dead was uncertain, but it was thought to be at least twenty, perhaps more than thirty…

My heart was clamoring like a fire bell as we turned away from the corner and started back. After a few quiet minutes I turned to the man I had thought to be Ben, and asked, "What did you say your name was?"

"It's Trevor Peaslee." He stopped and turned to me, offering his hand. I shook his hand in a dazed, mechanical kind of way. "Professor Trevor Peaslee," he went on, a little apologetically. "Of Miskatonic University. I am very pleased to meet you, Mrs Berling. In my time—you are remembered as a respected naturalist."

* * * *

The Notes of Benjamin Arthur Berling,
January 2, 2015.
Arkham, Massachusetts

I am not pleased with Peaslee's body. It is heavy set, and pallid; his small green eyes seem out of place somehow. I dislike his stubby hands. The brain however seems efficient. He was a scientist, after all. He is one still, if he survived the transition. Eventually I shall break him on the wheel of time, and take my own body back, if all goes as planned.

"Trevor Peaslee," as I must call myself now, lives alone in a small suite of rooms near the university. I find no indication of a spouse in the domicile, though there is a book of color photographs showing him with a woman, yet pudgier than he is but somehow it all has the look of a relationship in the past. That is well. I want no one coming here asking questions.

My own question for myself is, should I attend his classes, and attempt to teach? Just to keep up appearances…But also, I could almost wish for students, now, that I might teach them the distinction between the mind and the brain. It is something subtle and unsubtle at once. The brain is integral to the mind, as the ground is integral to running. But the runner is who he is…

I probably shall call in to the university and declare myself indisposed, if I can work these cellular telephonic devices, as they exist now. Not so different from what we anticipated—telephonic devices having been patented in 1876—but much more compact. Marvels, really. Many of Peaslee's body's physical memories remain. Quite possibly my appropriated nervous system will remember how to use the device; almost instantly I intuited the use of the domicile's incandescent lamps.

Inspecting Peaslee's mind psychically, I learned of the advances of his time; of television, of orbital mechanisms and jet planes and thinking machines. And the cellular telephonic devices in particular excite me. The compression of electro-machinery alone! I must study it under a microscope.

I feel no anxiety in recording my thoughts here. Anyone coming upon such a thing would regard it as raving or mere tale spinning. Even that remark would be so regarded.

I cannot help the feeling that I have achieved what should be reserved for gods alone. That I have achieved the transcendent, the supernal; that I am destined to succeed; that nothing can stop me, if I am reasonably discreet in my dealings with men of this time.

The question becomes, how am I to take control of the electronic amplification systems I need? The Yithians are quite specific about the device. But I must have sole command of it, if I am to open the way for the League. If I can complete my barter with them, I shall have all the riches of time—and they shall decide the future of mankind, for which I care not a whit. At any rate they are practical creatures, these primeval ones, and I doubt they destroy the ruck of humanity. Corpses are of no use to anyone but buzzards. But slaves are endlessly valuable. Eliminate the problematic element of mankind—perhaps a billion or two—and the rest will fall into line.

* * * *

The Journal of Glyneth Berling
August 10, 1878
Boston, Massachusetts

I have thrashed it out in my mind again and again, telling myself the man I think of as my husband must have gotten lucky in his prediction about this historically destructive tornado; or he had some advance knowledge from a meteorologist somewhere. But the details are correct. There is more he told me, in advance, than I recorded here.

Finally, it's the utter transformation of his personality—or rather, if he is to be believed, it is the replacement of his personality I must accept.

For he simply is not Benjamin Berling.

I have come to accept that he is Trevor Peaslee. And he has shown me things in the workshop that are in themselves either madness, or truth.

In Ben's workshop we activated an "electronic mirror" constructed by Ben, that records psychic experiences—in this case, the glass oval reproduced a memory. I beheld the moving image of a creature shaped like a cone with four snaking upper parts, the whole twice as tall as a human; it moves on a mucous-coated underside, the muscle contracting and expanding much as a snail moves on a single flexible foot. It's upper parts seemed serpentine, one of the "serpents" ending in what could be a head. Did not that irregular sphere topping the prehensile member have a row of eyes? I only glimpsed the creature, mostly the lower parts; I hope to write a fuller account of it in time. This, I am told, is a "Yithian, a member of the Great Race from the planet Yith." So Trevor informs me. Ben and Trevor, it seems, looked into one another's minds. And each learned something startling.

It's not difficult to think of him as Trevor, despite Ben's face and body; shaved, clean, with a completely different demeanor—gentle and receptive—Trevor seems like an entirely different person.

He describes himself as a researcher in a discipline this era does not yet know: *exobiology*, a "mostly theoretical exploration of the nature of extraterrestrial life."

"It was this fascination," he said, "that led me to being displaced in body

—and displaced in time, too."

After he said that, I insisted that we go to my desk. I would transcribe his story…Someday, I may provide this narrative to science, though perhaps in a discreet way. It contains claims—facts, if we are to believe Trevor—which are perhaps unsuited for much of mankind. Indeed, those who are believers in the creation tale of the Old Testament will be outraged. For Trevor speaks of Earth as more ancient than they'd ever supposed. And intelligent creatures here long before there could have been an Adam…

We went upstairs, I sat at the desk, filled my stylographic pen, and wrote down everything he said as authentically as I could.

"In the search for extraterrestrial life, exobiologists have only guesswork," Trevor said, as her paced up and down behind me. "There are indications that some primitive lifeforms might be possible on the moons of Jupiter; perhaps micro organisms exist within the soil of Mars. But we have not located any real proof of extraterrestrial life—and endless speculation is frustrating.

"Last year—in my time flow—my grandmother left me some documents written by her great uncle, Nathaniel Peaslee. She attached a note suggesting the documents contained something that might relate to my work.

"I didn't know what to make of it. All I knew of Nathaniel Peaslee was that he was an economics lecturer at Miskatonic—of all things!—and he'd had an extraordinary case of intermittent amnesia.

"Then, page by page, unable to put it aside, I read Uncle Nathaniel's account in his own words.

"As he tells it, his periods of amnesia were blotted with strange, alien remembrances. He thought it was hallucination, but he seemed to see a tantalizing imprint of an alien influence. He found subtle but persistent traces of a prehistoric race of intelligent beings, here on this planet. He stumbled over clues that led him to search for their lost library: the vault of memories.

He sighed. "You'll have to make a great leap, now, Glyneth. I am going to ask you to believe that during his lapses into amnesia the mind of my Great Uncle Nathaniel was displaced by an *extraterrestrial mind*, that had traveled in time to do it."

I stopped writing for a moment and turned to stare at him.

Trevor smiled apologetically—smiled with Ben's lips. "And—that's not all. This alien mind was one of countless colonists from the planet Yith; apparently they first projected themselves *mentally* from Yith; coming psychically they took over the bodies of mobile, plant-like creatures on Earth, modifying them—"

"Mobile plants?" I interrupted. "In what sense? Plants do spread, and move through seeding and…"

"No, I mean they were a sort of hybrid of plant and animal and they could—deliberately travel. They could move themselves something like the way a snail moves, and they had vehicles. They had a grand civilization—and they would become something called the Great Race. All this was hundreds of millions of years ago, long before mankind. Eventually, the Yithian civilization on Earth was mostly destroyed by another race of extraterrestrials. The remaining Yithians looked around for some other way to survive. So they sent their aetheric selves—their minds, their conscious essences—to travel in time; when they found a suitable host they ejected the original mind, and used the new form to explore the ages. They had taken over many bodies—choosing those positioned to access valuable data—and in this way they'd taken over Uncle Nathaniel's body.

"Nathaniel's own mind was drawn by the Yithians back in time to their era, where it occupied one of the alien bodies. Finding himself in a hybrid of vegetable and animal, using arms better suited for an octopus than a man—" Trevor chuckled. "—that was very hard to get used to. But my uncle was fascinated by the civilization of the Great Ones, and by the other time traveling minds he met there. He held on to that thread to keep his sanity.

"When the Yithians finished with him, they returned him to his original body—which at first he found repellent. But for a time, he couldn't remember most of what he'd experienced…just kind of fitfully.

"Looking for answers, he made his way to a certain Australian archaeological site deep in the Outback. There were hints in seriously outre old books that the records of the Yithians had been stored over millennia—and they fit with some of the fragmentary memories he had—leftovers from his lapses. Uncle Nathaniel found a site the archaeologists missed, and went there totally on his own. He found a way in…he was down there maybe days, scrabbling through a huge, dark, crumbling underground maze. The whole place nearly collapsed on him. But he found it. The library of the Yithians—a artifact. He was drawn to a particular book…a book he lost when he fled the place, one step ahead of something that whistled in the darkness.."

"It—whistled?"

"Kind of a doleful whistle, the way he described it. I felt a shock, Glyneth, reading that part of his story. Because I knew about a new Miskatonic expedition to Australia. Sounded like it was to the same area." Trevor groaned softly to himself. "I sound *crazy*, I know. Telling it, hearing myself—I sound like I was out of my damned mind to give any of this credence. But—what if it were true? I *had to know* if there were really traces of ancient extraterrestrials there…See, if I could find them I might be able to explore exobiology in an entirely new way. It might be the only chance in my whole lifetime to find proof of an alien presence.

"So—I did it. I spent most of my own money getting to the most desolate place I've ever seen. I didn't care to be ridiculed, so I ditched the expedition and went off on my own, the way my uncle did. There were hints in his manuscript as to the direction—and I got lucky, if you want to call it luck.

"I found the entrance to it but after a short trek down into the tunnel came to a stop on an impassible heap of gigantic stone blocks. The rest of the tunnel had collapsed since Uncle Nathaniel had been there. I couldn't go any farther down, and to tell you the truth, I was relieved. And I heard it too—that sick, off tune whistling from cracks between the old stones. A smell of ozone and something rotten—and there was this current of damp air…It was like it was pushing at me, as if it were alive, sentient. Curious about me. And not at all friendly.

"Wish I could impress you with a story that makes me sound brave… But I had to get out of there."

"I'm more impressed by honesty," I said. Wondering why I felt it necessary to reassure him about my feelings.

"…So I started running out, just blindly trying to get away.…when I stumbled on something. I literally tripped over it, just fell face down. I turned my flashlight and there, almost completely buried in sand, was this large metal-bound book. I carried it out and made camp. Looked the book over—parts of it were handwritten in English. Part of it was in ideograms of some kind. And it was an illuminated manuscript. There were illustrations. It was the book my great uncle Nathaniel had found in the buried vaults of the Yithian library. The English handwriting was the same as in the documents my grandmother had sent me. It was my uncle's handwriting. Just think of it—this thing had been there for hundreds of millions of years. Because it's a book he wrote in, when he traveled back in time—but he had gone back in time to an alien body. He didn't use his hands to write it. He didn't *have* hands then. He used whatever sort of digits a Yithian has. This was the book my uncle tried to carry out of the tunnels. And lost on the way. It's like it was waiting there for me, for generations…"

I was again tempted to doubt Trevor's sanity. "But—how would the book have lasted this long, Trevor? It would have crumbled into dust."

"It's not written on materials we know. It's written on stuff meant to outlast the planet! But—I was afraid the Australian government would claim the book before I had time to fully study it, so I found a way to hide it in a cheap aboriginal artifact sold to tourists—a small carved log—and I took it back to Arkham.

"I went over this thing for days and days. Locked myself in my place and pored over it. Parts of it were English accounts—some of Nathaniel's experiences with the alien minds he'd met while living as a Yithian. A few passages recounted his experience of what he called psychic dislocation. Other parts were written in that unknown language. I found similar images on the web, here and there—no one was quite sure what they meant…"

I was puzzled by his reference to a 'web' but I did not interrupt him.

"I kept on, and on, till I was half out of my mind from exhaustion. But I still I kept on, drinking endless pots of coffee, transferring the contents of the book, page by page, by scanning and typing into a computer file. Trying to interpret it. The illustrations helped but it was choppy…I was only getting bits and pieces.

"My mind whirled. I got into a state I'd never experienced before. like some latent memory was tingling in me; as if my consciousness was tugging itself away from my body. More and more I couldn't feel myself on the chair; could scarcely sense my fingers on the keyboard. Sometimes I felt myself floating above it—and seemed to see my body below, my head slumped on the desk.

"Then I would snap back into my body, and awaken from the dream—at least, I took it, then, for a mere dream. I would eat a little something, and go immediately back to work.

"Your Ben found me, on the fourth night of my obsession. I probably summoned him, without meaning to. All that focus on the pictures and ideograms in the book, my thoughts became visions and my visions projected into the aether—they followed courses dictated by the nature of the imagery. Visualizations of the Great Ones lead psychically to other minds seeking the Great Ones. Because the Great Ones have created a continuum for their own use in the fifth dimension: the realm of pure consciousness. There they created a kind of pathway, marked at intervals with projected signposts. A discarnate mind following those symbolic signposts would find its way to the Yithians—whose disembodied consciousnesses roamed freely in the stream of time.

"But—your husband found me first.

"Glyneth, did you see the device in his workshop that resembles a helmet? This was his own invention, and it was the door that opened electro-psychic possibilities to him. I found evidence in his workshop that the device works with certain arrangements of copper coils and crystals, suggested by ancient texts…"

"So all this time, he was not just madly tinkering—he was on to something?"

Trevor gave out an ironic chuckle. "Yes. But that doesn't mean he's not insane. The two are not necessarily mutually exclusive…especially when it comes to electro-psychics. And dealing with the so-called Great Ones…"

He scowled and I put my hand on his arm. "Are you alright, Trevor?"

"I…yes. The whole thing is a bit overwhelming. Sometimes I just have to…"

"Lay down and rest."

This time he lay on my bed, and I lay beside him—somewhat bold of me, but I could not help it. He needed me. I put my arm around him, and he seemed to fall into a restless sleep—the sleep of mental exhaustion. But not mental freedom…

* * * *

The Notes of Benjamin Arthur Berling,
January 9, 2015.
Arkham, Massachusetts

They came to me…as I slept they came to me…

I felt sick when I woke; I ran to the privy and vomited. But soon after, when my head was clear, the sickness was replaced by the flush of triumph.

The Yithians have come to me in my dreams, here in this time, just as they said they would!

I feared I would not remember the dream—but just as they promised it was as memorable as waking life. Their electro-psychic presence was palpable—and still remains so. A smell as of the ground burnt by a lightning strike is in the air around me.

And they showed me why I am here; why I am on the grounds of the Miskatonic University.

The device they have directed me to, is called the Superfast Laser Pump. It emits photons at a high rate of energy; a photon is a packet of sub-microscopic waves, I'm told; a particle which constitutes light in the electromagnetic spectrum. The superfast laser fires a bullet of light at another photon stored in a crystal; photons collide and destroy one another, and the destruction sends information to a third photon, with which it is entangled on what is in this time called the quantum level. This communication is instantaneous and carried out by means not understood even in this advanced age. But the Yithians indicate that the disparate photons exchange information through the fifth dimension; this is a dimension that communicates with our world and the plane of quantum possibilities, at once.

When a simple resonance device is added to the laboratory setting, the Superfast Laser Pump will open the way for the Yithians to come to a specific area. Washington DC—two places. The Capitol building, and the five-sided building they call the Pentagon.

"To take over numerous human forms, at one go, in a contained location, the Yithians will need my help; they will need the application of this laser pump, after certain significant alterations in it…

* * * *

The Journal of Glyneth Berling
August 11, 1878
Boston, Massachusetts

After breakfast, as we sat in the kitchen drinking coffee, Trevor asked me to once more shave off his beard.

"I would do it myself," he said apologetically, "but I can't stand looking in the mirror. I see someone I'm really starting to hate." He cleared his throat. "I'm truly sorry to hate your husband."

"You have my sympathy," I said. "I could scarce bear him." Feeling inexpressibly bold, I went on, "You're a much better man than he is. You'd… make a much better husband. For some woman."

His eyes welled up, a bit, at that. "Ah, but you know, the real Trevor, back home in my time, is not as good-looking as Ben. Trevor Peaslee looks more like Ben Franklin at forty than he does Ben Berling."

"I don't think I'd mind that at all," I added even more daringly. "It's a man's mind I find...*compelling*."

"There are...*things* you need to know about Ben. You see—I don't have his memories exactly, but, I've seen them—many of them." He hesitated, then, as if wondering if he should tell me all he'd seen.

I ventured, "I was wondering about that—if there were traces of memory in his brain..." I think I blushed. After all, Ben and I have had our periods of intimacy, though they ended some time before Trevor appeared.

"Neurologically speaking, there are what I would describe as *physical* memories." He frowned at the floor. "After spending time in the workshop, my hands, and some of my brain, seem to remember how to use his equipment." He smiled ruefully." I think I could now drive a horse and buggy fairly competently, too. Couldn't have done that, in my own body. But..." The smile faded away. "...most of what I've learned about him, I picked up clashing with him in the fifth dimension."

"There—I'm lost."

He nodded sympathetically. "Difficult to explain...But I'll try."

I suggest we again move to where I could write it all down. We adjourned upstairs.

This time, Trevor lay on my bed, to help him relax, and think. I hasten to add that I was seated at the rolltop desk, nearby, writing down what he was telling me, as best I could, as he lay there, hands clasped behind his head, his eyes closed, remembering aloud.

Some of his expressions are not entirely familiar to me, but I wrote them down as I heard them.

"Okay, Glyneth. So—I told you that I was in a kind of altered state from days of scarcely any sleep, fixated on the metal-bound book I'd found in the Australian ruins. I had visions of the Yithians..." Trevor took a deep breath. "Then, near dawn, as I was almost nodding out at my worktable, I heard a voice calling my name. It said, *"Trevor Peaslee, you feel yourself near leaving your body. Let go of it. Come with me. I will explain the book you have found; I will tell you what it means for you..."*

As I scratched this down, Trevor made a faint groan. I glanced at him, and saw his face contorted. "Trevor—can you go on?"

"Yes. I'm fine. Just give me a moment. Makes me feel a little sick remembering some of it." He cleared his throat and went on. "...I heard him calling me to come with him, and the voice was a lot like the one that comes from my mouth now! Like any man, Ben imagines himself speaking in his own voice, you see. I guess I went along with his suggestion because I was suddenly floating over myself. My mind was floating over my body. I could see the back of my head—then I floating farther and I saw my whole body slumped on my desk. I could see I was breathing.

"I wondered what I could see my sleeping body *with*. Did I have eyes, in some sort of skull? Did I have a brain? Was it some kind of subtle body, like the mystics talk about?

"I tried to see my aetheric form—to see whatever I was now; the spirit body, or whatever it was. I got scared—because I saw nothing there at first. I had no body at all! Then, I saw a flicker, like if you see a reflection of the moon in rippling water. It showed me the outline of my body, unclothed, semi transparent. Not very solid, but…it was there. Physically, I could just barely feel the body I was floating in. Emotionally though, I was all astir. I was scared, and my mind was racing. I felt the excitement of discovery… It was as if my body was made of thoughts and emotion and just a little bit of something else.

"That's when the room got dark. I couldn't see anything at all. But—I felt something near me. It appeared to me, little by little, like a photograph coming into focus. It was one of the creatures sketched in the book: a Yithian. It got more solid looking, and I could see one of those rubbery limbs beckoning; a "come with me" gesture. Then a point of light appeared beyond the Yithian; the light got bigger, and started to spin. It became a whirlpool of gold and red light. I wasn't sure I wanted to follow it, but I did want to see the glowing whirlpool better—something about that vortex seemed to say "there are infinite worlds inside me." And just wanting to see the vortex closer was enough to propel me toward it. The focused desire to move propels the disembodied consciousness.

"I followed the creature, and I felt the whirlpool pulling at me. Drawing me in. I didn't go *down* into the vortex, because it wasn't a thing that went down—it went *beyond*.

"I emerged into another place. I had lost sight of the Yithian. I wondered if it had lured me here to abandon me. Just—some cruel impulse. But by now I was too stunned by what I was seeing, too overwhelmed to really be afraid.

"I was seeing a infinite reach of space—a *skyscape*, is what I'd call it. There was no bottom or top to it. It was a skyscape made out of energy and possibilities and emptiness and colors—all coalescing in endlessly mutating orbs of light exchanging streams of energy; a skyscape of metamorphosing sphere that arose from a vast emptiness. And the emptiness was itself alive.

"Oh, the colors—most of the colors there seemed completely new. If I thought something was yellow or purple, I would change my mind, in a moment. No, that's *not* purple! That's *not* yellow! But it hadn't actually changed color.

"All coordinates became visibly relative. It's as if I could see relativity itself. A glowing orb that was way distant was all of a sudden nearby; when I perceived it as nearby it was also infinitely far off. Beyond all of it, the sky held stars but they were *jet-black* stars against a field of pulsing violet. Anyway—it was almost violet.

"And the endless spheres—maybe they were gigantic bubbles. Like a foam that couldn't make up its mind it was a foam. *But each one was as big as a world*—as big as Jupiter, or bigger. The spheres were reflecting one another, and they would spasmodically switch places, whipping back and forth. There were sounds that went with all these movements. It sounded like language at times, but it wasn't language. Sometimes the spheres seemed to *squeal* as they turned inside out, and then they looked as if they were struggling, really *agonizing* to restore their original shape. Till suddenly they found their way back to spherical. Moments later they turned inside out again. But some of them, when they failed to restore their spherical shapes, they'd fall apart, like they were spawning millions of smaller spheres. The smaller spheres would merge together in a way that seemed organized, even thoughtful, but I could tell it was just the physics of this place. Only, physics here was also thought."

He paused, and I looked at him. "Go on—I'm trying to keep up, Trevor."

"I know—I'm not making any sense. But I can tell you—this place was the fifth dimension. Oh, Glyneth—I wish I could show it to you. It seemed to be *one matrix*, yet as much space as substance, but I felt as if the space between things was alive and looking at me, and…." He sighed. "It's impossible to describe. Trying to grasp what I was seeing—my mind could not deal with it. I wanted to scream. I was afraid I was going to fall apart and just lose myself in all this, and that'd be the end of …of whatever I think of as me.

"Then I heard the voice—the one that had spoken to my mind when I was about to leave my body. It said, *You cannot understand this place. Simply follow me.*

"And that's when I saw the Yithian again—that fleshy cone, floating toward me, those boneless limbs sprouting from the top wavering around it. Light from every direction rippled across the Ythian, sometimes blotting it out so it vanished for a moment or two. But every time I saw the creature again it was a little nearer.

"I heard the voice reverberating in my mind again. *Come to me, my friend, I will carry you safely to my time.*

"I looked around—the glowing vortex was nowhere to be seen. So I moved toward the Ythian. The process of approaching an object in this dimension doesn't have the perspective qualities of the human world. If you approach a thing, it doesn't seem to get bigger. You just became suddenly closer—and the thing got more definite in appearance. More *there*ness to it.

"I was suddenly within reach of it, and I thought, *I'm being a fool, getting this close!*

"I peered at the creature's alien, three eyed face atop one of its prehensile members—and suddenly it went out of focus, and another face appeared. It was a human face, bearded man. Angry eyes, and mocking. It's the face I'm stuck with now…

"I cursed and tried to back away—but I wasn't clear on how to do that. And I was gripped, grabbed behind, then all around me. Ben's face really came into focus then, and I saw what was holding me; saw it as if I were watching from the cosmic mind that watches all things. I was gripped in ectoplasm stretched out from Ben Berling's disembodied head. The Yithian was gone. It had never been there. It was an illusion. There was just this man's head grown crazily big and getting even bigger. Eyes gleefully popping, his mouth kind of warping, stretching to open wider. It was like he was shaped more by his state of mind than his anatomy.

"His mouth grew bigger and bigger. I fought with what strength I could find but my aethereal body was weaker than his. He had experience here, in this dimension.

"I tried to *think* myself away from there. I thought maybe I could just *will* myself back to my physical body in the ordinary human world…back to my apartment, back to my desk.

"No. I was stuck in those tendrils of…I'm calling them ectoplasm. Maybe that's what they are.

"His mouth stretched still wider and wider. Inside it was a crackling blackness. Like darkness could be electrified.

"And then I was pulled in—he swallowed my entire being, anyway all of me there was in that world; swallowed my aetheric body like the whale swallowing Jonah.

"I flailed around, trying to get out. But there was no way out—just crackling darkness everywhere, stinging me. Like I was getting mean little electric shocks all over.

"And then I heard him thinking. Just phrases, here and there. *I have him now…He will go into the old husk, and I shall have a new, in his time. I shall have his form. He will have the world of gaslight and coal smoke and the devil with it all!*

"I was psychically linked with him, Glyneth—it was ugly. But I couldn't get out.

"Then I saw a pictures flashing in my mind's eye, like a slide show of his life, a sort of inner narrative twisted to fit his point of view. I saw your husband's memories: his growing up with an unfeeling father who sold him to be an apprentice at nine; whippings, harsh beatings from a man who seemed to have the face of a starved wolf. Ben ran away and got himself lost in Boston, until finally he was taken as an orphan by the Berlings. He became, outwardly, whatever they wanted of him. His adopted mother died, and after that his adopted father spent the days working and the nights with a bottle of brandy. And then he read about Franklin's experiments with lightning, and the miracles of Mesmer, and he wheedled his father into getting him every book that could relate to the invisible world of pure energy. And then—he met you, Glyneth. And he thought, *This woman is not without intelligence, perhaps she can learn to be of use to my work...*"

Interesting, hearing that—I might indeed have been of use to him. But Ben never did trust me with his work.

Trevor sat up on the bed, poured himself a glass of water from the pitcher on the taboret, and went sipped, staring into space. He had a tremulous horror in his eyes.

Finally he went on, "I saw all that, in his mind—and a lot more. And at the same time, he saw into my mind. He learned about my time; he learned about our technology. Our society. And when I realized that, it scared me—deeply. Because to me it's obvious the guy is damaged, Glyneth. Brilliant but damaged. He's a psychopath."

"I don't know that term, Trevor. *Psychopath.*"

"It means he's without conscience, without empathy."

I myself have suspected as much. "Trevor—how did you end up... here? In my world."

"He brought me here. I was disgorged from his inner world, but I was still all tangled in his coils, dragged along behind him. Like an animal on a rope. We traveled through another vortex—and into another kind of space. A sort of interface between the fourth and fifth dimensions. We were traveling along the surface of the stream of time—in our own little pocket of time. Like a couple of tied-together balloons, following above a stream of water, but going upstream. And—somehow I knew it was specifically time relating to Earth..."

"What did time look like, from there?" I asked. I felt awe, asking the question.

"Best I can do is...it was made of billions of intricate shapes forming and collapsing and forming; a seamless flow of construction and destruction. On the surface it was like a chaotic river of molten glass. I couldn't look at it long—it was something that wanted to wreck all my conceptions. When I looked away I saw the velvety violet background with the black stars in it.

Next time I looked back I saw something emerging from a shining anomaly, on the edge surface of the river of melting glass—something that might have been an Yithian. And I had the impression the Yithian was guiding us along. Ben was communicating with it somehow.

The League, I thought. It was something I'd heard in his mind. A faction of Yithians.

"Ben suddenly drew me down to the stream of time—there was a vortox, turning the way opposite the other had turned. I was thrust into the golden whirlpool… This time there was a going *down* about it. I felt like an infinitely heavy stone dropped into an infinitely deep well…

"Next thing I knew, I was here. In your house, Glyneth. In 1878. Waking up, on the floor. And I had Ben's body." Breathing hard, still sitting on the bed, Trevor turned to look at me. "There's something we must do now…"

I think my eyes must have widened. But I made no objection. Then he said, "We must go to Ben's workroom—now! Because I've started to remember more—other things I glimpsed in his mind. Things that might help us."

* * * *

The Notes of Benjamin Arthur Berling,
January 12, 2015
Arkham, Massachusetts

It was astoundingly easy. But I shouldn't be surprised. The Great Ones have given me guidance all along. They have timed this—an amusing expression to use, in this instance. *Timed.*

The Great Ones have lost some greatness; their ancient war has reduced them. And, too, I do not communicate with their racial leadership. Admittedly it is a cadre of Yithians who support me; it is a faction grown quite apart from the other members of the race.

The plan to take over a human nation, by taking over its leaders—by taking command of the United States government, and the warlords in the Pentagon, from within—was somehow offensive to the primary Yithian leadership. The League of Electro-Psychic Emphasis secreted itself away from the others. The faction made its own plans…

And the League found me as I was searching through the aether with my apparatus; they found me where few journey; where all journeyers are inevitably known to those who sense the fourth and fifth realms.

They found me—because they need me. This League of the titanic race of primeval worldmasters! It requires the assistance of Benjamin Arthur Berling!

Thus they sent me to seek out the little woman in the big laboratory.

Ellen Lo. Her name was on the door with several others. Her colleagues were not to be back in town until the end of January. First vacation and then, I take it, scientific conventioneering of some kind.

This the young man working at the front desk told me. He was a graduate student, I took it; a brown skinned fellow with long curly hair. He seemed admiring of me—naturally thinking I was Trevor Peaslee, who apparently has some status here.

He admitted me, and I found this Ellen Lo alone, in the laboratory just as the Great Ones said she'd be. She was a rather pretty little woman, perhaps of Chinese extraction.

"Professor Peaslee!" How brightly she smiled up at me. Or at whomever she supposed me to be.

"Ellen, how very pleasant to see you," I said.

She looked confused, then. I sensed I had not used the proper colloquialisms.

But she shrugged, and got up from her worktable, where she'd been frowning over one of those miniature foldable computers.

"So—you finally came to see the Superfast Laser Pump?" she asked. Fairly chirped it.

"Yes indeed." I had certain blueprints, a manual of sorts imprinted in my mind. I needed to confirm the imprints, familiarize myself before I could make modifications.

The device took up a barn-sized room with a very high ceiling; the special laser apparatus was glassy and chromium and so complex it had no clear shape to me, at first. But there was a keyboard and a screen at one end, and I had learned fairly quickly how to use such control interfaces. The League's imprints soon provided the rest.

The Asian woman lectured me about her beloved apparatus, and particularly caught my attention when she showed me the units that would hold the separated photons. That "cycling crystal box" could be useful on several levels, yes; it can constrain more than light. Another witticism— how they spring from me like sparks from a dynamo now.

When I felt I was ready, I made my suggestion. "Will you not go to the roof with me? You have shown me your pride and glory. In exchange I wish to show you something of an astronomical nature—with exobiological implications."

"'Will I not'?" She laughed. "You've adopted an interesting style of self expression, today, Professor. Dabbling in the drama department?"

"Precisely, yes, that is correct," I told her, bowing slightly.

"Ah ha! I won't make you break character. Is there a lunar eclipse tonight?"

"Something more dramatic," I told her.

"Cool! Roof access is this way."

She led the way—how ironic! Up the elevator we went, and then up a flight of metal stairs, then out upon the roof. She looked around, frowning. "Not good visibility."

"It's over here, right this way," I said.

We stepped over to the little wall around the roof, and without hesitating, I pushed her over it.

She fell gasping backwards, staring at me as she went. Perhaps four stories down, a little more? It could only have been a second and a half, but it seemed to take her so long to fall. I was able to enjoy it. Down and down she went.

She struck the ground, on her back, and lay still.

In haste I made my way to the laboratory, found her purse on a metal table, and located her key card. What a wonder are key cards! So much imprinted on a little magnetic strip. Credit cards, key cards, identification cards, tiny little black strips interrogating us.

Once I had her card, I rushed down to the front desk, where the graduate student was looking in a cellular telephonic device. I shouted that Ellen Lo had been raving about killing herself and then she'd run to the roof, and I was terribly worried. That's why I'd come—she'd called me and told me she was frightfully depressed...

The campus police came, and an ambulance. They seemed to believe my story.

I did make a mistake, however. Ellen Lo is not dead. They say she fell in a garden, in soft ground. Her body is largely intact but her brain injured. She is in a coma.

Well then! That should hold her. Later, I will go to the hospital, find may way in, and choke the last of her breath from her.

I have set the Laser Pump to the convergence suggested; I have added the apparatus suggested by the Great Ones.

In the morning, at the precise instant prescribed, I will open the door for the League. They will come to this time locale; they will gather aetherically over the Superfast Laser Pump. Modified, it now has a further application. It will project the first group of Great Ones from the League to one place—for in the morning the President speaks to Congress. Other League Yithians will be sent to quite another location: that curiously temple-like building they call the Pentagon. They await just beyond the curve of the horizon. The energy will reverberate from the ionosphere. The doors will open...

The husks of Congressmen and Generals and the President will be in place to receive new occupants...

Amusing to consider that the minds presently occupying those bodies will not be sent back to Yithian bodies, as once was the case. No. They will be flung willy-nilly into the aether. Where aetheric predators await like sharks in a sea.

I will perforce remain in this body—and the new rulers of this nation will give me whatever I like. They will reward me with the final secrets of the higher dimensions, and the river of time. All of time itself will open to me.

They warn me, now...

He will be here soon.

* * * *

The Journal of Glyneth Berling
August 11, 1878
Boston, Massachusetts

Trevor and I labored in the workshop for hours. It was a most peculiar experience. Here was someone who looked like Ben, who yet was *not* Ben, asking my help to try to investigate Ben, and Ben's apparatus.

In truth, with my help, Trevor was beginning to piece the writings, the charts, the diagrams and apparatus together. We instantly penetrated Ben's code—he'd written it in Latin, backwards! I fetched a mirror, and we transliterated. I was more fluent in Latin than Trevor and was able to translate what he could not. Thank God Ben was terse, and the diagrams detailed.

And now I'm in that same workshop, watching Ben—no, I mean Trevor—as he sits in a trance, a near-mesmeric state, wearing the helmet, electricity fitfully crackling about him...Power taken from the air itself. The air contains electrical energy and Ben used a vibrating whiplike device of his own invention that sucks electricity out of the atmosphere to power his experiments...

I wait, and still I wait.

Trevor told me it would take time to find Ben. He promised me he would come back. He even squeezed my hand as he made the promise.

"I will see what he is up to," Trevor told me. "I will come back—unless something prevents it. We will decide what to do. After all—here, we are always before whatever he is doing in the year 2015. Maybe there's a way I can stop him and...then stay here. I think I'd like that, if you'd like me to."

"You know perfectly well I want you to stay here. To come back. You, Trevor. Anyway you can."

"Then…I'll come back. And we'll make a plan. But I've got to try to find my way to him. I think he helmet will make it possible."

After Trevor entered the electro-psychic trance I had a terrible fear he'd not come back to me. He was entering an unknown world. Anything could happen.

I occupied myself in gaining a greater understanding of the equipment, and the process of disembodied journeying. I think I've almost grasped it.

My mind returns to its fears. Suppose something fatal happens to Trevor, in this trance?

How rapidly I've become attached to him. He is not Ben at all—and it's as if Trevor and I were born in different eras purely by malicious accident, but intended, all along, to be in the same one, together.

Oh! Trevor is awakening!

His eyes…

* * * *

The Notes of Benjamin Arthur Berling
January 12, 2015
Arkham, Massachusetts

It is done.

I was gone, in this time, but a moment, but it seems as if a great period of time has passed—the enormous psychic struggle took so much from me…

I am surprised at my feelings, now, about Glyneth. At the time, it was all cold fury.

I almost regret it, looking back, I almost wish…

But that is all foolishness.

* * * *

The Journal of Glyneth Berling
January 13, 2015
Arkham, Massachusetts

Ben stabbed me, quite deeply, under my sternum, with a sharp tool from his workbench. I fell onto the floor, bleeding inside. I knew I could not last long.

I had no doubt at all it was *Benjamin Berling*, who stabbed me. Trevor did not occupy that body, anymore…

My dear husband Benjamin stood looking down on my as I bled on the floor, the sharp implement in his hand dripping blood. He tossed it onto the bench and spoke a few words.

"Your friend came after me, Glyneth—he tried to force my soul out of his body! I suppose he planned to use my machinery, then, to return to you…But I was ready—I was warned he was coming. And I am stronger than he is. I have put him in the crystal box, my dear, where he circles forever. There is a wheel of time in that box—and your Trevor Peaslee is now broken on the wheel of time. I saw it all in his mind, as I took control of him—I saw his desire for you. I saw that you have been almost whoring to him. Hence, my wife, you will burn with the house."

Ben said no more. He went downstairs to lock doors, and set the fires. I could soon smell turpentine, and then smoke. I knew he would soon return to use the apparatus as the house burned…

I tore a strip away from my under garments, and staunched my wound as well as I might.

Then I had only one course. To crawl.

I crawled to the chair and pulled myself into it. The pain was monumental; it towered over my inner world. But I forced the helmet in place, and worked the controls. I established the transmission beam…

I couldn't quite make the transition through the helmet—I had not the strength left. I was trapped, until Ben completed the murder.

Ben found me sitting on the chair, clamped into the helmet; I was scarcely aware and nearly bled to death. My poor bandage was soaked and blood dripped town my side, onto the floor.

He laughed and called me an empty headed female for trying to use his device. He said I could never understand such complexities.

And then he strangled me. I did not have strength to resist.

But it was the moment of death—but not quite death—that liberated me to follow the transmission beam; that allowed me to be freed from my physical husk.

I separated from my body, and was elevated upon on the transmission beam; up and up I went. Not to heaven, but toward the aperture into the fifth dimension.

As I went, I could see Ben below me, as if from a great and increasing distance, as he removed the helmet from my body, pushed my limp corpse onto the floor, and took my place…Soon I realized he was now receding below me. The roof of the house became opaque; I could no longer see Ben. I glimpsed the flames at the rear of the building…

Quite suddenly, I was projected fully into the fifth dimension.

I was adrift, neither above anything, or below anything, but relative to everything. I looked about me—looked without having eyes, at least not the sort of eyes I can understand.

Though somewhat prepared by Trevor, still I had to struggle to retain my sanity, and tried to find some perceptual anchor. I discovered that if I kept calm and tried to sense my aetheric form, tried to feel it with my mind, some of the confusion drained away. I managed to learn movement in this abstract world, which was just as Trevor had described it: triggered by will alone.

But *where* should I go? I had no idea how to find Trevor, or his time. I might be lost here forever.

Then a shimmering anomaly appeared, near and yet far; and I saw Ben there, beginning to take shape. He was translucent; almost imperceptible. But he was there. Just enough.

I drew back, into the center of a warping cloud of possibilities. It made me tingle but did me no harm, and it seemed to hide me from sight.

Ben was not expecting me there, and did not perceive me. He soared in a purposeful way across the spaces of the transfiguring spheres, and I followed. Soon he descended, through a glowing vortex.

Adrift in a world of implication and geometrical transformation, I waited, uncertain—after a moment, I decided I had no choice. I followed.

I fell just as Trevor described it—like an infinitely heavy stone.

Then suddenly I was in a big room, larger than a barn. Here was much apparatus—including a near duplicate of the device in Ben's workroom.

There below me was a man in a chair, his head clamped into the helmet. I knew instantly this must be Trevor's body. It was shuddering, as Ben settled into it, like a man fitted into a suit of armor.

And where was Trevor? That is—where was…

As a scientist it is hard for me to say it. But after the metaphysical curiosities revealed to me, I will use the term. Where was his *soul*?

Then I remembered. *"Your friend came after me—but I was warned. I have put him in the crystal box, where he circles forever, broken in time."*

Trevor's selfhood, his conscious, was in "a crystal box"…somewhere near.

I saw the object: it was almost a cube; there were transparent wires, like cables of glass, entering it, and a complexity of crystalline forms around them.

I thought I heard his voice echo to me from there.

"Glyneth. Where am I?"

I looked back at Trevor's physical body. Settled into Trevor's husk, Ben, outwardly, looked like Trevor: A medium sized man, a bit plump, pale and blond, wearing the unpleasantly informal trousers, shirt and sweater they often wear in this time.

He set out, clearly in a hurry to fulfill a mission.

I kept after him, drifting above and behind. I found I could pass through walls, with a little effort. I was careful not to be too close upon his heels. I did not want him to sense me.

I watched, and followed, watching as he went to find the woman.

How did I know about her? In this form, glimpses are given us; at times glimmering crevices open between a maybe and a likely, and we see along trembling and temporary corridors of possibility. Extending out from Ben, in a corridor of likelihood, I saw an image of him standing over a woman in a hospital bed. Squeezing her throat. Who was she? Perhaps she was the caretaker of the laboratory.

Could I awaken her? Could I contact her somehow? Ask her to help me?

I drifted like an aethereal bloodhound along after him, kept on course by will alone. A whole angry cosmos of dislocation and disorientation wanted to tear me away from the pursuit. But I have always been a strong woman.

The hospital. I drifted in after him, down the corridors behind him, through a door

And I saw him bend over her, Ellen Lo: I saw it on the card near the bed. She lay there, mostly dead.

I saw him begin to do to her what he had done to me.

I saw that she was empty—she was just a husk. Her consciousness had left her. Was her body broken?

How to take the next step?

Then a bizarre and ungainly shape formed, only half there, in the shadows to one side…

A true Yithian. It spoke to me but not in English. It was not in language as we understand it. It spoke in concepts, in pictures. I was able to translate it into English.

Few of my folk are aligned with this man. Some of us have dignity, and will not debase ourselves. This man will open the door for the League, and in due course will come death for millions, in this timeflow. And slavery will come to all others.

My strength ebbs. I cannot fight this man. I have repaired the cellular linkages in this woman's brain; I was able to heal some of her body, but I am weak from the process. I could not save her from the death of her selfhood. The woman's consciousness is gone; her brain is empty…it is awaiting you. I can only show you the next step.

There: do you see it? The line of blue… Enter the blue line of force… and I will send it into this female of your race…

I saw a quivering, intermittent stroke of blue lightning, stretching from the Yithian to Ellen Lo.

Enter a blue stroke of lightning? Will it not destroy what remains of me?

Could I trust a conical creature, spouting rubbery limbs, one of which ended in a face?

Trust was the next step…

I followed the blue lightning, using my will and mental focus. My mind turned blue; mind burned with far too much energy. Then I was lying on my back…Feeling heavy, solid, achingly alive.

In a moment I was opening my eyes…I was lying on the hospital bed, staring up at the madman who was poised close to me—he had not Ben's face. But I knew it was Ben's hands tightening on my throat.

I clutched at the table nearby. There was a thick white glass vase with sagging lilies in it.

Energized by terror, I used every bit of strength I had and crashed the vase hard into the side of his head. It shattered.

He shouted wordlessly and fell over.

I sat up, and felt something tugging at me. It was a needle attached to a tube, thrust in my right arm. I pulled it free, and staunched the small wound with bandages laid on the table nearby.

Then I hid moved the vase and called for help. "My friend's fallen— he's hurt himself!" I shouted, as the nurses entered.

They stared at me. I have never seen anyone so astonished. They had thought me brain-dead.

It took these fuddled women some time to agree to release me. They argued against it, but I insisted. They found me a change of clothes left by a patient and they fit well enough. When they went about their paperwork, I slipped way, taking with me a ring of keys I found on a hook near the counter, and located a storeroom. There I found what I needed. Then I re- turned to the nurses, giving them the key ring as if I'd found it on the floor, and obtained my release.

But I did not go far.

I waited outside…and soon saw Ben walking stiffly out of the hospital. Ben—in Trevor's body.

What had Ben told the nurses? Had he let them accept my story, that he had felt dizzy—had fallen and hit his head, shattering the vase? It seems likely. Simplest.

His head was bandaged. Watching from the shadows as he paused on the walkway outside the hospital, I could see his mouth moving—I could read his lips. He was cursing. And he was talking to someone who wasn't there. Or perhaps they were merely unseen.

I followed him once more, this time in a physical body.

He went back to the laboratory—for it was approaching dawn, and he had work to do there.

The trek was perhaps half a mile past periodic steel posts topped by incandescent lamps. We traipsed, one well behind the other; his head probably throbbed as much as mine. I felt achy and strange; indeed my new body was bruised by the fall. I suspected there were hairline fractures in my left shoulder bone. But with each step I felt a little more comfortable in Ellen Lo's husk. Soon we'd reach the Miskatonic campus. Ben approached a big, stark, square building of white concrete and glass and chromium. I saw no one there at this late hour. A few lights were lit in its lobby, for appearances.

I hurried after him; once he heard me following, and turned, but I slipped behind a statue of the university's founder—what a grim faced man the founder had been! He seemed to scowl down at me.

Ben must have shrugged the sound off, for when I looked again he was at the door.

He entered the building, using what I now understand to be a key card; the door closed slowly behind him, slowly enough I was just able to catch it.

I waited, holding my breath, but he didn't look back. And when he'd gone up the stairs, I followed—not too quickly.

The laboratory door stood open. Inside, Ben, in Trevor's body, was bent over equipment below an enormous apparatus.

I crept up behind him; he heard, started to turn—and I threw all my weight upon him. Quite startled, he went down, though he was much bigger than I.

The syringe was ready in my hand—we have syringes in my century, and we certainly have morphine. Both had been easy to find in the hospital, with the nurses so distracted.

Remembering how he had stabbed me in the belly, I jabbed the syringe hard into the back of his right shoulder, stabbing through the clothing, and depressed the plunger. He yelled a curse and tried to shake me off—snapping the needle off in his flesh. He howled. And the drug had already gone home.

Ben threw me off and I scrambled back away from him.

He came roaring at me…then stumbled, beginning to stagger. He stopped, gaping at me, blinking owlishly. "Is that you, in there? The damned fool of a woman who…?"

He did not finish the question.

The lethal dose took effect, and he fell, limply, onto his face.

I crept over to him, and, my hands shaking, felt his pulse. It was irregular. Stopping. Starting…stuttering.

In a few moments, I knew, his heart would stop. I prayed there was enough time.

I had the other syringe, too. I waited…until Ben's heart stopped entirely. I sensed him sliding away from Trevor's dying body…

I laughed, and said, "Goodbye, Ben!"

Then I injected Trevor's dead body with the other syringe—adrenaline. I turned Trevor's body over and listened with my ear to his chest. Nothing. Then his back arched, his breast bone thumping my head.

And his heart began beating again…too late to save Ben, happily. My late husband had already spiraled away into the aether.

And still I was not done. I had a picture in my mind, an imprint from the my Yithian ally…

I shattered the crystalline box by swinging a metal chair. Trevor was freed…but unsure where to go.

The Yithian flickered into view…and guided Trevor.

It sent him home—to his own body.

* * * *

The Journal of Glyneth Berling
March 2, 2015
Arkham, Massachusetts

Trevor recommended this new journal as therapy; as another way to adapt.

We both needed a further visit to the hospital, after the events of that awful day. Trevor had a long needle broken off in his shoulder, and a concussion; I had painful hairline fractures and massive bruising, despite the partial healing the Yithian had given me.

How curious indeed to be in the body of a young Asian woman, in the 21st century.

I have wondered if Ben tried to go back to his body. Trevor assures me Ben could not have gone back to his body before it burned up in the fire—he'd have conflicted with his other time traveling aetheric self. He may have tried, but he'd have been destroyed by the attempt.

Sometimes I ponder the ugly fate of my own original husk—my body burning up along with the house. I shudder, involuntarily picturing it blackening, blistering; I try to turn my mind from the image.

I must let go of that Glyneth. I am another Glyneth, now, though for awhile I must pretend to be Ellen Lo.

"Now." I have come to revere *nowness*. I hope never to trade *now* for any other timeflow again. I wish to live in whatever now time gives me.

Yes, as a naturalist, I deplore this age of extinctions; the destruction of species after species of wild animal due to the blind expansion of a greedy civilization.

But still, I am happy, because I am with Trevor. He looks into my eyes and knows me for who I am. I see in his eyes the Trevor I knew in 1878, though then his mind had been imprisoned in Ben's body.

Trevor is plump, his hair thin, his eyes small and fingers stubby. That is simply Professor Trevor Peaslee. And I will always love him.

When we came back from the hospital, we took the 21st century variant of Ben's electro-psychic apparatus, and the modifications to the Laser Pump, and disassembled the lot in Trevor's apartment.

As we disassembled the device, I felt something draw my attention to the window. I peered out into the night and thought to glimpse, in a kind of mist beyond the glass, the dim shape of my Yithian ally. I felt it emanating approval. It spoke to my mind, wordlessly but clearly.

No more, it seemed to say. *The League is destroyed. Our era is time-locked now. No more from us. We shall pass into infinity...*

And then it was gone.

* * * *

The Journal of Glyneth Berling
April 7, 2015
Arkham, Massachusetts

Today, Trevor rented a very large safety deposit box in a bank vault. There we took the essential parts to Ben's disassembled apparatus.

And there, too, we locked away the metal shod book; the ancient codex found in the Australian ruins.

"Someday, when the time is right, I will give it to archeologists," Trevor said, as he turned the key in the lock.

"Oh yes?" I gave him a skeptical smile. "What day would that be, Trevor? When will humanity be ready for it?"

He sighed, and took my hand. "I don't know. I really do not know."

Perhaps Nathaniel Peaslee's book will never again see the light of day. And, this side of death, we are not likely to ever again journey to the hidden dimensions.

It doesn't matter. We have other worlds to explore together, Trevor and I. In one another.

A Tourist in Hell
by john shirley

Have you ever noticed how a great fire
makes the sunset finer;
it fills the sky with sulfurous ash
—makes a sundown's colors shinier.
Have you ever noticed how
a fit of fury makes a moment brighter;
it burns in the blood and somehow
makes our grip on life much tighter.
So it is when I choose to visit
the feverish plains of Hell,
what I envisage isn't only
the will of the dark angel;
No—I am gladdened like a tourist,
on seeing the Grand Canyon;
or perhaps it's like harvesting
a field of wild abandon.
You see, I'm just a tourist in Hell
merely touring Hades itself;
There's a comfortable hotel
for a tourist in Hell.
How lovely the dancing flames
that trim the river of fire;
sweet is the smell of burning names
from the eternal pyre.
Pleasant to have our picnic
beside the lake that roils with hate;
where seething regret's intrinsic
to realizing "it's too late!"
We drink an unctuous red wine
from the harvest of the season:
from the crushing of the grapes
of the failure of reason.
And then my dear it's your turn
to add to the infernal light;
How pretty when I feed you to the fire—
how charming my delight.

Nodding Angel
by John Shirley

Beth watched her Mama pat the top of the grave down with the rusty shovel. "But Mama, how'd you know he was a bad person? You just met him."

"I knew because of the angel." Mama glanced up at her. "Didn't you see her?"

"No. I didn't. I don't know what it means, that nodding angel. You told me once but—I'm not clear in my mind."

"Girl, don't be simple. You're almost seventeen. You have come into the woman's time and bled to show it. You should be able to *see* the angel. And in this family we know about the nodding angel. You were told."

"I was told when I was little, and I didn't understand it. Aunt Dora never spoke about it. I've never seen no nodding angel, neither, not anywhere, nor over no one."

"She never spoke of it? She's ashamed of our chosen way, is she?" She leaned on her shovel and glared, shaking a wisp of white hair from her eyes. "That woman, she's truly your father's sister—and it's well she died."

"Don't say that!"

Mama's voice rose to a strange mix of a shriek and a whisper. "It's well she died, I say! She connived with the judge to take you away, and got away with it too, those years and years—I should've…" She shook her head. "It's well the lung fever took her."

Beth felt a stinging in her eyes; a hot ball of anger in just under her ribcage. "Dora was good to me. She kept me in shoes and sent me to the schoolhouse. I don't know nothing about all this." Beth peered deeper into the woods, where lengthening shadows were reaching out to clasp the older graves.

"All you need to know now is the dance, and the song. I showed you how. Now you dance and sing, and then we'll go back and have our soft drinks. I got that orange soda pop you like."

Beth truly did not want to dance and sing here. It didn't feel like a good thing to be doing that funny little dance on a grave, singing in the beech woods, at late summer dusk, in her bare feet—Mama insisted on the bare feet. "I don't think I can do that. You need to do it, Mama."

Mama made a snort of exasperation. "It *must be done by a maiden*. Why can't you do it? Ain't you still a virgin?"

"I still am. Yes." She didn't know how to explain her reluctance Mama would accept it. Mama was a small wiry woman, but strong in every way, and would not accept anything she didn't want to hear. She would not want to hear from Beth that doing the dance, singing the song on the grave—that it would be crossing a bridge that would crumble into a big hole the moment she got over, and there was no way back.

"This man…" Beth looked at the grave. "How'd you do it?"

Mama sniffed. "With the pickaxe. One good swing from behind and it's done. Not much more than punching through a punkin' shell."

"And all these others?"

"Mostly the pickaxe." She seemed to reflect a moment, then added, "Poison once, and twice a butcher knife."

"And Daddy?"

Mama looked away; her mouth worked like she was chewing for a moment. Finally she looked defiantly back at Beth and said, "The pickaxe. The angel was there, girl, clear as a neon sign, nodding right over him. So I had to do it. And I was glad to. He talked of taking you away, and selling you to them slavers. He was a wicked man. You know that."

Beth didn't say anything. She had suspected, seeing these graves for the first time today, that Daddy wasn't plain old gone away, like she'd been told. He was dead, killed like some passing stranger chosen by Mama.

Now she knew.

From two years old, Beth had heard had her father was wicked. Mama had said he had been planning to sell her into white slavery, give her to men who would misuse her. But she had begun to doubt the story, after Aunt Dora took her—Dora being so kind, and daddy's sister. Still, even now, it was easier to believe he was evil than that he wasn't. Thinking of him in one of these graves, it was better if he *was* evil; that her Mama only killed what was evil, like she said.

All at once, Beth ached to see the angel. Maybe that would help. If she could just see the angel that once…

"You will see the nodding angel, come the time," Mama said confidently, as if she'd heard Beth thinking. "We always do, the women of this family. *Then* we know. We know what we're here to do." Mama closed her eyes. "The nodding angel is beautiful, and she smiles like heaven shines." Her voice was growly with emotion. "She appears over the person's head, and I look at her, asking the question without having to say it right out…" Mama broke off, opened her eyes, and wiped some sweat from her forehead with the back of her hand, leaving a streak of grave dirt.

An owl hooted. It was early for them to be out.

Mama went on, "…And the angel points down at them, and smiles, and nods to me, like to say: *Yes they're evil, they're bad, they must die.*" She flapped a gnarled hand at the other graves in the twilit woods. "Now, girl—this digging and filling, it's got me breathless. But the rule says I got to do that alone. You do your part now." Mama sat cross legged on the ground, close by the grave, letting go of the shovel so it tipped, made a slight ringing sound when it hit the base of a tree. "You do the dance I taught you, and sing the song, while I rest."

Beth held back. She could just run off….

But Mama looked at her in that warning way she had. Like little pilot lights in the back of her eyes.

So Beth stepped onto the grave, and did the brief dance. It resembled dancing a box step with an invisible man. And she sang the brief song, as Mama sat there, breathing raspily, waiting.

"We know what you was," Beth sang, in that slow old tune Mama said was from Scotland. *"We know what you done. You see now what you was, you see now what you done. Angel she smiled and she said yes; it ain't no more and ain't no less."*

Just like that, over and over, three times exactly.

Mama was frowning at the woods. She didn't seem ready to stand up yet, so Beth stepped off the grave, and asked softly, "Who sang over daddy's grave, when you did him?"

"My sister Lorraine," Mama said dreamily. "I wasn't a maiden no more, 'cause I met your daddy—so I needed her. Just that one time helping me, then she run off and married. I had to wait for you." She chuckled. "I knew you'd be a girl." She fell silent for long enough that the shadows reached noticeably farther. Then Mama sighed. "Had to wait so long to see the angel nodding again. Then you came home and that long haired fella come walking by. And it's no accident he came along. You were sent to help me and he was sent to die. Now—help me up." She stretched out a hand.

Beth stared..at the angel appearing over her Mama's head. For a blink of time it seemed like the angel had a lean furred face, and goat's eyes. But that face melted away, and there was only the beautiful woman's face, with blue eyes and golden hair and a smile shining like heaven's light. Beth felt a sudden sureness; an unprecedented conviction within herself.

But she had to ask the question. *Should I?*

The angel nodded in reply and pointed. And Beth nodded back.

Then she picked up the shovel, and hit her Mama with the sharp edge of the shovel blade, in the side of the head.

A rush of pleasure went through Beth, when the blade struck; a pleasure that filled the world.

Mama slumped, and Beth jabbed the shovel blade into the spindly neck to be sure. She did that again and again, till the metal had gone all the way through.

When Beth was done, the angel faded slowly away, still nodding.

Beth dug the grave, and did the burying, and did the dance, and sang, and went to see if that young man up the road would take her, so she could have a baby.

She would need someone to do their part. It wouldn't be such a long wait. A small girl could be taught to dance. The women in her family just about always had girls.

And the angel would always need someone who could see her nodding.

Calaphais and the Demon Malchance

by John Shirley

The merchant Calaphais was coming to an agreement with the seller of dates, Mustapha of Caesarea, when their negotiations attracted the notice of the demon Malchance. A fiend of the air, Malchance had blown in on an ill wind, a sour meteorological note, provoking the village camels to lift their heads and snort, the village dogs to sniff the air and whine, and its old women to cringe into their robes, making the sign against evil.

Seeing the crones make the sign, Malchance laughed to himself as he drifted invisibly by. He waved back at the women, though they were unaware that he was fluttering his unseen fingers. He regarded the sign against evil as a species of greeting; he regarded it thus ironically, yet deep in the folds of his inmost nature he took an obscure comfort in seeing it.

On an impulse—he was a creature of impulse and curiosity, little else—Malchance tarried to observe the traders. Calaphais, a man with a pointed black beard and red and blue turban, the colors of his turban signifying his spiritual sect, was sitting on a carpet in the silken pavilion of the date seller, pretending to argue about the price. In fact, Calaphais knew that this white-bearded Mustapha, whose hands were beginning to crook with rheumatism, had recently lost his eldest sons, one to a feud not of his making and one to the ague; that without his sons to oversee the date-pickers, his harvest was diminished. Some other man might have used this intelligence to lower the price he would pay for dates, knowing Mustapha for a desperate man, but as the wife of Calaphais had once said, while she lived, "He is not 'some other' man." So Calaphais now allowed himself to be persuaded that he must pay much more than he Mustapha had secretly hoped…

Malchance was both bemused and irritated by Calaphais's generosity. Malchance regarded generosity as aberrant, even perverse behavior. It incensed him when men behaved unnaturally, though if you had interviewed him, and he were inclined to honestly answer, he could not have said why. Of course all attempts to interview demons are prone to return only perverse responses, unless the demon is bound by some magical sigil, some unbreakable imprint of Solomon's, and even then their replies are of little value, since they understand so little themselves. Calaphais had once read an account of a mystical interrogation carried out by the magus Belafelonce, who had bound a demon, Repulsivoraq, to reply "truly and without deception," and it was truly and without deception that Repulsivoraq replied, to Belafelonce's question regarding how many angels God commanded and where one might reliably encounter one, "You may as well ask how many zebras are green and blue, and how one may see an ape take to wing. No such exist except in the mind of man. There is no God but Vengeance; those beings who exist are but you transient ones creeping below, the Hungry Mind of the Harsh Glare above—and the wilderness of sublime beasts such as myself, between…" Belafelonce believed the demon, supposing the creature knew more of the ultimate reality than he did himself, but this is both true and untrue at once, like so many other things. Misdirected in this fashion, Belefelonce thereafter went awry, and came to a bad end.

But it is the demon Malchance who concerns us, and it was he who followed Calaphais from the tent of Mustapha of Caesarea, to the oasis near the village where the merchant's caravan awaited him. "I have a bad feeling upon me," Calaphais said to his jet-black camel driver, Norigula, when he found him in the shade by the murky pool. "The whole way here I smelt death, though no carrion was apparent; I labored to walk, as if there were weighted chains on my ankles; now my own camels shy from me, and when I look around I see only the tattered appearance of the trees, the offal on the ground by the goat slaughterer's camp, the flies and the dust. I can see nothing more—where once I saw beauty."

"You have a malady," said Norigula, backing away. "The plague is upon you. God be with you. Find another to be your camel driver."

But it was not plague that had hold of Calaphais—he was merely feeling the effects of demonic breath on the back of his neck. So full of ire and spirit-bile was Malchance, that his proximity alone was enough to curdle fresh milk, or a man's soul.

Demons, however, are a bit more than a collection of malevolences. They are sentient creatures, and as such, each has a personality, characteristics, peculiarities. Malchance had three dominant peculiarities: impulsiveness, curiosity and a dislike of unpredictability in the world around him. He liked to be the very soul of unpredictability himself, but could not abide it in others. Men and women were on the whole predictably prone to be fractious, selfish, gluttonous, dishonest, proud; a demon's role, as Malchance saw it, was to fan these small flames, so that feuds and wars, those delightful displays, were combusted. It was Malchance's cousin Miseruppulis, who had cultivated the very feud that had taken Mustapha's son from him. Human predictability made these little triumphs possible. But from time to time Malchance encountered exceptions, like Calaphais. Following him to the oasis, he had looked into Calaphais's memories, and saw that he had been smitten with an errant fantasy, as a boy, of an encounter with the divine, which had induced in him this anomalous behavior, so that consistently through life Calaphais had behaved benevolently toward other men, and, against all odds, had somehow thrived.

This unpredictability set Malchance's teeth on edge –for though he was an astral being, make no mistake, he had teeth—and his natural curiosity drove him to try to get to the bottom of Calaphais's deviancy, so that he could uproot it.

And so Malchance followed Calaphais as, troubled in mind, he walked out into the desert to pray, the demon mulling the satisfaction of his curiosity. When Calaphais—still feeling himself dogged by an unknown misery—had reached a hummock on which a tuft of brown grass shuddered in the wind of the dusk, Malchance drew into himself drifting grit and bits of seed and drifting camel hair, so that this detritus took on the shape of his body, and in this way he made himself known to Calaphais. His appearance was of a lean winged biped, with wings of leather but shaped like pinions of vultures, with four eyes arranged into a diamond-shape on his bristly head, a drooping multifanged mouth wide across his torso, extremities ending in three-pronged talons.

Calaphais drew back in alarm, asking, "Is this indisposition in me bringing about hallucination?"

"You see what you see," said Malchance, his words coming from the wide mouth across his belly. "You will not for long question your senses: I will shortly make myself known to you in terms you cannot deny. Pain is a convincing witness."

"It is the indisposition itself," Calaphais marvelled, "revealed and voluble!"

Malchance bowed—demons are not without a sense of style. "It has come to my attention, Calaphais of Alexandria, that you are an anomaly. Anomalies in the natural order torment me. I cannot abide them. I could dispose of your own case by simply murdering you, in a trice. But it occurs to me that if I can show you the error of your ways, you would be of great use. You are received as a wise man into the tents of sheiks and the palaces of kings—you could counsel these potentates to war."

"You are very good to offer me a choice," said Calaphais, clasping his hands to still their trembling, "but I must regretfully decline."

"You decline too soon—I have not yet begun to persuade you!" declared Malchance.

So saying he sprang forward and took to the air above the cringing Calaphais, his wings raising a dust devil with their beating; he seized the merchant by the neck with his lower talons, and drew him into the sky. As Malchance jerkily rose, he had no more need of visibility, and he allowed the grit and detritus to drain out of him; by the time Calaphais was as high in the air as the top of a palm tree, a local shepherd, spying him up there, perceived only a man flying upward, spasming like a fish on an unseen line as he ascended into the air, seemingly propelled skyward by his twitchings.

The shepherd fled in horror, but Calaphais could make no escape, and soon gave off his struggle, resigning himself to death. Death, however, would have been a kindness, and kindness is not something disbursed by devils. Instead, Malchance flapped yet higher, to just beneath the clouds, flexing his talons to induce greater discomfort in his prey. The demon had sunk his claws into the soft flesh under Calaphais's jaws, not quite crushing his throat nor yet severing arteries, but producing much bleeding and extreme discomfort.

Calaphais writhed in voiceless agony, for what seemed ages, though in fact it was 77 seconds.

Then Malchance let go his hold and Calaphais fell, turning end over end, the pain momentarily lessened but replaced now with the terror of plunging from on high toward the spinning, stony land below. He might have been relieved at this opportunity for a quick death, but his instinct over-ruled his good sense, and he clawed at the air as if to find a hold in vapor.

"Now!" Malchance demanded, spiraling down beside him. "Will you submit to my program for your preservation from aberration? Will you prey upon, conspire against, and undermine your fellow man?"

This entreaty only served to restore Calaphais to himself; his soul took counsel with something higher, and he found his self control. Inwardly drawing away from terror, though he continued to tumble earthward, he responded, "No! Death is for me a union with the Beloved! I rejoice in it!"

Snarling, Malchance swooped to sink his talons into Calaphais again, claws this time digging in about the unfortunate merchant's spine, stopping his plunge nigh to the ground, the arrested descent giving Calaphais a terrible wrench, so that he screamed in pain. The demon began to ascend once more, tightening his grip on his victim's spine, giving it a vicious twist now and then, to induce greater pain and finally agony. The word agony is bandied about a great deal—few actually experience it. Calaphais did.

Malchance eased his grip a bit and stopped his wrenching, so that agony subsided to mere excruciating pain, and Calaphais hung from his talons, gasping. "Before I recommence your torment, mortal," said Malchance, answer me this: "What is this Beloved you speak of? How will death do ought by release your soul into the Harsh Glare, where it will be consumed by that rapacious, that cruel light?"

Calaphais thought at first that the demon was making sport of him, trying to sew doubts—but some intuition, perhaps refined by his close proximity to the demon, the presence of Malchance's mind like a dark, foully membranous umbrella, informed him that the demon was genuinely puzzled.

"Why…" Calaphais found it necessary to lick his wind chapped lips, to spit out the blood that was beginning to seethe up from his traumatized insides, before continuing, "Why the Beloved is called… by some…God. The usual…usual notions of God are inadequate—this is no mere person. Nor does it ordain the evil that takes place upon the Earth. God is more like an endlessness of mind. But it wishes us well and calls us back to it."

"What? What do you mean, back to it?"

"Once all beings were part of the pleroma, the body of this Beloved, but Time came about, and flung us from the Beloved, the sparks of our being falling to Earth…or to the airs above the Earth…The Harsh Glare only seems so because of your nature…Oh it is hard to speak, here, demon…my throat closes with blood. I cannot continue."

"Why should I let you continue with lies? I have looked at the Harsh Glare, and I have seen nothing but searing hostility!"

"Because…" Calaphais paused to spit blood. "You are capable of seeing only hostility. If your head is turned to the south, you see only the south. Turn your head to the north, and see…" He began to gag, and spat out additional blood. He gasped for air and managed, "…and see the north…"

Malchance snorted. "I have heard some of the older daemonae speak of something beyond the Harsh Glare and they sound a note of sadness as if they wish they could return there—but I have always known they are trying to get rid of me, they're working against the competition, trying to send me to my destruction! And I note they do not try to return!"

"They cannot bear the…the suffering…it would require. Purification…painful…"

Unconsciousness was bearing down on Calaphais, and Malchance gave him an extra clenching of talons, so that the wave of agony would wake him again. Calaphais cried out a Holy Name, imploring, sobbing, but never cursing.

"Still you keep up the charade!" said Malchance. "Well now…I could torment you thus for hours, perhaps days before you died; I could take you to a mountaintop and slowly pick you apart. The idea has merit! It has appeal! The tang of your suffering, more distilled, would be a spicy delight!

But still could you end all discomfort if you will submit to my will, and destroy your fellow men, who are, after all, but ephemeral, grubby little primates!"

"Do…as you choose," Calaphais wheezed. "I will not submit. Even a thousand years of torment could not…measure against the joy of reuniting with the Beloved. It is as nothing…nothing in comparison…"

Malchance snarled in frustration, sensing that Calaphais was moving into another state entirely. He had reorganized his inner state, so that he was detached from the physical pain, he was oriented to something else—something that Malchance could not quite distinguish. Something that was beyond Malchance's senses, as the highest notes of a violin may be unheard by an old man. "What is this? You dare to withdraw within?"

"I…have merely shifted my attention to something else…a change of…inner polarity…The pain continues but…I am outside it!"

To Calaphais, who had trained inwardly for many years, it was as if the pain induced by the demon's claws had become an edifice, an architectural expression, a spiky, grotesquely designed temple to the god of Despair. Normally a man in terrible pain resides within the edifice; Calaphais had stepped outside it. He could still see it, looming above him. But he was not within its baleful influence.

"We'll see if you can continue to remain outside it!" Malchance cried.

Malchance then flung Calaphais high into the air—yet he kept ahold of him: Malchance's talons were still embedded in Calaphais's flesh, but were now unreeling, outward, on lines, on wires of ectoplasmicksis, that hardened but resilient astral tissue, so that Calaphais was like a kite on a cruel string, with Malchance the kite flyer. When gravity took hold and Calaphais began to fall, Malchance ceased extending the sticky lines from its extremities, and spun about, swinging Calaphais around in taut circles, a considerable distance from him, wheeling him this way and that, cackling gleefully like a wicked child, nearly tearing the merchant's spine from his back—and it would have torn away, too, had not Malchance reeled him back in, clutching him close once more.

"There! Now how do you feel! Was not the pain almost infinitely increased?"

"Nothing is infinite but the Beloved—I reached the far frontier of the pain and stepped beyond it," Calaphais responded, his voice weak. For he was close to dying.

"Bah! You are a stubborn one, that is all! But I shall take you on yon mountain top and shred you, cell by cell, and then we shall see how well you hold out!"

Malchance descended to the rocky, icebound mountaintop, and flung

Calaphais upon it, breaking his legs. Calaphais groaned, but quickly found his inner orientation, and once more stepped outside the grotesque temple of pain. Malchance could see that Calaphais was dying. He might keep him alive, so to torment him longer, but there was something about the game that was deeply unsatisfying—Calaphais's refusal to identify with his suffering seemed to suck all the joy from the act of torture, for Malchance.

"Poor Malchance!" the demon muttered, sadly. "I am cheated!"

"My soul is about to leave this broken...shell..." Calaphais rasped. "Come with me, to see...come with me...follow me...see if I lie..."

"A man who is deceived does not know he is lying," Malchance growled. "But now I see it is too late to keep you here...at least I have ended your aberrant life. Now there is one less troublesome exception... Now your soul rises to be consumed by the Harsh Glare!"

Malchance watched intently, though he had observed the phenomenon many times, as Calaphais's soul sprang from the top of his head: the rough outline of a man, elaborated in light. Usually these souls were faint, filmy, tenuous things, scarcely there at all—but Calaphais's soul was considerably more substantial than any Malchance had seen before. This further anomaly, and the remarks Calaphais had made—and made sincerely, Malchance knew—piqued the demon's curiosity. And since curiosity was one of his driving attributes, he was driven to follow the soul of Calaphais, as it ascended upward. He would watch from a safe distance, he told himself, as the soul was consumed by the Harsh Glare.

Upward, upward, the soul went—or rather, outward. For the light that demons called the Harsh Glare encompassed the world, in every direction, not simply "up."

Malchance gave chase, like a hawk pursuing a smaller bird, up and up. He had tried, before, catching these souls and eating them—it could be done with some souls. Some were slow and ragged and easily caught. There was little taste to them. But others were rapid and slippery, could not be grasped as they ascended...

Calaphais's effulgence rose through the atmosphere, to the edge of the void, where the overarching shimmer of light—a particular light visible only to spirits–was always in play. When Malchance approached this radiance, turning his eyes toward it, he quickly recoiled, hissing—a harsh glare indeed. He turned instinctively away...

But curiosity spoke up again. Why not go a little farther, and see this impudent, transitory Calaphais consumed by the Harsh Glare? It would be amusing to see him burst into flames like a moth at a candle.

Malchance tried to look away from the Harsh Glare, but continued to ascend, following the fleeting, flitting form of the soul of Calaphais...

He turned his attention to Calaphais, who appeared to be singing a song with his mind as he rose…

The pain continued to mount for Malchance as he ascended—yet Calaphais, he saw, was not burning up, but was becoming more and more substantial, as if the light were entering, combining with him, refining and restoring him, making him more what he already was at the same time as bringing him into intimate relation with itself…

"Calaphais!" Malchance called. "How comes it that I am in pain, I feel my wings begin to burn—my pinions are smoking, seething away!—and you, by contrast, are enjoying this place, are flourishing here? I demand an answer!"

"You are turned to face south, my poor friend!" shouted Calaphais back, from close above. "Face north! Look inward and outward at once! Assume that all you thought true was wrong and look to see what is—and you will be set free!"

Malchance watched Calaphais rising, the soul's effulgence increasing, its joy redoubling; and the demon realized, then, that the real reason he had chosen Calaphais for torment was envy; was a secret suspicion that Calaphais had indeed known a secret…a secret Malchance ached to know.

So Malchance ascended further, gazed into the terrible illumination that had been called the Harsh Glare, and threw aside all assumptions of knowing, but only looked, simply looked…

There came a flash of intense light around Malchance, then, and he was incinerated—outwardly. His outward form was instantly burned away, but inside, as the ashes drifted down, was revealed a small creature, winged and vaguely human, a creature without memories or, as yet, a name. But this inner fetus was able to ascend into the light, to bask in it, to listen to the voice that called it closer, so that it might begin, might seek a new adulthood.

Calaphais, meanwhile, in a higher place, was greeting old friends and ancestors. Soon, however, he drew aside from them, for a time, to pray for the soul that had once been hidden inside the demon Malchance.

✗

The Egregious Error of Werner Witherbye

by John Shirley

He found her as the iris bloomed
and the morning sunlight swelled;
He spotted her as Spring rites loomed
And sighing pines were felled.

She stood upon a hunter's run,
red blooms about her growing;
Her hair gleamed like a dawning sun—
his desire too was glowing.

He doffed his hat, knelt on the sward,
begged the music of her name;
he swore he would draw forth his sword
to protect her from all shame.

Quoth she, "I am called Erizand,
I'm a maid of Sere Legee;
I've seen ought but this forest land—
how I long to know the sea!"

"Maiden, I am Witherbye—
Call me Werner if you please;
I'll escort you low and guard you high
as we journey to the seas."

Her eyes alit, she trusted him,
And they traveled to the west;
they tarried at a lonesome inn:
devils carved upon its crest.

He gave her golden wine to drink
in a goblet he'd prepared;
she felt her heavy head then sink—
his hands upon her hair.

She was no more a maiden
when he'd done his wicked deed;
He was base and he was craven:
when planted he his seed.

But a seed may grow a blossom
or may grow a briar thorn;
and Erizand woke before him,
on that rainy April morn.

Pain and blood awoke him:
and he beheld a demon's claws:
the beast laughing as it choked him,
and gripped him in its paws.

She stroked her scaly demon,
her soft white hands atwitch;
she said, "My foolish young one,
you have soiled a maiden witch.

"To fly far from my family
was e'er my girlish dream;
to flee away from destiny
was my naive scheme.

"Now I know what mortals are,
my fate must be embraced;
but you will scream and you will char,
for all that I'm disgraced."

She instructed her familiar,
an artist at its art;
The cad watched in a mirror
as its blades exposed his heart.

The servants heard the shrieking
and fled into the fields;
the old inn walls were creaking
as if they too would yield.

By parting flesh and cracking bone
was Witherbye revealed;
until his quivering soul alone
was finally unsealed.

Then the demon plucked his soul
like an oyster from a shell;
saw that it was a lump of coal
—to stoke the fires of Hell.

And so ensued the endless doom
for Werner Witherbye;
his suffering woven on the loom
of predatory lies.

Let all men who would deceive
—and think only of their glands—
learn that soon they too will grieve...
in the claws of Erizand.

That Ambulance Again
by John Shirley

"It's that ambulance again, Allie," said Syd as they drove home. They'd lost a good deal at the casino, which always made him feel a little sick inside, and they'd each had a couple of cocktails over the limit. Two middle aged people, Syd thought, who should know better. "Same one following me every time we've been to the casino. Twice a month for three months—same vehicle number on it, same guy at the wheel. That albino guy."

"He never actually bothers us. Some guy, who owns an ambulance—and he's crazy, is all. He'll forget about us eventually."

They stopped at a red light and Syd watched the ambulance in the rearview. The albino was pale enough to look like a ghost the dim light. "Maybe you're right, he's just crazy—but crazy can be dangerous." Syd reached under the dashboard, pulled the revolver out of the holster bolted up there.

"Syd—what the hell are you going to do with that?"

"It's just to scare him off. I'm going to ask what the hell he's doing."

"Syd, don't!"

But Syd was already out of the idling car. He walked with the gun behind him back to the ambulance waiting for the light.

The passenger side window rolled down and the albino—just an ordinary white haired, red-eyed albino—looked calmly out at him. Seeming, if anything, a little amused. "Yes sir?" the man said, in a reedy voice. "Can I help you?"

"You can tell me why you follow my car from the casino every time we go. Been going on a long time. It's creepy and it's getting old."

The ambulance driver shrugged. "I'm followin', mister, because something bad's coming and you're gonna need me here, whatever it is. I always know when something's coming. You'll both need it. Even if I can't save you."

"Something bad. What the hell are you talking about? You threatening me?"

"Oh no sir. As for what's coming, and exactly when—I don't know what and when. Except...when you're driving back from the casino. Something will happen. Could be anything from a sinkhole opening up, or a truck hits you, or something falling off a building on your car. All I know about it is that in involves your car." He leaned back in his chair, staring at his hands on the wheel. Softly he said, "I have a responsibility 'cause...I always know..."

"Okay, that's enough!" Syd pointed the gun at the albino. "E-fucking-nuff! Over! Done! You do it again, next time...and I'll...bang!"

He lowered the gun and stalked back to the car. Climbing behind the wheel he said, "You were right, Allie, he's crazy."

The light had turned green and was now turning yellow. He accelerated through it.

He glanced in the mirror. The ambulance was following, pretty close. "And there he is again!"

Syd accelerated, really booking now, and the ambulance followed. Its lights came on—and Syd stared at the whirling red and blue lights in the mirror.

"Don't stare into the rear view at this speed, Syd, you're going into the wrong lane, you're gonna to hit that truck! Syd, look out—!"

That was the last thing she ever said.

* * * *

The ambulance driver walked up to the burning vehicles and had a look. The truck driver had blood on his forehead, but seemed okay. But the other car was burning. They were both already dead in there—a blessing they didn't have to burn to death—and there was a lot of blood splashed around.

"It's funny," the albino murmured. "It was that way with all the others, too. They're looking into the rear view—and they hit something. Sometimes a wall, sometimes they go off a bridge. It's sure funny it works out that way. Well—same as always. Nothing I can do for dead folks. But I can always be there if they don't die. That'd sure be a change..."

The ambulance driver turned away, got into his ambulance, called in the wreck, and then drove away, heading to a bar across town. There was someone there who was going to drive home in a few minutes. They would need his help.

You See Me as You See Me
by John Shirley

You see me as you see me
when I'm seen as you suppose;
You gaze on bonny babies
who become two squawking crows;
You see me as you think me,
as you imagine me to be;
You glance upon a tree-trunk:
it grins with gnarl and glee;
You see me as you dream me—
your mind flitters here and there—
You see me as a dragon
in the autumn-misted air;
But I am forever stealing
my appearance from your thoughts—
I'm draped in your myth-making
(whatever you've been taught);
You see me as a leering goat:
fiery horns and seven eyes—
for I gladly shift my form to fit
imagination's guise;
You see me in a journal
of the arcane and the weird:
I am the writhing tentacle;
A ghost with living beard;
It's well that you imagine
all the faces you devise;
I'd rather you didn't know me—
best you simply don't get wise;
were you to see the chaos
that plots and wishes ill,
and know it for projection—
I could no longer eat my fill;
This way I feast on all of you
who lift candles in the night:
I seem safer when I'm written
—but then I snuff the light...

And I'll Burn Like a Vampire in the Sun

by John Shirley

I can hear the crash
that made the bruise
of sunset;
I hear the weeping
of wind through the trees;
And the thought
that you might
at last choose
to return to me...?
my cruel lover,
it drives me
to my knees

> *[chorus:]*
> *God help me, she's coming back to me*
> *Oh God, will I never be free*
> *Oh no, it's too late for me to run*
> *I'll burn like a vampire in the sun*
> *like a vampire...*
> *I'll burn in the sun*

I hear the rodents
patter on
the cabin roof:
arrythmia
of my beating heart
I run inside
to pack my
belongings
but again
the endless night starts

And I hear
the nightbird's hopeless longing
and yes I know

it's just trying to warn me
it urges me
to pack my few belongings
and the murmur of the river
agrees

> *God help me, she's coming back to me*
> *Oh God, will I never be free*
> *Oh no, it's too late for me to run*
> *I'll burn like a vampire in the sun*
> *like a vampire...*
> *I'll burn in the sun*

Then gravel crackles
at the coming
of your car
As the horned owl
slowly
blots out the stars
there's no escaping
from your
homecoming
there is no escape
ever
at all

> *God help me, she's coming back to me*
> *Oh God, will I never be free*
> *Oh no, it's too late for me to run*
> *I'll burn like a vampire in the sun*
> *Yes like a vampire...*
> *I'll burn in the sun*

Swords of Atlantis
by John Shirley

For Imaginary Friends

⚔

PART THE FIRST
The Swords of her Heart

CHAPTER ONE

Two young men were running through a dimly lit, frigid tunnel, their panting breaths and skidding boot-steps echoing back to them. The faint light came from outcroppings of glowing rock, its dull green shine reflected in iced-over stalagmites. The Voorhi were in close pursuit of the two Hyperboreans and getting closer, the roars of the subhumans beginning to overtake the echoes. Long legged and slender, Brimm was a few paces ahead of Snoori, his squat, hirsute, and gasping companion. They ran so quickly they passed through their own clouds of visible exhalation.

"They're gaining on us!" cried Snoori, gasping before going on, "Can you do nothing magical?"

Lungs aching from exertion and subzero air, Brimm ransacked his memory for a spell he could apply to the circumstances. Though Brimm had apprenticed to Urgus, he had been driven out by the angry sorcerer before his education was complete, with the result that he was only a patchily trained spellcaster. He could deploy Klockel's Avalanche Invocation to stone elementals, but incautiously disturbing rock spirits would bring a ton of rock on him and Snoori.

The tunnel dimmed ahead; the enormous bare feet of the shaggy Voorhi slapped louder behind them as they began to catch up. The beast-men would surely tear them apart before cooking them. The dimness became shadowy, bringing to mind Filkin's Instant Torchlight. The Voorhi disliked strong light, and despised flame—hence their only illumination was fluorescence. But Instant Torchlight required kindling to start a fire…

Still, there was a possibility—

As if tripping over the thought, his feet chose that instant to lose their traction; he slipped and fell, skidding on the icy floor of the tunnel. Wheezing, Snoori skidded to a stop beside him, helped him stand, and they both instinctively looked back at the Voorhi; at the hunched, ape-limbed halfmen covered with long filthy yellow fur. The creatures would be upon them in seconds behind…

Brimm drew his slim silvery sword but instead of pointing it at the Voorhi he touched its tip to the stony floor, and called out, *"The Fire of the Air Obeys Filkin and Brimm!"* At the same instant he visualized the appropriate rune and directed his internal energy down his arm, into the sword. Light flashed along the slim blade—and burst upward, like a small volcanic explosion.

The Voorhi shrieked, and bumbled into one another as those in front came to a sudden stop, momentarily blinded and afraid.

"Ha!" Snoori said. "I knew you—oh damn." For the flame had shriveled and vanished into the stone, for lack of fuel.

"Come on!" Brimm shouted, and they turned, sprinting down toward the distant oval of blue where the tunnel opened onto daylight.

The mystic fire having vanished, the Voorhi roared at one another, and took up the chase again. They were gaining once more, one bound from bearing their quarry down, when Brimm stopped again, hastily visualizing the rune, calling out the spell, sending the energy down to the rock—terror made his mind wonderfully well focused.

The mystic fire erupted upward, the Voorhi again scrambled backwards, and the two Hyperboreans sprinted to the opening. Even so, the slap of the pawlike feet could be heard as the Voorhi sprinted after them. There was only time to leap, feet churning the air, into the windy void.

Moments later Brimm and Snoori were tumbling into a thick white blanket of new-fallen snow, and rolled head over heels, over and over, a good distance to the valley floor.

They came to a stop in icy cold and bright sun. Brimm lying on his back, gasping at the Northern Lights, Snoori face down, coughing into the snow. The Voorhi, at least, would not follow them into daylight.

Snoori groaned, and turned over on his back. "That was not a dignified retreat, Brimm," he remarked, and sputtered out clots of snow.

"Ah. Something we can agree on."

They remained there, coated in snow and breathing hard, until at last Brimm got to his feet, dug his sword out of a drift, and started trudging toward the saddle-yaks they'd tethered a few hundred paces down the valley.

"Wait!" called Snoori, wiping snow from his beard as he caught up. "Maybe we shouldn't give up! You've got that fiery spell to drive them off—we can search the tunnels for the gold again! We must have missed it! The Voorhi *do* hoard gold, the rumor is quite definite—"

Brimm stopped, and glowered at Snoori. "*Rumor?* You told me you'd confirmed it, that a treasure was assuredly there!"

"Ah—as Uncle Bloor once said, what assurances are there until one grasps the gold or embraces the maiden?"

"Were you not the friend of my childhood, I'd skin you and use your hide to warm myself!" Brimm turned and stalked away.

Snoori sighed and followed, shaking his head. "How sad you make me."

A few minutes trudge, then Snoori shaded his eyes and peered into the distance. "Do you have money for ale, and some dinner? I am quite without funds. It appears we can't even sell the yaks. It looks as if they have been eaten by a tusk lion…"

* * * *

"And precisely why should I go with you to Atlantis?" Brimm asked, scowling about him at the dingy tavern. "You talked me into attempting to loot the den of the Voorhi and nearly got me killed. Perhaps I should I blame the wine we drank that night. Sober, I would never have listened to your ridiculous notions of beast-men hoarding gold."

"I still think we gave up on the Voorhi too soon, Brimm." Snoori wiped ale froth from his ginger beard and went on. "The Voorhi probably had the gold hidden under those enormous heaps of dung."

"Then it can stay there!" Brimm leaned back in the teetering wooden chair, toying with his father's old dagger—he held it between his long index fingers, its dulled point not quite penetrating his pale skin. "In truth, it's more likely the only thing the beast-men hoard is fleas. And I nearly froze in those mountains."

"It wasn't so very cold."

"Bah! You were born with your own coat of fat and fur."

"It's not *fur!* I'm simply gifted of a little more body hair than some men. You're merely jealous, you with your skin like a small boy's." Snoori pouted at his flagon of ale and Brimm glanced about the tavern. There were but two others in the low-ceilinged, sag-floored old tavern: an old man in a bearskin cloak muttering sadly over a goblet and the heavy-browed, greasy woman who brought the ale. She licked her lips and winked at Brimm when he glanced her way.

Brimm shivered, partly from the night's chill and partly from pondering what he might have to do to pay for a pallet in the tavern loft. "How about a fire, innkeeper?" he called. "It's fearful cold in here."

"Why, you have your candles!" she said, her voice creaking at her own wit. "But you may have a hearth fire, if you pay for its making! A mere two groats—if you carry in the firewood!"

A shared leg of tough mutton and two ales had depleted Brimm's resources. He had not even a groat left. He might use Filkin's Instant Torchlight to start a fire in the fireplace—but there was not a stick of wood in it. And he had no wish to make the crone run to the Guardians of Order crying, "Witchcraft! Devilish sorcery!" Some in Hyperborea tolerated sorcery. Some did not.

Snoori looked up at him, his flaring mustaches lifted by a smile. "You wish warmth? Then let us journey south! Atlantis is far to the south, just west of the Pillars of the Gods, and everyone who trades there basks in the glory of the sun!"

Brimm snorted. "Some are *sacrificed* to the glory of the sun, from what I've heard of those southern lands."

He shrugged. "In Atlantis they're more likely to be sacrificed to Poseidon. Occasionally someone is chained to sea rocks as the tide rises. Crabs as big as calves eat them." He raised a finger to forestall Brimm's inevitable reaction. "But—! We need not run afoul of priests and their acolytes! Remember, as a boy I went to Atlantis with my uncle. I have seen it with my own eyes! And truly it is *such* a pleasantly warm place—hot springs bubble through the island. The very ground is warm to the touch!"

Watching the cold plume of his own breath quiver the candle flame, Brimm tugged his father's tattered red velvet cloak closer about his slender shoulders. The thought of going to a warm land had a certain appeal. He was bone tired of Hyperborea, no less weary of Hypexa, Hyperborea's sprawling and most malodorous port city. He had been tired of both for most of his twenty-two years. He had been raised in the shipyards of Hypexa, though his mother—who had given him his fine-boned features and onyx eyes and shiny jet-black hair—was said to have been Thracian. Brimm looked like a foreigner in his own land and was often treated like one. He felt no loyalty to Hyperborea's ice-bound mountains, its rocky shores noisy with querulous sea birds and walruses; he felt no bond with the blond ruffians who made up its seafarers. Was he not refined, a man of the world—had he not studied with Urgus himself, in far Keltia?

He shrugged ruefully, amused at himself. In truth he'd seen little of the great world, beyond Keltia and a settlement on Aquitania. There'd been a few other ports along the rocky coast of Keltica Gaullia. All squalid, muddy, foul smelling.

Atlantis, by contrast, was said to bristle with magnificent castles painted in leaf of gold. He had seen the Atlantean triremes as they snobbishly passed Hypexa by, grand triple-decked ships of mahogany trimmed in ornately carved ivory, with scrollwork touched up with gold; each bore a figurehead of Poseidon gazing at the horizons with eyes of burnished emerald. The sun was indeed said to be friendly on the vast island of Atlantis, and the women were rumored to be friendlier to men of the north than their own mincing, decadent husbands.

Yes. Atlantis had a certain appeal…

But Snoori planned a skulk into some Atlantean fastness after "easy treasure," and in Brimm's opinion, if ever treasure had ever been easy to find, it was already found and spent.

Still—Brimm was a Svell, son of Hosly Svell, with a blood-born obligation to take to the sea. Brimm's name, in fact, was Brimir Svell—his first name meaning "rover." But most called him Brimm the Savant—a nickname not used with by some with irony, thanks to their doubts that he was truly a savant who had studied with Urgus. Yet, it was so. It was also true that he had been expelled after seven seasons, not quite two years, for breaking into the great sorcerer's Arct Scrolls. Did Urgus praise Brimm for his acumen in discovering the secret room? Did he appreciate Brimm's cunning in persuading the guardian—hippogriffs love fresh fish—to admit him into the Arct Chamber?

No! Instead, the intractable old sorcerer had cursed him for his temerity, smiting him with blindness in one eye and a painful limp, a curse lasting an entire year. The maladies had passed away at midnight on the anniversary of his expulsion. A torment, yes, but it was the dismissal that hurt more.

However, Brimm could once more see with two clear eyes; he could stride with steady steps, and just as important, he was one of the few living men schooled to keenness with an Atlantean piercer. His father had taught Brimm well, as Hosly Svell had been taught by his own father; for Brimm's grandfather had made his fortune as a mercenary employed by King Squen, Lord of the Fifth Kingdom of Atlantis. Brimm's father insisted that the slender, finally turned, silver-hued "piercer" was the only sword of its kind north of Atlantis—and few piercers remained in Atlantis itself, the metal's secret having been lost with the death of its forger. The blade was his father's only patrimony to Brimm, apart from the cloak and the chipped old iron dagger. Hosly Svell gambled, drank, and whored away his shipbuilding profits, yet had affected to look down upon Brimm for being cast out of his apprenticeship.

Brimm sighed. It was true, Father had traded his last thing of value, a solid gold Babylonian orb, for Brimm's place in the halls of Urgus, and Brimm had squandered his chances.

Brimm, Urgus declared, had been defeated by his first real battle. "You have been defeated by your own youth. It is the first bridge to win across, and you were driven back; undone by clinging to boyhood. You never crossed the bridge, Brimir Svell."

There had been nothing for it but to prove himself in other tests, in other places. Even one-eyed and limping, Brimm won three duels with experienced warriors. A Kelt and two Hyperboreans went down before the piercer. They were strong, fierce, and slow men with clumsy broadswords and axes of iron. He had carved them up almost at his leisure.

But the duels had left nothing but a sense of sickened obligation. Urgus had sent Brimm home with a bag of silver pieces—and Brimm doled it out by the handful as compensation to the widows of his felled opponents. He had no funds now, and no desire for mere dueling.

Fighting as a mercenary, perhaps defending ships from occasional pirates—that he could do with a will. But thus far the shipmasters had looked on him and laughed. He was tall and lean, more like a willow than an oak; he carried a weapon that, to their eyes, looked like a slim saber made of some light metal better suited for jewelry; a blade sure to break at the first clash. Fragile the piercer was not, he explained; it was in fact stronger than iron, and sharper than iron ever could be.

But they only laughed and waved him away. He felt as if in dismissing his sword, they dismissed Brimir Svell. He seemed too much like his sword, slender, bendable, more like an ornament than a man. Lying on his deathbed, his own father had waved him away. "Take the sword, take your great-grandfather's dagger, take my seafaring cloak, take this silver piece—and go your way, my son."

Brooding over such things awoke pangs within Brimm. He shook his head. Best not to think of it. He needed something to keep his mind busy…

"Very well, then, Snoori. What is this new absurdity you call a plan?"

Excitement in Snoori's eyes joined with reflected candlelight as he leaned forward to whisper eagerly across the table. "On the north side of the great island of Atlantis rise impassible cliffs made of sheer green glass coughed up from a forgotten volcano—but there is one place where rise city ramparts, jutting right over the sea. This is the outer, northern wall of Poseidonia. It is a small realm, one of the ten kingdoms of Atlantis. It is circled with fields and orchards and streams jumping with curious but delicious fish. And there, in an old palace, waits the beauteous Cleito, a princess who has offered ten bushels of gold to any ten men who will become the Swords of her Heart: the champions who will destroy a minor demon set in place by an addle-pated old sorcerer—a sorcerer long dead. But this minor demon remains! Now, all one has to do is join this band, help them slay a demon and they each will receive a bushel of gold and…" He paused dramatically. "…a helmet full of pearls!" He cleared his throat. "Oh, and the bravest of her champions will win her hand—that's just by the by. Why do you look at me that way?"

"I cannot believe you are once more babbling on about winning the hands of princesses!" Brimm shook his head in disbelief. "Gods! How many times at the temple of edification, when you should have been learning your letters, you maundered on about such myths! Nubile princesses awaiting you in some foreign prison!"

"But I have heard the tale of the Cleito from many a sailor! Just yesterday I had it from the captain of a certain ship. He assured me that it's all quite true! And even if it is not all true, Brimm—why, there are ten kingdoms in Atlantis, each with a king who sits at the Atlantean council—and each king needs good men! We could carry spears and bask in the sun and drink the king's wine! Meanwhile—what harm to visit Poseidonia and see if the treasure for the ten is indeed on offer?"

"We have no means to get to Atlantis, even should I agree on so foolish an expedition," Brimm grumbled. He sipped the dregs of his ale and put his empty flagon down in disgust. "We are now entirely without funds."

"Brimm, I am the friend of your boyhood, one of the few who could bear your prideful ways. Would I invite you along on an adventure—an adventure guaranteed to bring riches—had I no means to get us there?"

"What means do you have?" Brimm asked suspiciously.

"Ah…as to that…I have made arrangements with the very captain I mentioned! He needs mercenaries to protect his ship. He needs them tonight, so badly he'll take anyone, even you and your pretty sword! He assures me there will be free food, wine every night, and we may sit at our ease the whole way to Atlantis."

Brimm shook his head. "We'd be fools to trust him."

"Why must you be so cynical? There are trustworthy people in the world, Brimm! They at least are not mythological. Anyway—what else is there for us now?"

Brimm winced. Painful though it was to admit it, Snoori was right about that much: they had few other options. Except, perhaps, laboring—actual *work*. Probably in a tanner's shed.

At that thought, Brimm shuddered.

He was without funds, and he ached to put Hyperborea behind him. Somewhere, in another part of the vast world, fortune awaited him. And Atlantis was said to abound with treasure. Furthermore, there were said to be ancient sorceries at work there. Perhaps he might add to his store of spells…

"Very well," Brimm sighed. "I can think of nothing better."

And so, tugging their cloaks tightly about them, they set out to the harbor. Brimm continued to ask questions; Snoori continued with glib responses. They wended their way through the maze of alleys and backstreets, stepping over offal and reeking puddles, until at last they came into sight of the sea.

Leaning into a sleety wind from the east, Snoori led the way to a vessel at the very end of the docks. A single guttering torch lit the aft, where the captain was muttering with a large crewman.

"Captain Zenk, it is I, Snoori! My companion and I are ready to embark!" Brimm and Snoori made their way over the gangway, heads ducked against the wind. "We shall protect your vessel on the long voyage to Atlantis! Let us seal the bargain with a glass of wine!"

Zenk spread his arms as if they swaggered up to him, as if they were old friends. "You are quite welcome here! But look yonder!" Zenk pointed to the prow.

They turned to look, and the row-master cracked them firmly on their heads from behind, using a long oar as a club, striking them both with a single vigorous stroke.

* * * *

"Snoori, you have turned me into a galley slave," Brimm said bitterly. "Had I more slack in my chain I would strangle you with it." He bent his back for another sweep of the oars, feeling the sun burn another layer of skin from his exposed skin.

"It was not my doing!" Snoori protested. "Did I not take the same knock on the head?"

"*Did you not* tell me that you were confident of the captain—twice, on the way to the harbor! *Did you not* insist that he could be trusted? You repeated it most earnestly—twice, as we took ourselves to the harbor."

"Ah, yes—but there are risks in embarking on a life of adventure. The search for plunder and charming women is a dangerous one."

"You're an idiot. And I'm an idiot for trusting you." Brimm sighed. "I suppose I wanted so badly to get away from Hyperborea...and there seemed no other options, at the time..." A whip snapped and he bent more industriously to the oars.

The sun was high, and they were overdue for their watery noon gruel. Great green waves lifted as if to stare into the galley, and then sank back; clouds curdled darkly on the horizon; dolphins followed their wake, making mad laughing sounds at the two rows of chained men, as if to say *We are free to leap, to cavort, and you must hunch in the sun on a sweat-stained bench.* The manacles were hot from the sunlight, burning Brimm's wrists.

When the galley rose on an almost mountainous billow he glimpsed a green-skinned Nereid, naked but for a filigree of foam. She was riding one of the dolphins as it arched from the sea; she too laughed at him before vanishing into the billows.

"I was astounded, Brimm, to awaken and find myself chained to the rowing bench," Snoori said, as they lifted the oar for another row. "Surprised to find you there too of course," he added, putting his back into rowing as he saw the burly, bow-legged row-master approaching with his whip.

"Or perhaps I might not strangle you," murmured Brimm, as if savoring a new concept. "Perhaps I'll strangle that great whip-bearing ape instead, then take over the ship and leave you chained at the oars. That might be more satisfying."

"Brimm, Brimm, you abuse me! The winds have been fair, we are indeed headed toward Atlantis, and we haven't had to row *constantly*."

"We have rowed most of four days—that feel like four years! My hands are raw. My back is aching. Sunburn blackens me. I am abased! I am a scholar, not a slave!"

"...And they do give us wine in the evening."

"That swill? The rank spoilage from their kegs." He was constantly sick to his stomach but couldn't tell if it was from the stew made from fish offal, the sour wine, the ever-thickening stench of bilge—or the galloping waves. Up the face of one enormous wave they sailed, down another, up and down perpetually. Brimm remembered sailing beyond sight of land with his father, when a boy, to deliver the hulls of ships to Keltia and Iberia, and he had fared well enough; but as the son of the shipmaster he had lolled in the shade of the sails, taking lessons in navigation and cordage. Now he was fallen to the lowest station of sailing men, apart from the cockeyed boy who emptied their stool pots. Chained at the oars in front of him were aging cutthroats, scooped from the gutters of Hypexa; rowing behind him were several witless farmhands, caught by a thump on the head just as he had been.

If it had been a trireme, at least he'd have been under a deck cover, sheltered from the sun. But this was but a *pentekontor,* a two-masted, square-sailed vessel rowed by fifty men, twenty-five to a side; there was a slightly raised deck between, and the shade of the sails scarcely reached Brimm and Snoori.

A shadow did fall over him then—that of the row-master. "Keep rhythm, dog!" snarled the row-master, and on the word "rhythm" snapped the very tip of his whip betwixt Brimm's shoulder blades, not so hard as to damage the muscles of a useful slave, but with an exacting flick that stung like a wasp, doubly painful because it struck sunburned skin.

Brimm hissed between clenched teeth, and fell into rhythm. It was not easy to work an oar with Snoori at his side. Snoori was broad shouldered but short-legged, coming not quite up to Brimm's shoulder. There was a saying that a tall man and a small man could not row well together, and now he saw that it was so.

As he struggled to sweep the oar with Snoori, Brimm noticed the ship's captain, Zenk—a swarthy man in a red turban and yellow silk—making his way to the prow of the vessel, now and then missing stride as the ship rolled. What held Brimm's gaze was the sword borne awkwardly in Zenk's yellow sash. It was Brimm's own piercer.

The Atlantean piercer must be used properly. The tubby, oafish Captain Zenk wouldn't be able to cut a melon with the blade, Brimm was sure, let alone an enemy.

"I'll show you how that sword is used, you strutting boar," Brimm muttered, watching him.

But first he must lay his hands on the blade—hands confined by iron chains. He had already tried magicking them off with Knudsun's Efficacious Unchainer, but judging from the lack of results he had failed to memorize the spell properly. His erstwhile master, Urgus, had hectored him for his "lackadaisical, feeble, haphazard efforts at memorization" and not for the first time Brimm feared Urgus had been right about him. Of course, he had never envisaged himself in chains. Why then learn an unchaining spell? He had not anticipated Captain Zenk.

But other spells had a certain fascination for him…Knudson's Divulger of the Feminine Mind, Lurania's Guaranteed Charisma Enhancer, Urgus's own Summoning for the Smiting of Enemies…But suppose he persuaded an elemental to smite Captain Zenk? How would it get him out of these chains? It might end up sinking the ship and him with it.

Hence, he sighed and waited. Time seemed to slow; it dragged by, measured only by the steady creak of the oars. At length a spindly, coughing rower chained near the prow gave a final gasp, lunged against his chains, and collapsed. The spindly rower's brother, who had been kidnapped with him, cried piteously out for help. The row-master took a quick look, unchained the spindly man, and tossed him headfirst over the side. His brother sobbed, and was beaten for it.

Brimm decided he would complain no further, aloud, in a whisper, even within himself. It was a waste of energy—and he had come to this vessel of his own accord.

He must wait for his moment.

* * * *

Fatigue and monotony and rising temperatures melted the days together. Two weeks passed, with no opportunity for escape. When a strong following wind pushed them rapidly enough, they were allowed to walk the decks a few at a time, to keep their muscles from cramping up and becoming useless. But even then they were kept on long chains, like hounds on leashes, and watched closely by a hulking much-scarred Hyperborean brute armed with a spiked hammer.

Once as he worked the oar, it struck Brimm that the sea's vastness, its mountainous waves, was the measure of his mounting desolation. He felt he was close to crossing into an infinite sea of despair, from which he could never return. Despair, he called out to the conventional gods of his people: that triumvirate of giants, Apollon, and his sons Boreas and Chione. Again, and again he called to them.

They did not respond; neither by omen or vision. He had no sense of their presence at all. They never had responded to his prayers. Was it because he had never sacrificed to them? Or was it because they did not truly exist?

Brimm recalled that Urgus had jeered at the usual gods, deities like Wotan and Apollon, saying that they were mere egregores, phantasms created by the human mind. Urgus insisted that there were only a handful of authentic "titanic beings"—that was his term for them—like the goddess of fertility, and the Red Lord of war, and the sea king whom the Atlanteans called Poseidon. Even these were intermediary entities, godlings, emanations of the Unnamable Lord above all, the secret god over-arching all things, whose true name was known to but a few, and who, at any rate, held himself remote from mankind. Below the intermediary godlings were the elementals, mysterious entities who thrived in either earth, air, fire, or water. And below the elementals were wandering spirits, who sometimes showed themselves to mankind and could occasionally be treated with, and even commanded...

But Urgus himself had claimed to worship only the Unnamable Lord. He did not practice rituals of submission to the Titanic Beings. "It is best to be unnoticed by them," he said.

"Oh, Unnamable Lord, I call to you," murmured Brimm, as he struggled with the rising sea of his despair. "You whom Urgus spoke of only by touching the Sign of Nine Points—can you not help us, this once?"

To his disordered senses it seemed, then, that the sun briefly swelled, and flared in the sky. But Brimm only hung his head, sure that madness was creeping up on him.

Soon after, when the row-master had gone to the other side of the ship to harangue the portside oarsmen, Snoori whispered, "Brimm—you see the storm clouds there, off to the west?"

"What of it? They are not coming this way."

"But what if they could? What if they changed their minds? Did you not tell me you learned a spell to draw a storm?"

"Why..." He almost lost rowing rhythm, considering it. Did he indeed remember the incantation? Had he the energy of spirit required to summon an air elemental? "Perhaps. If I ponder it. But—were I to summon a storm it might well send us to the bottom in our chains. What good would it do us?"

"Look yonder—to the south. Do you see that streak of dark gray and blue?"

"That cloud bank?"

"I have been to Atlantis, you remember. It was just once, trading with my uncle. That streak of gray and blue on the horizon—why that is the ramparts of Poseidonia—one of the ten kingdoms of Atlantis."

"The land of your mythical 'Poseidonian princess,'" Brimm sniffed. "We will see the docks, from our chains on this vessel, and no more of Atlantis than that."

"Just so. If the captain fetches up to the docks of Poseidonia, within the island, he will never unchain us, unless we are to be sold into even worse conditions. But—if the ship is urged by a storm, and carefully driven, why there are sandbars just under those ramparts. My uncle's ship ran aground on them. In about an hour, with the diminishing tide...."

"We would capsize in these waves and drown."

Snoori sighed. "Perhaps you're right."

"But on the other hand..." Brimm was in a desperate mood. "...if indeed we merely ran aground. Then..."

* * * *

Dusk was upon them when the sails were raised, and the rowers were given their thin fish stew. The other rowers were bemused by the murmured incantations of the lean Hyperborean with long black hair, the sunburn turning his pale skin the color of ripe cherries. Clearly, he had surrendered to madness. Only one of them, an old, blue-dyed Pict, recognized Brimm's hand-motions as magical passes. The Pict only shrugged. He had tried calling on his own gods, but it was useless for they reigned far from here. It appeared to the Pict that the Hyperborean's hand-motions only succeeded in making his chains clink.

Yet Brimm was scarcely aware of the chains, or the galley to which they bound him. He was in a state of mystical trance, the deep inward focus that Urgus had taught him; in his weakened state his spirit energy was not at its most potent, in the somatic sense—but fury too is tinder for a blaze, and he had an abundance of fury. He expanded the flickering prism of his emanation, and drew on the electricity in the air to expand it further. He then extended unseen fingers, long wisps of spirit energy, toward the flashing, brooding storm to the west. His unseen fingers beckoned, as did his physical fingers.

Brimm spoke the name of the aerial elemental, Zirrish: he who was known to revel in storms. Muttering under his breath, Brimm promised two ritual sacrifices, the lives of two men, if Zirrish should bring the storm hither and turn the ship with precision to the sandbars. Brimm promised to glorify Zirrish in legend, so that the fame of Zirrish would multiply a thousand-fold and more men would sacrifice to the wondrous rider of storms at sea, and great would Zirrish's power grow...

There was a pause. A tenseness suffused the air, as if the elemental were pondering the offer.

Then—thunder responded, from just overhead.

For a moment Brimm thought the thunder a rebuke. But the waves from the west rose, rearing up as the storm changed directions; black clouds rushing toward them on long crooked legs of blue-white lightning.

Onward the storm came, with unnatural haste, and Captain Zenk gave orders to shorten sail; it was no use, the ship's hull itself was driven like a sail ahead of the powerful winds, and men cowered in terror as ragged bolts of lightning flashed about them and the ship plowed a new furrow in the sea, turning to the southeast, toward the sandbars beneath the northerly ramparts of Atlantis...

Snapped from his trance by a flash of lightning and a wall of pelting rain, Brimm struggled with his own rising fear. Already lightning had struck one of the two masts, set it afire; already the ship's timbers were working, intermittently spitting water. The aft was lifted, the prow dipped, the vessel surging headlong toward the cliffs of Poseidonia. Oars snapped off; men groaned and cried out, each to his own gods.

"This was a ghastly mistake!" Brimm said—but Snoori didn't hear, he was huddled with his head under his arms, terrified of the lightning and the high, sharp-peaked waves looming over them; the onrushing cliffs of quartz-sparkling stone ahead.

Faster the ship sped, faster, far too fast, Brimm was sure.

He opened his mouth to implore Zirrish to desist—before he could speak they struck the sandbar. The ship creaked; a timber somewhere screeched as it split part.

But they'd struck the sandbar at just the angle called for. Everyone on board was tossed and jolted, slaves in their chains howling with terror at the impact, the burning mast snapping to fall cross the oarsmen, who hastily frantically it into the sea.

But the ship held together, taking little brine-water, and, in a double handful of seconds the storm diminished, pounding thunderously away like one of the great angry mammoths that yet roamed upper Hyperborea. The darkness thickened, but the galley steadied. Waves still battered its hull and the tide had only just begun to drop. Reavers and scavengers might come upon them, Brimm thought, and make short work of the crew to take its cargo of furs and northern iron and Hyperborean ale.

The ship must be pulled free of the sandbar. As the waves slackened, crewmen brought out levers and tools to force the vessel off the sandbar.

As Brimm had calculated, the row-master and the Hyperborean brute hurried to unchain the oarsmen—their collective muscle would be needed to free the ship. They were to work at the incentive of snapping whips and unsheathed blades.

Unchained, stretching his limbs with the row-master's whip cracking, Brimm saw his chance. The row-master and the brute were turned away, shouting at other men, and the captain had gone to the rail to assess their position—Zenk standing only a few strides away, with his back to Brimm.

Energized with rising anger, Brimm took three long strides, and snatched his silver piercer from the captain's waistband.

Zenk turned in startlement, just in time to receive the sword's thrust through his breast. He stood there, swaying, dying on his feet, as Brimm shouted at the sky, "Zirrish! I offer these, my enemies, to thee!" He added a few arcane words, dedicating Zenk's life-force to Zirrish.

Captain Zenk gawped down at the blade plunged to the hilt between his ribs, and then sank to the deck, eyes glassy. Brimm pulled the blade free with an expert motion.

The row-master roared and rushed at Brimm—but Snoori tackled the whip-wielder's bowed legs, knocking him to the deck. Brimm stepped up and with a swift stroke, struck the slaver's head from his shoulders, again speaking the words of sacrifice to Zirrish.

Still enveloped in magical energy, Brimm was able to see the ghosts of Zen and his oar-master rising from their still-quivering corpses. The phantoms looked about them with terror, mouths screaming soundlessly, and then were caught in a net of lightning-fire, and drawn up, wailing with the voice of the wind, into the receding storm clouds…

Brimm turned, saw that the ship's freemen crew were rushing furiously at him: the captain's second, the keeper of cargo, the rigging men and sail stretchers, and two burly carpenters, brandishing staves and hooked long-knives. The Hyperborean brute, too, hefted his hammer and came along for the kill. They were all old cronies of the two slain men, and they knew, too, that if Brimm was not killed and quickly, a full mutiny would be in the offing. Snoori snatched up the very whip that had cut into his back— he snapped it smashingly at the crew, driving them a few steps back. "Keep back or I'll whip your eyes from your heads!"

Brimm turned to the freed slaves, who were gaping about them, just now comprehending the new possibilities. "Take anything you can wield and strike them down," Brimm shouted, "or you'll be back in chains tomorrow! Fight and you can loot the ship!"

Eyes widening, mouths twisting into ghastly grins, the slaves caught up hefty pieces of shattered oars and rushed at the outnumbered crew, battering the startled crewmen, driving slivers as long as a man's arm into throats and bellies. Two slaves went down to gutting knifes; a third had his head knocked into mush by the Hyperborean brute. But five crewmen were smashed quickly to broken corpses bleeding on the deck.

The Brute turned and swung his spiked hammer at Snoori, who leapt aside to keep from being instantly pulverized. Before Brimm could intervene, the captain's second, a burly, black-bearded man in a turban, leapt over a dying man and charged at Brimm, his wickedly curved longknife upraised, ready to hack down at Brimm's forehead—the burly second exuded the strength to split Brimm's head like a melon.

Brimm let him stride close—and at the last possible second slipped to the left, ducked under the curved knife, cut deftly upward with the piercer as his attacker rushed helplessly past. Brimm felt the impact as the piercer drove into the muscular upper belly, but the weapon was so sharp it went quickly up through a lung and into the second's heart. Brimm just had time to tug his weapon free before his staggering enemy fell dead.

He turned to see that most of the freemen were dead, most of the slaves alive, but they huddled back from the Hyperborean brute's spiked hammer. The brute was swinging the hammer in wide arcs, keeping them at bay, and on the next pass trying to connect with Snoori—forcing Snoori to back away. He had snatched up one of the curved long-knives but it was too short to cut past the hissing hammer, and it was all Snoori could do to dance out of its reach. Snoori leapt back as the spikes swished past his face, driven to the aft rail.

Heart hammering, a red mist in his eyes, Brimm waited till the brute's hammer was on a backswing—then he rushed in, ducked easily under the iron spiked mallet as it was arced toward him. He drove the piercer up between the big, swinging arms; he struck quick and deep, into the brute's throat, slicing the artery. It spurted blood as the man shouted in fear, and staggered backwards—the brute fell back through the hatchway, into the cargo hold.

And Brimm muttered again to Zirrish, offering up another life. He only owed Zirrish two, but why not curry favor, should he need Zirrish again. He added, "That makes three, an additional gift for the great Zirrish!" The wind about Brimm whispered words he could not understand, and hissed in pleasure…

The other slaves gasped at the Brute's demise—and then cheered. They rushed headlong at three remaining crewmen, who unanimously chose to vault over the rails into the sea.

Brimm felt a sick exhaust come over him. He swayed, and gagged. But he kept to his feet, took a deep breath, and searched about till he found his old dagger and cloak in a box at the prow—the row-master had used the one to pick his teeth and the other to wipe his sweat.

Snoori emerged from below as Brimm clasped the cloak about him.

Brimm noted a sizeable bag of coin in one of Snoori's hands and a javelin in the other. Snoori hid the bag with his body, as the crew, behind him, began to argue with one another about dividing the spoils. "Brimm, ho!" Snoori called. He hurried to the prow, and covertly handed the purse to Brimm. "Hide this under your cloak." Brimm tucked the agreeably plump bag of coin away, and, as he wiped blood and sweat from his face, he wondered aloud, "What do we do now?"

They both looked across the deck, where a one-eyed Hyperborean oarsman, mane and beard of flowing red, roared in triumph as he put a wounded crewman to death, and urged the freed rowers to declare him their new captain. He extolled himself as a former pirate captain, wise in the ways of the sea. He had killed three crewmen himself, he declared. "And if we are to share in this ship's loot, we must move it from the sandbar and make haste to a friendlier port!"

Snoori shook his head, and murmured. "Brimm, I have no wish to serve under that rogue, nor do I wish to fight him for the ship. The Atlantean navy must be aware of the ship by now, surely they'll try to take it…"

Brimm was torn. Here was Atlantis, within reach. But here was a ship stuffed with loot. And suppose the Atlanteans deemed the mutineers to be pirates? They might well set upon the galley.

And he didn't like the way that red-bearded pirate was glowering at him with his remaining eye. "I don't trust that rogue either. And we did set out to reach Atlantis…and so…"

Before the ship's new captain could decide their fate, Brimm and Snoori were over the rail, dropping feet first into the sea. They were scarcely under water before they found footing in the shallows and lurched across the sandbar, the waves up to their chins, with the confidence of true Hyperboreans. "Come," Snoori adjured him, as they trudged in sodden clothing up to the cliffs. "I have been here before, they knew my uncle, they certainly admit us, and we will find a tavern, dry clothes, a fine meal, in Poseidonia! We will tell them we were with the crew!"

Snoori led the way to a high, stone stairway cut in a zigzag up to the notch at the top of the cliffs. The three escaped crewmen were already halfway up the cliff, Brimm saw. The sight made him uneasy.

"Fear not!" Snoori said. 'They will say nothing about us! They will assume we've gone with the ship!"

As Brimm and Snoori made their sodden way up the stairway Snoori explained that a foul wind on his first journey here had brought his uncle's vessel onto the very same sandbars at low tide, and with his uncle he had gone up the stairway to the well-defended gates, the two of them seeking aid for their grounded vessel. Snoori's uncle was a trader who had business with Atlantis, so in due course the small ship was pulled off the sandbar and brought into the harbor to the south.

But the two wet, bedraggled escaped slaves who presented themselves now at those same gates seemed to the Poseidonian guards more like undesirables. Especially as three actual crewmen of the galley had come up first, and told their stories, pointing to Snoori and Brimm as mutineers.

And so…

* * * *

"From a slave galley to a dungeon. Thank you again, Snoori."

"I was *astonished* the guards didn't remember me, Brimm! Of course, I didn't have a beard then and they spoke only to my uncle…"

It was early morning, something Brimm surmised thanks to the thin dawn light slanting through the dungeon's single high window. The morning light illuminated a sweating stone wall slathered with a slick green growth. At the base of the wall a rat-sized cockroach scuttled to a crack in a corner. The air reeked of urine and moldy straw.

"Telling them we're here to set the Princess Cleito free…" Brimm shook his head. "They winked at one another, over that. I could almost hear them thinking, more buffoons who believe that idiot tale!"

Snoori sighed. "How much do you think was in the purse they, ah, confiscated?"

"I only glanced in it once. A good deal of silver, and gold. Confiscated, you said! Ha! We'll never see it again! Those four guards will be retiring to country farms, soon enough…" Brimm shook his head sadly. "A small, fickle fortune—with us and gone."

Snoori cleared his throat., "I've always wondered why you don't simply *conjure* gold, Brimm. I was afraid to ask, you're so surly when I innocently wonder about magical things. But—*if* you could conjure it up here, we could bribe our way out!"

"There is no such spell that actually *works* to conjure gold out of thin air, Snoori. At least, none Urgus told me about. If there were, I'd have used it long ago. Why am I explaining this to you? You know, there is enough slack in these dungeon chains to strangle you with…"

"You wouldn't murder the faithful friend of your youth! You're not so crass!"

They were slumped on the damp straw, their arms numb from a night in heavy chains, and Brimm had spent hours wracking his brains for a suitable spell that might free them. Once more he berated himself inwardly for not learning a spell for unchaining.

And once more, he was bereft of his sword. How long before that bastard of a jailer sold his precious piercer?

"A sword, oh a sword," Brimm growled. "I much prefer a good solid blade to magic. The piercer always works. One can use it to shave, as well as cut throats; it can be used to stir a pot, or to pry at a stone wall."

"Are you becoming delirious?" Snoori asked, as if merely curious.

There was a rattling at the door, which then squeaked open, and a bear-like man in a yellowing tunic came in: the jailer, carrying a lantern in one hand and keys in the other. He led the way for two men in gold-threaded gray-black livery. One of the men was red faced, gray bearded, and hawk eyed. His beard was coated in fragrant unguents; Brimm could smell it the instant he came in. The other was younger, clean-shaven, but he had the raptor-eyed look too. He was probably the bearded man's son. Their eyes were set off with kohl, an eyeliner fashionable amongst the moneyed in these Southern climes, and their earlobes chimed with small bells. Brimm thought their affectations rather decadent.

The younger man raised a vial of perfume to his nose to allay the reek of the dungeon as he approached the staring prisoners. He looked doubtfully at them. "I am Fress—this is my father Remnon. We are the king's sacred retainers. Are you the vagrants who asked to serve the princess Cleito?"

CHAPTER TWO

Brimm and Snoori gazed down upon Atlantis.

Their weapons returned to them, along with ill-fitting helmets of rusty iron and oaken rims, Brimm and Snoori now stood beside Remnon and Fress and gazed down upon the fabled land of ten kingdoms.

Atlantis was not a continent; yet it was enormous, a very big island shaped like an off-center diamond; a land big enough to be divided into ten distinct fiefdoms of various sizes. The kingdoms were now ruled by the descendants—or so the rulers claimed—of demigods who had ruled Atlantis after its establishment by Poseidon.

Several of those kingdoms, including Poseidonia, Eumalosa, and Poseidonia, spread out before Brimm and Snoori as if on a map, their detail only slightly muted by the morning mist. The two amateur adventurers stood upon the, clay-brick road along the upper edge of a high prominence just under the walls of the city. The mossy wall of settling stone was splayed along the upper stone rim overlooking succeeding valleys that receded to the south, each flatter and lower. In the lowest valley were several circular inner canals, perfect half-circles curved one within the next.

On Brimm's left, to the east, the cliffs of Atlantis parted, and the quite narrow cleft admitted a deep inlet from the sea. The inlet was wide enough for three ships abreast and flowed into a channel connecting the ring-like concentric canals. Dug out centuries before by legions of laborers, the canals contacted each of the kingdoms; thus, each King had his own port.

On the beetling bluffs overlooking the inlet stood loaded catapults. At this distance they seemed to Brimm like insects poised to leap. Mechanisms like gigantic crossbows, ready with tree-trunk-sized bolts, stood beside the catapults, pointing out to sea as a warning to would-be invaders.

Within the natural outer battlements of Atlantis countless warships, and merchant vessels comprising every sort of galley, were anchored along the canals. Others moved with stately ease to inner Atlantis, propelled with slow deliberation by galley oarsmen.

The remainder of Atlantis was lost in the haze of distance, so that Brimm wondered what curious little kingdoms hunkered there behind their stony boundaries.

Nearer, terraced orchards and fields of velvety green hugged the canals; rustic castles of wood and stone—none coated in gold—rose atop stony bosses of land encircled by hamlets wreathed in a haze of dun smoke. Low walls of crudely erected black stone divided fields and borders.

A blue cone, truncated at the peak, rose above the mists in the far distance. A slumbering volcano, Brimm supposed.

Nearer was another doorway to the underworld of Vulcan: separated from the canals by a curving causeway was a dark lake within the crater of a long collapsed volcanic vent. Hot vapors yet rose fitfully from its inky surface; sulfurous bubbles burst there to exhale a yellow mist that rose to blur the sun into a coppery oval. Overlooking the lake, in the shadow of the outer rim of the island, rested the partly tumbled ruin of an ancient palace.

"There lies the palace erected by Blessed Poseidon, in honor of Cleito!" said Remnon, pointing at the palace with a trembling finger. Remnon now wore the livery of King Merz: gold sea dragons embroidered on flat black silk. His speech was High Atlantean, a variant of the cruder language spoken by most of those who lived and wandered 'round the Great Sea—but the accent seemed quaint to Brimm.

"Cleito, you say?" Brimm frowned. "But surely that is the name of the princess we are asked to rescue? It cannot be the same one, if that is the palace of a Cleito she lived centuries in the past."

"Of course, it's not *her*, oaf!" declared the younger retainer. "She is the great-great-granddaughter, and then some, of Poseidon's mortal love. She is Cleito the Ninth."

"The eleventh, Fress!" his father corrected irritably, wincing.

Fress scratched his head. "I thought it was the ninth. Are you sure?"

Odd, thought Brimm, that Fress did not know such a salient fact. He gazed uneasily at the palace. The rectilinear, blocky ruins seemed to squirm in the rising vapors of the lake. "We're of course honored by the opportunity to serve the Princess…but perhaps, after all, we might simply sign on with good King Merz—we should be happy to guard his majesty's palace."

Remnon compressed his lips and shook his head. "King Merz has all the help he needs—except at the old palace of Poseidon, yonder."

"Does King Merz have a harem?" Snoori asked, trying to make it sound like innocent curiosity.

Remnon shot Snoori a glare. "You will never get close enough to his palace to find out, I assure you!"

"The sun tilts low, Father," said Fress. "We'd best be off."

"Yes. The eight who've already come are drinking good wine and devouring sausages as they await us. With you two, we have the Ten Swords of her heart, and we need delay no more. We'll take a cart from the stables to the cliff road!"

Their guides strode toward the stables. Brimm hesitated, holding back, and caught Snoori's arm. "Snoori—perhaps we might dash down the hillside here, and find another employer in some other kingdom."

"I haven't eaten since yesterday—and they spoke of sausages and wine! Besides—the treasure!" Snoori hurried after them.

Sighing and pondering the insatiable demands of friendship, Brimm followed.

* * * *

What remained of the repast set out for the Ten Swords of Her Heart was scattered across a block of fallen stone outside the palace gates. Brimm and Snoori managed a small meal from scraps and the dregs of several bronze goblets.

Remnon and Fress waited impatiently until they finished, then waved them into the Hall of Supplicants, where the rest of the Ten had gathered…

The Hall of Supplicants was a high-ceilinged chamber alive with shadows and echoes. Twitching yellow light from a few torch sconces scarcely penetrated the darkness. The sound of their boot steps echoed back to them as Brimm and Snoori strode to join the others waiting at the high metal doors at the other end of the hall. The cracked blocks of the walls were carved of red granite; the pilasters along the walls were trimmed in red coral and volcanic glass, some of it fallen about the bases of the square columns. In a panel along the upper walls glittering porphyry was carved to represent the waves of the sea. Dust, webs and rubble hid the corners of the marble floor.

The squirming shadows hid most of the sagging ceiling; Brimm could faintly make out a patchily intact mosaic of something like a giant squid, watched over by a bearded man wearing a diadem. Poseidon?

The eight soldiers, raggedly assembled before the high doors, seemed to be from everywhere but Atlantis. There were two northern nomads, with their high cheekbones, dark skin, almond eyes; they were clad only in rancid beast-furs, their weapons hammers of bronze and stone.

There was an ebon warrior of the far south, his face ornately decorated with symmetrical scars. Clad in a long red robe, he towered over the rest of them, but his flint-tipped spear was longer than he was tall. Beside him was a painted, intricately garbed, ruddy-skinned warrior wearing a headpiece resembling a feathery snake—he hailed from the far western continents where, according to Urgus, rose mighty civilizations centered around stepped pyramids. Squatting at his side was a blue-dyed Pict armed with a stone-tipped club and a bronze dagger. The company included one sleek, armored warrior of Ur who wielded a short, curved iron sword and stubby spear, his bronze helmet topped with the silver disk of the moon god. His face was masked.

The other three looked to be ragtag vagabonds, perhaps Mycenaean, peering fearfully about them as they hefted cast-off Atlantean battleaxes.

The door before them was of the same silvery metal, Brimm judged, as his own slender sword, but less polished. The door panel had once been inset with gems, but they'd been pried away by thieves and only scratched indentations remained.

The palace was in large part a ruin; everything about it spoke of disuse and abandonment and fear. A rankness caught at Brimm's nostrils, carried by a faint draft from under the slightly bent metal doors. Rotting fish?

"So, we leave you now to your holy task!" declaimed Remnon portentously. "Once we have gone, the doors will open and you will behold Cleito! You will see the sea demon that holds her in its clutches; this is the fiend you must defeat! There are many of you, and thus you are likely to win the day! We have shall go and, ah, count out the gold and pearls, to be divided among you—and now—"

"Hold!" Brimm cried out. His doubts were gathering force—he had noticed Fress's curious smile quickly hidden under his much be-ringed hand, at the mention of counting out gold and pearls. "No need for such haste!" insisted Brimm. "Indeed, Fress there looks doughty enough and wears a fine sword! Why should he not join us and partake of the treasure? Surely, we are to have casualties. There will be enough gold for those who remain!"

"Ah, no," Fress said, blinking at Brimm in alarm. "My sword is purely ornamental. It's for ritualistic purposes only. Mere costumery! Not even sharp!"

"I shall loan you my dagger!"

"No, no, I thank you! You see, the door of the throne room will open quite soon, of its own accord, and sadly, Father and I are not permitted to remain!"

Remnon cleared his throat. "And now, we must bid you goodbye! May the good fortune of the gods attend you all!"

"Stop!" Brimm called, his voice harsh with warning. "You shall not depart! If we face this, so shall you. We have need of your knowledge."

Remnon took his son's upper arm and tugged him back from the door. The two retainers backed away. "That is not possible. But—again—best of luck to you all!"

"Stop them!" Brimm growled. "There is something wicked afoot with these two!"

Snoori nodded. "I too mistrust them."

The Ten exchanged frowns and turned dark looks upon the Atlanteans who continued to back away, both of them smiling and bowing as they went. Suddenly the black warrior from the South made two quick bounds and took up a stance behind the King's retainers, his spear poised to attack. Remnon and Fress came to a sudden confused halt. Brimm drew his sword and joined the black warrior—and together they herded their protesting guides to the metal doors. Which at that moment creaked themselves open.

Forcing the protesting Atlanteans along, the Ten stepped forward, for, despite their doubts, none of them were cowards and all still hoped treasure might be found.

They were in a smaller room now—it was high ceilinged but a third the size of the Hall of Supplicants. Brimm saw no throne. Nor were there torches; a flaring, dipping blue light emanated from vents low on the walls. There were no furnishings, no columns, only a ripe fishy stench, and a few cobwebbed mosaics on the walls. The mosaics showed Nereids and mermen frolicking in the waves beneath unfamiliar astrological configurations. The floor—at least, nearer the door—looked to be coated by some brown and gray crust. Then Brimm realized its coating was the dried residue of old blood on white marble.

The high metal doors closed behind them with a clang. Brimm spun on his heel and saw there were no handles, no knobs, no visible means of opening them metal doors. The warriors stared at the doors at the Pict tried to pry them open, to no effect. Each man murmured and cursed, each in his native language.

"Father, what has happened?" Fress wailed, clutching his groin as if to prevent his bladder giving way. "This is not seemly—this is not possible! The door opens not from this side!"

"Silence," the old man muttered. "Let me think. There must be some means…"

The floor began to quake—and a metallic grinding noise brought everyone to stare at the far end of the rectangular chamber. There, the dirty marble floor was separating, gradually parting, halves shunting aside into slots in the walls. The stench of oceanic decay was palpable now.

"It has begun!" Remnon groaned.

The Ten stared in dull amazement as a shimmering pool of indigo was gradually revealed, its shuddering surface giving off more of the sickly blue light. From the center of the pool, gratingly lifted by some hidden, rusting mechanical device, rose a throne on which was seated a strange but beautiful woman. Her throne, almost too big for her, was of gold-streaked marble arrayed roundabout with broken coral branches, streaming water as it rose. On her head was a crown of coral tipped with emeralds, dripping with sparkling water. She herself was the color of green olives, her full lips crimson; the whole of her large pupilless oval eyes were speckled with gold like polished opal; long, slick green-black hair flowed over her bare shoulders; her small hands, nails crusted with ruby dust, rested placidly on the arms of the throne. She wore an iridescent gown that clung to her firm breasts but just beneath her bosom the gown greatly expanded, fanning out widely below to hide her hips, her legs, wetly draping the entire lower part of the throne.

"Behold!" Fress said, his voice a squeak of awe, shaking hands clutched before his face. "Princess Cleito! The sacred consort of Poseidon!"

"And…you may as well know," said Remnon grimly. "That is Cleito herself—not her descendent, despite the tale we prefer to spin. She was mortal, and there was only one way she could live on, without the blessing of Poseidon. She must fight for her food! For when she strayed from Poseidon, he cursed her…and now you—" He pointed a long-nailed finger at Brimm. "Have cursed us all! At least my son and I would have lived—but now, we shall perish with the rest of you!"

"Only seems fair, really," Snoori muttered.

Remnon turned toward the immortal yet eldritch princess on the throne before them—and fell to his knees. "Cleito!" cried the king's retainer. "Take these others, but spare my son and your faithful servant Remnon! We have brought you many a succulent hero—as did my father and his father before him!"

With the suddenness of a seizure her mouth popped open, as if in a convulsion, exposing a toothless purple orifice writhing with slick, fluttering tendrils. She emitted a prolonged, ear-splitting screech comingled of hate, horror, and hunger. This was her only reply to Remnon.

Then her gown, which Brimm now saw to be made of living skin, parted like a wet curtain and her true form was revealed. Her neck, her shoulders and bosom were all that remained of the princess; below it, she was a giant squid. It was almost as if her humanity was an excrescence growing from the top of the creature: ten heavy, mottled and suckered gray limbs now reached eagerly toward the soldiers of fortune. Eight of the wriggling tentacles bore circular suckers, while two longer limbs, equally prehensile, were tipped with dexterous club-shaped appendages, as it is with all giant squid. The princess's cephalopodan lower half was disproportionately bigger, far larger than her upper half, and yet perfectly melded with her upper body. Where her ribcage should be was the thing's head, regarding them hungrily with two black discs, eyes big as a plates and black, so very black, black as polished onyx.

The men backed away—but the tentacles stretched out, longer and thicker than Brimm would have thought possible.

The squid-like part of her now tilted back, raising up to expose a gigantic beak where the tentacles converged, snapping hungrily at the warriors.

Several of the warriors screamed like frightened children; Fress bolted to the doors and pounded on them, squalling in fear. Remnon threw himself face down, babbling prayers.

Suddenly, fast as a striking cobra, Cleito's tentacles whipped round the two northern barbarians, lifted them screaming into the air, and drew them near. She thrust first one, then the other into her opened beak, which elongated as needed for her feasting. Weapons raised, the warriors reacted with moans and cries of fury.

In seconds two sickening seconds she sucked the flesh away from the Northmen—and then the beak opened to spew out their bones, their armor and leather, the greater part sinking away in the pool. Yet a few scraps flew past the edge of the pool so that a fresh, bloody skull rolled to thump into one of Snoori's boots. With an unmanly yelp he kicked it away into the pool.

More tentacles surged out, and Brimm dodged the flashing tentacles. He ducked, then struck with the piercer as the limbs whipped past. He struck home, and black blood oozed, but the limbs did not slow their grasping. He tried frantically to remember a spell he might use against this abomination, but the castings he knew needed concentration and time—he was given no time for anything but sidestepping, ducking, and slashing.

Crying out in many languages the warriors backed away from Cleito, waving their blades—but her sucker-lined lower limbs, as much supernatural as fleshly, plucked the warriors up one by one. In seconds she stripped the mortal flesh from their bones, spitting out weapons like a man spitting out gristle from his dinner. As the beak drew men in and crushed them, chewing them up, the princess's scarlet mouth worked in sympathy, as if she too were chewing.

The black warrior shouted in defiance and threw his spear hard at the upper parts of creature on the throne—but fast as a darting barracuda, a tentacle caught the weapon, reversed it, and sped it neatly back so that it impaled the warrior's neck, splitting his throat. Then as the black warrior stood swaying, clutching the spear haft, the other tentacle lashed round his ankles and dragged him, thrashing and gurgling, feet first to its giant beak.

The survivors hacked furiously at the tentacles—one big man with a battleaxe cut partway through a suckered limb and Snoori chopped at the wound with the head of his javelin. The limb fell apart, but another grew quickly in its place.

Faster and faster the limbs flashed, the beak gulped—and soon seven shrieking men were gone. The room was unnervingly quiet. And the spear of the black warrior was there, now lying on the edge of the pool…

A tentacle hissed toward Brimm, and with it another, so that they were coming from both sides. Brimm ducked, slashing, backing away toward Remnon, just out of reach of the tentacles. They stretched out, adding to their length, poising over him…

"Snoori—help me feed it this old fool!" Brimm bent, dragged the weeping, slobbering old retainer to his feet. With Snoori's help Brimm heaved Remnon toward the tentacles.

The offering was accepted—Remnon was caught up and crammed screaming into gaping beak.

Fress wailed, "Father! Oh, spare me, great Cleito!"

But at the same time other tentacles reached for new prey. Heart pounding, Brimm used his flexible, razor-sharp piercer to good effect, just managing to deter the undulating limbs.

Only a few of the Ten remained. The warrior of Ur, though darting and spinning adroitly, was next to be caught…

"We're her next morsel unless we can find a way out!" Snoori yelled, slashing at tentacles to keep them back.

A club-tentacle shot out, wrapping tightly around Snoori's legs and tugging him screaming across the floor toward the great snapping beak.

"Drag your javelin point on the floor, Snoori, to slow it down!" Brimm called, as he turned and ran to Fress.

Snoori did as he was bid, and the javelin point caught in a crack in the floor, as Fress cringed away from Brimm waving his ceremonial dagger and, squalling, "Stay away!"

Brimm kicked the dagger away; it rattled into a corner. He picked Fress up in his arms, dragged toward the struggling Atlantean to the pool. "Let me go!" Fress sobbed.

The princess was still chewing at the man from Ur, whose armor slowed the marks of her mastication, the strong metal so far resisting her, the metal squealing with the grinding pressure. The creature's beaked head shook the struggling warrior, like a wolf trying to break the neck of a rabbit. The armor began to break up—the squid-beak spat the armor out in several uneven chunks. The warrior had drawn a knife, slashing at the black orbs of the monster's eyes—Cleito howled as a knife struck home, and the great beak opened. The warrior pushed off against the cephalopodic body, breaking free, even as Brimm caught Fress by his ankles, swung him about and threw him with all his strength at the gnashing beak.

Fress was caught in midair air by a great appendage—and was quickly crammed, howling with terror, into the creature's maw. Snoori was in midair himself now, half strangled by another tentacle, throwing the javelin at the princess's bosom. It missed, clacking off the throne.

Brimm caught up the black warrior's spear—and then the tentacle dropped Snoori, as if suddenly disinterested.

Cleito had fed to repletion, Brimm realized. It was as he had hoped. She needed ten men to feed upon, and ten she had consumed.

Laughing hysterically, Snoori thrashed in the pool and Brimm reached out, helped him onto the rim, dragging him away from the tentacles.

The cephalopodan part of Cleito was covering itself now, receding under the gown of skin. The throne was beginning to rumble, to lower once more into the pool. The princess belched hugely, and tittered. Brimm thought to see a febrile misery burning in her eyes. And he saw something else: a hand reaching out from between tentacles. The man from Ur, still protected by armor, still alive, but weakened, perhaps losing consciousness…sinking down into the pool. Perhaps destined to be eaten later, a snack for the abomination.

"That's one too many," Brimm snarled.

He aimed the black warrior's spear, and threw it with all his might. The spear flew straight and true, past truncated tentacles, to drive itself into the princess's head, between her opalescent eyes. She shrieked and twisted, spurting black blood; squid ink gushed from her undersides.

Still the throne drew down, and she vanished with it, in a swirl of black effluvia.

Then…

Someone came spluttering up to part the surface of the pool. A woman. Was it the princess—released?

It was not. There was armor clinging to her, though she had lost her metal mask: it was the warrior of Ur. Not a man of Ur, after all. All along—a woman.

Brimm had heard of warrior women, but had never met one, except for a single shield-maiden who was indistinguishable from the other reavers but for lack of beard. This warrior woman of Ur, though rough edged, was fair. He watched her in fascination as, spitting out blackened water, the woman swam to the edge of the pool, impatiently pushed his proffered hand aside and clambered out. She was cut here and there, oozing blood that reddened her wet undergarments. Sucker marks showed on her shoulders.

She stood up, and Brimm appraised her. Her natural color was bronze, her eyes dark, her jet hair cut short. Her face showed a stark, robust beauty—a beauty unmuted by her cold anger as, gasping for air, she eyed the two staring men defiantly.

"Well?" she demanded. "Is there treasure—or is there not?"

"Well, as to that," Snoori said, scratching his head. "I am not entirely certain."

"It was all a lie," Brimm said, quite firmly, still gazing in wonder at Ur woman. "There is no treasure."

They were silent then. Brimm glanced toward the door and wondered if they were doomed to be trapped in this charnel chamber forever.

"Will Cleito come back?" Snoori asked, staring at the bubbling pool. "She came up short a portion of her meal!"

"She all but swallowed me," the Ur woman said, turning to look at the pool. "Perhaps she had not quite eaten her fill—but she has had enough."

"She will be back, if she lives," Brimm murmured, noticing another roiling in the pool.

But behind them, to Brimm's profound relief, the metal doors creaked slowly open.

Brimm and Snoori and the warrior woman turned to the doors—then Snoori bent down, plucking up a purse that had been spat from the creature's beak. Brimm recalled seeing the purse on Remnon's sash.

"Ha!" Snoori crowed.

The woman found a dark green cape dropped by one of the warriors, wrapped herself in it, and snatched up a short sword as they rushed toward the door. Brimm caught up Fress's ceremonial dagger. Surely it would be worth something...

They hurried out of the throne room, and were soon gasping in the sweet open air outside the ruined palace. The woman of Ur slashed a hole in the cape, and thrust her head through it, draping it over her bloody, torn garments.

After the shrieking chaos they'd faced in the palace, it seemed eerily peaceful out here, Brimm thought. Somewhere, a bird called; the sea surged, a reminder of Kraken, and the will of Poseidon. And below them, away toward the channel leading into Atlantis, galleys slid unhurriedly along glassy canals. "As if all that we have just seen hadn't happened..."

"My creaking bones and bruised limbs testify," the woman said. "It happened."

"Too truly," Snoori said, looking at the blood splashed on his boots.

"even warriors—eaten alive!"

Brimm gave a dour smile. "You don't regret the deaths of Remnon and Fress?"

"Not in the least! The were scum! And speaking of scum I would wish to clean myself of blood and squid effluvia, and put the memory behind me. Let us think of it no more…except for…" He looked more cheerfully at the clinking sack in his hand, small but promising.

Brimm looked frankly at the woman. "I am Brimm, this is Snoori—and you?"

She glared back at him, frowning. "I am Selinn. That is enough for you to know."

"Selinn of Ur," Snoori said. "A charming name. But not very informative."

Brimm nodded. "I'd like to know how you came here, Selinn of Ur."

"Like any other warrior," she snapped. "I heard the tale of the Ten—and the treasure." After a moment she shrugged, and added, "A seer of my temple said that I was called to find certain things in Atlantis. When I heard the tale of Cleito, it seemed an omen."

"And in Ur? Did no one object to this adventuring?"

She scowled. "You know enough. More than I should have said."

Brimm shrugged and turned to Snoori. "So much for your Cleito, Snoori, and so much for seven brave men. And the treasure that never existed at all!"

"Don't be so sure of the treasure!" Snoori opened the purse. "Ha! Six pearls and a double handful of gold. Didn't I tell you?"

"Didn't you…" Brimm stared at him. "You call that a treasure? I could still strangle you—with my bare hands."

"Suppose we find an inn, and I buy dinner, would that put you in a better mood?"

"*You* will buy dinner? Most generous! But we will split that purse—I'll pay for my own dinner."

"We will split it *three ways!*" Selinn declared, hefting her short-sword.

Snoori sighed. "I was afraid of that. So it shall be."

Brimm nodded. "Come along, the both of you—I see smoke from a far hamlet. Let us find some Atlantean realm other than Poseidonia…"

"Yes—why not!" Snoori chuckled. "We can find work here! The birds of sing a cheery tune—let us make Atlantis our new home!" He looked sidelong at the warrior woman of Ur. "Selinn can take her share of our small treasure…and accompany us to the next realm, if she chooses."

"For now," she said grudgingly, "I'll go with you. I need to salve my wounds somewhere." She looked suddenly at the ground. "Did you feel the rumbling under us just now?"

Brimm nodded. "I thought to feel something. Perhaps Poseidon is unhappy with us."

"Oh, that small shaker? It happens all the time here," Snoori said. "Nothing to worry about. This is Atlantis! Surely, we've seen the worst of the place. It must improve! What else could go wrong?"

And so, determined to leave the foulness of Cleito's temple behind them, they set off at a good pace along the crumbling old cliff-side track, searching for any trail at all that would lead them down into the heart of Atlantis.

* * * *

At Cleito's palace a dim figure shaped of dirty-gray mist drifted out through the open doors. It seemed to pause, giving out a mournful sound that was something like air blowing through a subterranean passage. It coalesced, taking on a little more form, almost a human body, not quite a silhouette; its head lifted as if sniffing the air. The spectre's shape was indefinite, but seen in the right light, the ghostly form might roughly sketch the outline of a woman.

It held as still as its tenuous body could, snuffling, listening, attentive. It muttered.

The birds stopped singing.

The spectre listened and snuffled again—then it drifted slowly down the path that Brimm, Snoori and Selinn had taken.

⚔

PART THE SECOND

Swords for the King

CHAPTER THREE

It was late afternoon, and long shadows stretched out like eager ghosts from the three wanderers as they trekked stolidly down the path, ever deeper into Atlantis.

The track took them through a grove of date palms, where they paused for a mild repast; they soon set off again, crossing a stream misty from a steaming hot spring; onward, through a meadow of enormous sunflowers, taller than any of them, looking down upon the travelers as they passed; between long hummocks of volcanic rock, where multicolored reptiles flashed sinuously and vanished; past soil-covered barrows, each with a slab of runically etched stone…

On and on, through a narrow, arid stretch of crumbly red volcanic rock broken only by occasional baobabs and quiver trees…

The ground soon became softer, verdant with high grass—and then the path ended in a partly crumbled black-stone wall.

"A wall," Brimm said, "might mean a settlement near."

Snoori, ever the first to feel peckish, was inevitably first to scramble through the rubbled gap in the low stone wall, into the little kingdom of Eumalosa. "How I look forward to an inn and dinner!" he called.

But no inn was apparent, Brimm saw, as he and Selinn climbed in turn through the much-used gap in the wall. Here was a forest of curiously primeval trees, most of them unfamiliar to Brimm. They rose from a dense, dark-green growth of mist-draped shrubs. The woodland exhaled an intoxicating odor of antiquated mulch and unseen blossoms. A dusty pebbled road traced along this side of the wall, then suddenly curved to dive into the forest.

At the turn of the road stood a stela: a chipped, engraved slab of sandstone leaning under the weight of centuries.

Snoori was puzzling over the cuneiform inscription as they caught up with him. "I hope it doesn't say we're about to be killed, or eaten—or both. "Brimm and I always seem to encounter declarations of that kind."

Selinn squinted at the worn inscription. "This writing," she said, "is of Sumer, and is known in Ur. The high priestess told me the writing originates in Atlantis—long ages ago Sumer and Ur were colonies of Atlantis."

"And now?" Brimm asked.

She shook her head gravely. "We do not kneel for the Kings of Atlantis."

"Can you read it?" Brimm asked, a little embarrassed that his skill as a savant did not extend so far.

She nodded. "It says, *'Here is the place where I, Eumalos, twin brother of Mneseos, founded his kingdom, and here I declare this land good, unto the stream Poiseidon's Tears. May it be a blessed gift to my mother, Holy Cleito.'*"

Brimm shuddered at that name. "Cleito again." He thought back to what he'd learned of the history of Atlantis from Urgus. "It's said there were five sets of twins, born to Poseidon and Cleito, ten boys in total. They became the first ten kings of Atlantis's ten kingdoms. One of the kings was Eumalos. That was long ago, a thousand years and more, if any of the story is true." He turned casually to Selinn, hoping to impress her. "The direct descendent of Eumalos, Squelos, son of Squen, was king in that realm."

She only shrugged, and started briskly down the pebbled road, which wended between tall evergreens, their tops bending, straightening, bending in a sea breeze coming through the channel.

Brimm hurried to catch up with Selinn, striding beside her but not too close, and noticed she carried the short-sword carried firmly in her right hand. He paced along beside her, humming a Hyperborean folk tune. She simply marched on, saying nothing, glancing suspiciously at the trees now and then. He liked this woman, despite her taciturnity. He respected her courage; he admired her rough-edged beauty. He wished to be, at least, a friendly traveling companion to her. What would it take to make her trust him?

Snoori caught up with him. "Strange there are no guards on the road."

Another ten steps, and the woods opened out to show, up on a ridge perhaps half an hour's walk up ahead, a high wall of wood, a palisades on a raised base of hardened clay.

"No need for guards on the road," Brimm said. "You see the palisades around the town? Guards patrol along the top, I have no doubt, and see much from there. We will speak to them soon enough."

Beyond the palisades rose the squared-off central tower of a castle, itself trailing wood smoke in the same westward breeze. Would that be the keep of King Squelos?

Hoof beats from the forest brought them around—and Brimm beheld a creature he had never encountered before. He had seen donkeys, and equids slightly larger than donkeys miserably confined to the hold of a ship— but he had never seen a horse. This one was a great gray charger, with more than the heft of a bull, snorting as it drew up just short of them, its furious black eyes glinting, whinnying in disappointment as they stepped back just in time. A trained warhorse, judging by the villainous look in its eyes—it would have enjoyed trampling the wayfarers.

Brimm's hand had gone to his sword—but then the man on the charger, and the six other men riding up in chariots pulled by smaller, horned equids, had encircled the wayfarers. They were burly, swarthy men, with bronze armor and braided beards that reached to their sternums.

There was a quiver of arrows on the horseman's broad shoulders, a bow in his hand, an arrow already nocked—and pointed at Brimm. The gray charger's master was in proportion to his mount: thick-bodied, wide shouldered, lantern-jawed. He had braided black hair and dark brown, oval eyes. Tied over the back of his horse was a freshly killed buck still dripping blood.

"I am Breeke," the big man rumbled. "I am Lord of Breeke manor, and kin to King Squelos. These men are my huntsmen. Now you will tell me who you are, and what you do here."

"My lord," Brimm said, taking his hand from his sword and instantly going down on one knee, ducking his head in respect. The man was not only keenly dangerous but a nobleman, a person of force in this kingdom. "I am Brimm the Savant, these are my companions, Selinn—"

"*Temporary* companions," she amended sharply, making Brimm wince.

"And Snoori." He glared at Snoori, who was gaping at Lord Breeke's horse. It stretched its snout out, bared its teeth—and snapped at his face. Snoori stepped back and dropped to one knee. "What creature is this who bears him?" he whispered

"In my land they are highly regarded," murmured Selinn, admiring the creature. "It is a horse."

Brimm said, "Lord, we have come from far lands in the hopes of serving the…" Not knowing the politics of Eumalosa, he hesitated. For all he knew Breeke might be an enemy of King Squelos. "Those whom you serve in this place."

Breeke chuckled. "A cautious man. And one who claims to be a Savant." He lowered the bow and arrow but did not put it away.

"Oh, but he is!" Snoori enjoined. "He studied under Urgus himself!"

Brimm winced again. Urgus might be a name to conjure with here—or a name to curse with.

"Urgus. I have heard the name. A Northern necromancer of some kind."

A necromancer Urgus was not, strictly speaking, though occasionally he had truck with the dead. Sorcerer was a better description. But Brimm knew better than to correct nobility, at this juncture.

"If you are a wielder of magic, Brimm the Savant, perhaps the King may take an interest in you. He mumbles about such things from time to time. The queen dabbles, I believe."

"For myself, I wish to serve the King of this land as a warrior," said Selinn.

The hunters laughed, and Breeke snorted. "You look like you've been in a fight, it's true. Perhaps with a particularly fierce raccoon?"

"A squirrel!" one of the men jeered. He was a particularly hefty, beefy-faced man.

Selinn drew herself up. "I will fight any of you squirrels!" She slashed the short sword once through the air, spun its grip in her hand so that it ended up pointing at the last man who'd mocked her.

The gray charger reared back, but Breeke was laughing now. "Ho, Spund, but you are to be struck down by this runaway from a—"

Before Breeke could say 'whorehouse'—the word was forming on his lips—Brimm stood up and interjected, "My lord! This lady is a princess of Ur—and a warrior woman! I have seen her fight! She's like an incarnation of the fire goddess! Such a one would put her enemies off guard—and then take their heads from their shoulders! A valuable asset to any fighting force!"

"As am I!" Snoori put in.

"You are a princess too?" called the jeering rider. The others laughed.

Selinn scowled. "Fire goddess? I serve the moon goddess alone!"

Brimm sighed. If they survived, he would speak to her about a more diplomatic manner.

"We shall see about her skills as a fighter," Breeke said, putting his arrow back in its quiver—perhaps to show he was not afraid of a woman. "But she is not equipped for combat at the moment. We shall let her have a little armor. You will march ahead of us into Mnemos—" The *M* was silent, the name pronounced Nemos. "And there we will have you cleansed of vermin and you will be fed. Tomorrow perhaps we shall learn if you can fight."

* * * *

"In truth," rumbled Lord Breeke, after taking another pull on his spirits of wine, "I am bored with the same faces—my men, the courtiers who fawn over the king, and my own clumsy servants. You three are at least interesting; your foreign accents are amusing. Your ways are amusing also. Perhaps this one..." He nodded toward Snoori, "...would make a good Fool for the king's court."

Snoori's eyes flashed at that, and he sat up straighter. Then he caught Brimm's glance and set to scowlingly finishing his ale.

It was the evening after their arrival. To Brimm's surprise—considering how they'd been treated heretofore in Atlantis—they had been taken to a chamber with clean straw, washing tubs of warm water infused with cleansing tonics. They were given woolen tunics, and, for Selinn, the addition of a bronze breastplate and helmet. The helmet was an open-faced casque, trimmed in silver and figured with fish scales. The servant delivering the armor remarked that it had been made for a boy, a nephew of Breeke's, who had died in a Tyrrhennian battle.

Now, Breeke gazed with hooded eyes at Selinn, seated across from him, her new armor glimmering in the torchlight. She had helped herself to the stew but not to Breeke's wine. She toyed with a half cup of very weak ale, and looked pensively at the dented table.

"The armor of Ranaeus fits you well, woman of Ur. My nephew was too young to go to Tyrrhenia. Too young for battle. His father said he was unmanly, so Ranaeus took offense and insisted on going." Breeke gave a wintry smile. "His father...my older brother...is the King." He chuckled. "And the king can never be wrong. Or can he?" He looked at Brimm. "You are supposedly a savant—what do you say?"

"I say that even a savant does not know who is wrong or right without first learning much of them, my Lord," said Brimm.

"A clever answer. You will certainly learn something of the king to-morrow. He is curious about you. He has troops about Ur—that mayhap is the reason…" He glanced at Selinn, and chose not to finish the observation.

"Will Atlantis make war on Ur?" she asked, with her usual directness.

He shrugged. "Perhaps, perhaps not. If you are indeed a princess—un-likely as that seems—you will strive to keep the peace. Our soldiers have occupied every land, thereabout, except Sumer, and Ur itself. It seems our High Priest has some superstition that keeps them from it."

"He is wise. Ur is protected by the moon goddess," she said. "All spir-its of the night sky are hers to command."

"I thought Ur had a god of the sun," Breeke said.

She sniffed. "One of those too. He is over-rated—like all males. The best of us worship the moon."

A servant woman filling a bowl of mead laughed at that, then remem-bered herself and quickly withdrew.

Breeke finished his spirits of wine and began on the mead, scooping it up with his goblet. He drank deeply; mead slopped on his chin, and tunic. A manservant stepped in and discreetly dabbed at it with a cloth.

Lord Breeke looked into his goblet. "I myself have only returned from Tyrrhenia this season, for the winters are kinder here, and the troops need rest. But perhaps I may get to know your land next…princess." He frowned, and pushed his goblet away, as if recognizing that drink might have loosened his tongue. "I bid you a restful night—and good fortune tomorrow." He stood, and, swaying, walked stiffly off toward his own bed-chamber.

After a moment Spund stepped up to the table, his considerable bulk cast a big shadow. He pointed at Brimm with a dagger. "It is apparent that my lord is bored with you. Go hence to your sleeping chamber, and get what rest you may."

"What is your rank, to give such commands to me?" asked Selinn, with a particularly imperious disdain.

"I am chief of guards, and a war-master in battle, woman! No more of your impudence—tomorrow you will be seen. The King may choose to employ you, or feed you to the servants of Poseidon and Baal, depending on his mood."

"Very good," Snoori said. "We shall not disappoint him. Nor shall we waste Lord Breeke's mead." He stood up, took the bowl of mead in his hands, and drank it down in one long draught, as Spund watched with a palpable disgust.

No servant came to wipe the mead from Snoori's chin, so he wiped it himself with the back of his hand.

In an outbuilding of the castle grounds, their chamber was of wood and wattle, sealed by bitumen. The chamber was in a large well-house built over a cold spring, and thus chillier than most of Atlantis. But the brazier glowed, providing sullen red-tinted light, and they had been given woolen cloaks.

Snoori staggered in first, threw himself face down on a pile of straw, was snoring almost before the straw-dust settled about him. Brimm sat on the floor with his back against the wall, near the brazier, his right side cold, his left too warm, and watched as Selinn, her back to him, stretched out in the farthest corner, her breastplate softly clanking.

After a moment she asked, in a low voice, "How did you know I was a princess?"

"I didn't! Although perhaps your mien suggested the idea. I wanted them to treat you with respect. Surrounded by armed men it was easier to use lies than swords. And sorcery needs preparation."

"I don't need you to protect me."

"I will keep that in mind. Surely a princess does not go wandering off at the whim of a seer? What truly brought you here?"

"I have no reason whatever to discuss my past with you."

Brimm was stung. But he said, "Just as you like."

* * * *

Brimm was exhausted but unwilling to face sleep—he could feel nightmares about Cleito clamoring to be released. He saw again her semi-human face; the black orbs of the giant squid, its beak sucking and chewing and spitting ...

Sometimes, on the walk from Cleito's palace, he had seemed to sense someone following. Looking back, he saw only misty shadows rising from the murky soil.

He looked about, found a piece of chalky stone in the wattle, and pulled it loose. He used it to mark out an intricate rune that Urgus had taught him—one of the first sigils he'd learned on coming to the sorcerer's caverns.

This you will need, said Urgus, *because my work sometimes draws unclean spirits, with whom I will not trade or truck. Yet they hover about, waiting for a chance to drink the life of the unwary...*

The sorcerer's remarks had been uttered with methodical languidness, but they'd made Brimm's flesh creep. He memorized the sigil with his full attention.

The sigil completed, Brimm lay down by the brazier and resigned himself to a fitful sleep. Selinn stirred, sighing in discomfort. Brimm closed his eyes, and said, "Take off the armor, Selinn, and you will rest more easily. I will never try to take liberties with you, on my sacred word."

She did not respond, nor did she shift to remove her armor.

Brimm slipped into sleep, and into precisely the nightmares he'd feared. Cleito…

* * * *

As Brimm slept, some part of his spirit seemed to hover nearby, as if retreating from the nightmares that troubled the rest of his inner self. He found himself enjoyed with the hovering spirt, and watched his own body twitch and mutter, as some part of him dreamt of Cleito and her feeding. This detachment of spirit was something common in students of Urgus. It had its benefits.

Shortly, Brimm's disengaged spirit noticed a mist seeping under the doorway. The mist took shape: the outline of a woman sketched in an unwholesome vapor, its face obscured.

The spectre drifted toward Brimm's sleeping body—and then came to the sigil. It stopped, and backed away, as if blown by a sharp breeze.

It seeped back under the door, and was gone.

CHAPTER FOUR

When Brimm woke, he saw that Selinn had at last set her armor aside. She was snoring softly, deep under the straw.

He stood, and stretched, and went to a wooden bucket of water, where he cleansed himself as well as he could.

Then Snoori burst into the room, thrusting the heavy wooden door aside so it sagged on its leather hinges. "I have vomited copiously," he said, rubbing his head.

"Thank you for the announcement," Selinn said, sitting up and picking straw from her hair.

"Regret follows the tracks of excess, Snoori," Brimm said, quoting a Hyperborean saying.

Snoori belched and clutched at his belly. "But even so, I must face the king—and something…Something I don't want to know about. That big oaf Spund hints, and gloats about it, but won't tell me…"

"Yes—we face our 'welcome' to Mnemos," Selinn said, showing a glimmer of humor for the first time.

"Let us go and discover what Spund gloats about," Brimm said, as Selinn put on her breastplate and casque.

"What is that?" she asked, nodding toward the sigil on the floor. "I put it there to protect us from hungry spirits," Brimm said, shrugging. Indeed, he had dreamt—was it a dream?—of a spirit who had come, and had turned away from the sigil.

She picked up her sword and sheathed it. "I doubt the effectiveness of your northland runes. You would do better to sacrifice to Inanna."

"Is Inanna your moon goddess?"

"Of course not! That is Nonna. Inanna is not Nonna." She tightened the straps of her cuirass. "Do we have breakfast?"

"Do not speak of breakfast," Snoori groaned, turning away.

Presently a stooped old woman brought them flatbread, venison and a jug of water—Snoori choked down a little bread—and then Spund called them to the courtyard.

* * * *

Spund and Breeke's huntsmen marched Brimm, Selinn and Snoori into the square. Selinn had her sword and armor; Brimm had the piercer. Snoori had chosen a javelin, of several weapons offered him, perhaps hoping to skewer his enemy from a safe distance. He was not a coward, but he liked good odds.

Shields had not been offered them.

Spund halted them a few steps inside the courtyard. "Wait here," Spund said. "Do not move."

The morning sunlight hadn't quite reached the courtyard. Torches were set in corner sconces, their light guttering over the crowd and reflecting from the bronze helmets of guards leaning on iron-headed pikes. The ground was of beaten red clay; the high palisade walls to the right and left were of oaken posts black with bitumen. Across the courtyard from Brimm the outer walls of the king's citadel were made of black volcanic stone.

A dark balcony of gray rock and wood jutted from the wall over the gate. It was a little below the top of the walls, and still in shadow. Two servants in white tunics were placing large glass lamps to either side of the balcony as a short man in a sea-green robe, wearing a crown of gold and red coral, strode out to look down upon the courtyard. A tall woman in silver and red strolled out to sit by his side. Their faces were difficult to clearly make out in the jumpy lamplight.

"Behold King Squelos!" called out a crier in dark robes, stepping into view behind the king. "Hail your Sovereign and his consort!"

A markedly unenthusiastic cheer rose from the crowd.

"Kneel!" Spund snarled, giving Brimm a shove. Brimm staggered, then steadied himself, silently vowing that he would make Spund pay a deep and painful price for his disrespect. Already, on this journey, he had been struck from behind and made a galley slave; he had been needlessly arrested in Poseidonia and thrown into a dungeon. He had been deceived into quite nearly becoming meat for a monster. No further abuse would be tolerated without a demand for payment. *Soon.*

But just now…a sovereign with the power of life and death gazed down upon him.

Thus, Brimm knelt, as did Snoori and Selinn.

The king flapped a limp hand. Somewhere a drum began to thump, and brass chimes were clashed and jingled.

"Now stand and wait your turn!" Spund commanded. They got to their feet, and Brimm looked at the crowd, perhaps four hundred people huddled near the walls to right and left. Those closest—sitting apart in sedan chairs, and attended by bald servants in skull caps—were decorated in elegant face paint and long, dangling gold ear rings. They wore soft, shiny brightly-colored tunics, their braided hair and beards gleaming with pomades of butter and coconut oil and glinting with crystal beadwork. The bulk of the crowd, craning to see from behind the sedan chairs, wore crudely dyed woolen tunics, and rough boots of animal hide. Some yawned; others waited eagerly.

The wooden gate in the stone wall swung open…

But nothing came through the gate. Not yet.

Then, came squeaking sounds. A two-wheeled oxcart creaked into the square; it toted a large cage of thornwood containing three hunched men; grimy, scarred, wearing only loin cloths, their eyes haunted and angry as they clutched the crooked wooden bars. One of the men was black; perhaps he hailed from the continent to the South. The other two, with olive eyes and brown complexions, seemed Atlantean.

The ox stopped in the center of the square as if familiar with the destination, and from behind the cart stepped two priest-warriors in bronze masks, visages of Poseidon and Baal-Samin, the metal faces permanently frowning in judgment. They called out to their respective gods, one facing the nearest entrance to the sea, on his right—the ocean was out of sight but always made itself felt, in Atlantis—and the other looking to the sun. The crowd called out in response, the women warbling. Brimm understood only a phrase or two of the invocation: "From blood to fire, from fire to sea."

Brimm glanced at Selinn, saw an angry look on her face—she looked like a hawk guarding its nest, in that moment—and he saw that she had her sword at ready in her hand.

He drew his silvery piercer. Snoori, his face pale, clutched his javelin close to him.

The priest-warriors cut through leather knots shutting the back of the cart, and the three men climbed stiffly out, blinking in first sunlight creeping over the walls.

The priest of Poseidon went through the big doors into the castle, returning seconds later with three weapons carried in his arms like cordwood. Two were pikes, one a rusty ax. He passed them out to the three men, spoke sharply to them—something Brimm couldn't clearly hear—and backed away.

"If…those men are our adversaries, today," Snoori ventured, "why, then we'll have little trouble…"

The priest of Baal-Samin turned the ox and led the cart back through the gate. The priest of Poseidon called out gruffly to the shadows within the fortress.

There was a pause. And then…

Two giants shuffled forth. Each was head and shoulders taller than Brimm; each seemed to be only semi-human: partly man, partly beast.

One of them, the taller of the two, had the head and the long sharp horns of a gray-black bull, a furry dewlap hanging from under his jaw. The other was thicker, broad chested, with enormously long arms that nearly reached the ground—he had the head of a ram, with great curling horns. The hips and groin of both were girded in bronze and leather. Their feet were shod in heavy boots with wooden soles. The bull-headed giant carried a great hammer, iron and wood; the other carried a short spear.

"The minotaur!" Selinn breathed. "And his minion, the Goat Lord!"

The crowd cheered, welcoming their familiar champions.

"These will be our adversaries, once they've finished with those three men," said Brimm. "But I suspect they are neither minotaur nor goat god."

As the two beast-headed gladiators strode closer to the three cowering men from the cart, Brimm confirmed his suspicion. Looking closely, he perceived that the "minotaur" was actually a man wearing the hollowed, mummified head of a very large bull, its eyes cut away; a "transformation mask" completely enclosing the man's head and strapped to his shoulders. The ram's head was that of a great ram, also strapped on. Brimm saw eyes gleaming madly through the eye-holes cut in the masks. Some of their height was due to the strapped-on beast heads, but he judged both to be remarkably powerful, bulky men, and eminently dangerous. Could the audience not see through the illusion? Doubtless they preferred to believe.

Brimm looked to the rear—and Spund sneered at him. "There is no escape, northlander."

It was true. A double line of armored warriors stood behind Spund, their line bristling with pikes.

A roar and a shriek—Brimm turned to the square and saw the ram-headed fighter already trampling one of the Atlanteans, crushing the fallen man's ribs under his wooden boots; hairy fists, at the end of unnaturally long arms, suddenly coming together, crushed his victim's head. Brain matter spurted like yolk from a smashed egg.

"This does not bode well," Snoori sighed, as the priest of Poseidon called out for the god to accept this sacrifice.

"The fool stumbled and fell," Selinn murmured. "We must not."

Brimm was trying to recall a rune—Urgus's own 'Unmanning of Enemies'. The spell required drawing it on the ground, then chanting—what exactly? He almost remembered...

The other two prisoners from the cart were jabbing their weapons at the minotaur, who was easily blocking their jabs with the leather wrapped shaft of his sledgehammer.

The ram-headed warrior rushed the black prisoner, bent double, his thickly calloused knuckles taking the place of front hooves.

"He moves like an ape," muttered Selinn.

The ram butted the black man hard, knocking him into the other prisoner, so they both went tumbling down. The minotaur timed his hammer stroke neatly—it took a long swing to bring the great hammer up, over, and down, in the time the Ram Lord knocked the two men off their feet—and the sledge struck deeply into the black man's back, smashed through spine and chest, and kept going, crunching into the Atlantean beneath. The fallen men mingled their screams. The black man's shriek cut short, and he was left gurgling; the other man's scream went on until the minotaur swung the hammer in its long slow powerful arc one more time. The scream grew louder as the hammer neared.

Then the shriek was cut short with a startling suddenness.

The crowd hooted and clapped in approval. Drums banged and chimes jangled. The priests called to their gods.

The king waited expectantly, now turning to look at Brimm and his companions. And suddenly Brimm remembered how to cast Urgus's "Unmanning of Enemies."

He went down on one knee and used the tip of his silver piercer to scratch the rune into the flattened clay. Now, if he could chant the spell correctly...

Spund swaggered up and scuffed away the rune. "No magic, coward!" He pushed at Brimm with his foot. "Go! Take your turn with the Minotaur and the Lord of Goats!"

Brimm straightened up, glared at Spund—and saw a curious mist churning behind the big chief of guards. In the mist formed a shape he recognized: the specter who'd visited his chambers. It seemed to feel his gaze and slipped away into the foggy shadows.

Mists often swirled in Atlantis, and imagination gave them strange shapes—and Brimm shrugged the ghostly shape away. "Very well, Spund. Just tell me this—does your king forbid dueling?"

"Dueling? You may now duel the minotaur!"

"Oh, but it's you I'm thinking of. Afterwards. I plan to kill you."

"Ho ho! Sadly, I will not have the pleasure—you will not live so long! Now go!"

Selinn, looking very much a proud princess of Ur, was already walking toward the minotaur, short sword at ready.

Brimm growled to himself, nudged Snoori, and they walked up to stand beside her.

"Well, it's been a short life but an interesting one," Snoori said, hefting his weapon.

"These creatures work together," said Selinn softly—as they spread out on the fighting ground to face the minotaur with his bloody hammer, and the Ram Lord with his bloody boots.

"They do indeed," whispered Brimm. "Sidestep the ram, then rush the minotaur, cut where you can, and back away before he swings the hammer."

Selinn nodded. "It may befall better if we keep him between us and his companion."

Then the Ram Lord rushed at them, head lowered for butting.

Snoori yelled a Hyperborean imprecation at the Ram Lord and jabbed with his pike at its neck, then sprang aside when it turned his way. He evaded the creature by a hair's breadth, even as Selinn and Brimm charged the minotaur, the warrior-woman to the right, Brimm to the left. She made quick high-pitched yips at it, lightly slashing to draw the giant's attention. The minotaur began to swing the ponderous hammer her way, but she was already dancing back and then Brimm darted behind, aimed the piercer with a desperate precision, and sliced deep into the soft flesh back of the monster's knee, cutting through its hamstring.

Crimson blood fountained and the crowd cheered in bloodthirsty rapture.

The minotaur howled in pain, throwing its mummified head back. Then, crippled leg buckling, it tipped over onto its back.

"Look out, Brimm!" Snoori shouted and Brimm caught a peripheral blur of ram horns from his right. He threw himself aside and rolled, as the Ram Lord charged by on all fours, knuckles cracking the clay.

Gasping, Brimm got to his feet in time to see Selinn vault onto the Ram Lord's back, wrapping one arm around the base of its goat-head mask, stabbing under the leather straps with her short sword. The blade plunged deep and the Ram Lord bellowed, pawed at his throat and skidded to a teetering stop.

In a split second Brimm realized that the Ram Lord was going to fall hard on Selinn—and the giant's great bulk was enough to shatter her.

He couldn't reach her in time…

But Snoori was there, stepping in, grabbing the wrist of her sword hand, pulling her free as the creature fell.

The two of them tumbled clear of the Ram Lord.

Another roar from the crowd—and a growling snarl from the minotaur as it struggled to get up on its good leg, using the hammer as a crutch.

Unwilling to let the minotaur rise, Brimm rushed in, dodged a swipe from the giant's club-like fist, and stabbed the piercer through the eyeholes of its mask, driving the blade with all his strength.

The minotaur screamed and let go of the hammer to clutch at its head, falling back writhing in the dust.

Then it shuddered…and lay still.

Brimm looked for the Ram Lord—saw Selinn stabbing down hard, severing the thing's spine.

Removing his bronze mask, the priest of Poseidon walked stiffly up to the dying minotaur. He was a bald man with angry black eyes and a neatly cut beard; he wiped sweat from his bearded face with the back of his hand, stared down at the creature, then turned angrily to Brimm. "You have killed the son of a god! This is blasphemy!"

The crowd gasped and muttered.

"Rubbish, priest! That thing has no kinship to a god!" Brimm called out, making certain it was loud enough for the onlookers to hear.

He strode to the minotaur, pulled his sword free, then used it to cut the straps on the mask.

"Stop!" the priest hissed.

Brimm tugged on one of the great curving horns and pulled the bull's head away. Beneath the mask was a face that was scarred and filthy, its beard cropped short—but quite human. And now, it was staring in death.

Brimm threw the reeking bull's head aside and turned to see that Selinn had exposed the face under the Ram Lord mask. The face was, in fact, *not* quite human. It was somewhere between ape and man, with a receding jaw and sloping forehead. Thick black brows grew together over glazing, sunken eyes.

"It's one of the Other Men," Brimm muttered, walking over to Snoori and Selinn. The three of them gazed in dull amazement at the dead subhuman. "I thought them all dead."

"A few such cave-dwellers remain," Selinn said. "I have seen them in the mountains north of my land. A dying race. They will soon go the way of the furred elephants."

"You have killed the son of a god," insisted the priest stubbornly. "He became the son of a god when we declared him so!"

"That makes no sense at all," Brimm said. But it was useless arguing with priests. He raised his voice and called to the crowd. "If I have killed the son of a god then the gods have permitted me to do it! Who could fly in the face of their will?"

The crowd muttered; some seem to speak in assent, others damned him with the sign of the horn. The priest glared at him, then looked up at King Squelos, as if to ask him for a judgment.

I've got to steer them another way, Brimm thought, and turned to Spund. "You! Spund! We owe our royal hosts another fight! Come—I challenge you! You have impugned me! Now defend your right to demean me—or skulk away like a coward!" He turned to the king. *"And let the vanquished surrender his blood to the Gods of Eumalosa!"*

Spund clenched his teeth—and looked up at King Squelos. "My Lord?"

Squelos nodded gravely, and called out in an oddly high, fluting voice, "Strike him down if you can, Spund! You have been challenged in this place of ritual combat! You can do no other!"

"And anyway," put in the queen, her voice lower than her husband's, "I am bored! The other fight was over so very quickly!"

The King nodded at her in sympathy.

Spund grunted, drew a long heavy scimitar, and charged at Brimm

—who was then turned away to watch the king and queen.

Brimm, however, both heard and *felt* Spund coming. The fight with the two false demi-gods had sharpened his senses, and now his sorcerer's intuition was keen. He ducked under the big slicing blade, feeling the air of its passing, and stabbed upward up deep into Spund's armpit.

Spund screamed, dropped the sword, and clutched at the wound as Brimm danced out of reach.

The crowd whooped in delight.

"Pick up your sword, Spund!" Brimm shouted. "You have two hands!"

Spund spat a curse at him, but snatched up the sword with his left hand, swung it in a high arc and brought it down hard—right where Brimm had been standing a split second before.

Brimm had leapt backwards in a move his father had taught him, coming down on his feet neatly, leaning forward to balance the backward motion, and now he slashed at Spund's forearm.

The piercer cut deep—and Spund howled.

Brimm danced back, shifting his weight from foot to foot, waiting—and Spund obliged him by charging again, coming at him like a rhino, head down, sword extended.

Brimm was surprised by his adversary's quickness, and had to throw himself down to get out of the way, shoulder-rolling tautly, coming up before Spund realized he'd missed his target.

The chief of guards was blinking in confusion, staggering to keep standing, spurting blood from two wounds.

Spund turned, raised his weapon—and the spectre that Brimm had glimpsed earlier in the mist now reappeared; it came from behind Spund to dart at Brimm's eyes.

For the first time he saw the ghostly face clearly: *Cleito*. She gave out a soul chilling hiss as she flew directly at him.

Startled, Brimm stumbled back, and had to twist his entire body, fast and hard to one side, to avoid Spund's blade. It stabbed through his tunic but only grazed his skin; the tip of the scimitar drove into the clay. Instead of pulling it loose, Spund grinned, grabbed Brimm by the throat, yanked him close and started to squeeze.

But Brimm had his weapon ready—he drove the piercer up under Spund's chin, between the bones of the big man's jaw, through his tongue and up into his skull.

Brimm twisted the blade, and Spund stiffened, coughed blood, spasmodically letting go of Brimm's throat. Brimm had just time to roll aside before the big man fell.

Only now feeling the full wave of fear that had crashed over him with the onset of Cleito's apparition, Brimm got to his feet, wrenching his blade free. Rubbing his throat, shuddering, he watched till he was sure Spund was dead.

The crowd was chanting a local word that Brimm did not know—but it had the sound of raucous approval.

The two priests looked at the crowd, then at one another. The priest of Baal-Samin shook his head at the other, who shrugged. They then went to Spund, intoned to the sun and the sea, offering his fading life as their gift, as if they'd planned the whole thing. Then they turned to walk with what dignity they could muster back into the citadel.

Brimm looked up at the king, and went to one knee. "Great Lord and King! Queen of the realm! You have lost a chief of guards! Allow me to offer my services, and those of my companions! Any one of us is more than enough to take his place! We only wish to serve you."

He was afraid Selinn would interject, "*Temporary* companions." But instead she went silently to one knee before the king. Snoori knelt too, and the king nodded.

"Come into the citadel, then!" he called down to them, standing. "We will speak further. Oh, and I declare you the winners of this ritual combat."

"Is there any sort of reward that goes with that?" Snoori asked, to Brimm's intense annoyance.

"I don't know," the King said. "No one else who has met the minotaur and his companion has ever survived. I shall give you a nice glass of wine and perhaps some sheep and bulls."

"That seems appropriate," said the queen brightly, taking his arm. "Come, Squelos. I am famished."

CHAPTER FIVE

The king and queen of Eumalosa were already enjoying breakfast when the stooped, white-robed seneschal led Brimm and his companions into the feast chamber. It was a big oval room of volcanic stone and wooden columns, lit by brass oil-lamps on the big oaken table, and high narrow windows which admitted but little light. Wooden platters held fruit, some of which Brimm had never seen before, and meat cracklings.

Brimm, Selinn and Snoori had been cleansed of blood and dust, and had surrendered their weapons to a heavily armed and quite hairless eunuch. Brimm regretted letting them take the piercer, not merely because it was precious. While he was *reasonably* hopeful the king would not give the command to have him slain today, Brimm had his doubts. The priests could have privately petitioned Squelos to punish Brimm's so-called blasphemy.

But as they approached the royals, Squelos looked up at them with only mild interest. "Who is this? Oh—you!" He wiped his mouth with an embroidered napkin.

"Ah yes!" The Queen poured herself some wine. She picked up the gold cup and eyed Brimm. "I almost didn't recognize you without Spund's blood on your face."

But she was smiling as she said it. That was a good sign, wasn't it?

Brimm bowed to the king's consort. Then it occurred to him he didn't know the queen's name. "Thank you for your hospitality to us...great queen."

She was a dark, lanky woman of perhaps four decades, with straight black hair snipped sternly off just above the shoulders. Gold paint outlined her eyes, beneath her precisely clipped bangs, and her eyebrows had been plucked away. She wore a white robe trimmed in gold thread. A handsome woman, her prominent nose somehow adding to her royal mien, she resembled images he'd seen of women belonging to the royal clans of northern Ifri, the seemingly endless continent not so very far to the south: a place of vast deserts and trackless jungles and grand rivers and lakes that were said to rival seas. Likely she had been a princess of Ifri married off to Squelos.

Brimm bowed to her, then turned to the Squelos. He was a squat man, with large dark eyes, more light-skinned than the queen, bearded but otherwise apparently hairless.

Brimm cleared his throat. "I regret the necessity of having had to kill a useful guardian, great King. I do not engage in casual dueling, and often bear a tepid slight, even the occasional understated calumny. But Spund insulted me repeatedly, and abused me, when I came here only to seek your service."

The king plucked a bit of gristle from his teeth and flicked it onto the floor. "Any armed stranger who comes here is normally taken into custody, and thereupon enslaved or sacrificed or, in some instances, inducted into my army. You are however too useful to sacrifice—it wouldn't look quite right, either, as the low-castes and even the nobles seem to approve of you."

The queen set her cup down and nodded. "And I'm told that this woman…" She peered at Selinn. "—claims royal blood? She does have the look of the nobility; perhaps one of the families along the Euphrates. Slavery would thus seem inappropriate." She looked at Brimm and Snoori, with an expression of distaste. "And these two are her guardians?" She gave a small shrug of regret. "We cannot make them our slaves."

The King gazed at Selinn for a moment, his nostrils flaring, then he shrugged and gave an assenting grunt. "I suppose you are in the right of it, Maitha. Hence, you three will all be of service as functionaries of my army and the citadel guard."

"What does a *functionary* do?" asked Snoori, blinking. Brimm rolled his eyes. Snoori remembered to add, "…O Great Lord."

"I have a thought or two in the matter," said Squelos urbanely. "Perhaps this one…" He waved an emerald-bedecked hand at Brimm. "…this one can take Spund's place. It's the usual thing when a man of Spund's rank is dispatched in a fair fight. I shall dispatch a messenger to the guards." He took up his cup and tossed back a draught of morning wine. He belched, and said, "You there, servant! Bring these three some wine."

They were brought three cups of morning wine—in cups of brass, not gold—and drank gratefully, for the tension of combat still lingered.

"And as for your rewards, why, you shall each have a cow and a couple of sheep, perhaps one or two other beasts."

"Can we sell them, Great Lord?" Snoori asked, guilelessly.

"Why, certainly, if you do not wish to breed the sheep, though it can be profitable…" Squelos shook his head in wonder. "Why am I speaking of animal husbandry with this man?" He dabbed at his mouth. "More relevantly, I shall have the under chieftain of Guards instruct you in your initial duties, this very afternoon. Do finish your wine and go away, please."

"Not so hasty, Squelos," Queen Maitha broke in. "I've heard that this reed of a northlander is a sorcerer! That is what Breeke tells me!"

Brimm bowed to her once more. "I am in fact known as Brimm the Savant, a humble student of sorcery hailing from Hyperborea."

It was now Snoori's turn to roll his eyes.

"Are you indeed a savant of sorcery?" Maitha leaned forward with greater interest. "Well then! Can you be of assistance to a man who is unable to sire children?"

Squelos's brow darkened and he clacked his cup down. "Or a woman who is not fertile!"

The queen looked at him her husband a slight frown, feigning puzzlement. "But Squelos—there is your harem. They too have not—"

"Silence!" barked Squelos, throwing his cup at the aging servant. "We have no need of such aid! If he's a sorcerer he is to apply his magic to the reading of omens—and perhaps to…ah, I have it! The calling down of storms upon the enemy!"

"Oh—he can do that!" Snoori said with a burst of enthusiasm. "I've seen him! When we were—"

"*Snoori,*" Brimm interrupted sharply. "There is no need to boast. All my arts are at the King's disposal." While it was in his mind to profit from being a court advisor on sorcery, he knew that unrealistic expectations could be disastrous. Events could take an ugly turn for a man who disappointed a king.

"Good, good," Squelos growled. He waved impatiently at the servant. "Where is my cup, damn you! Bring me more wine!"

"Perhaps," said Maitha in a bored, dismissive voice, "you might wish to return to your quarters—you will be summoned in good time."

The three companions bowed as they backed away, then hurried from the room.

* * * *

Of the ten kingdoms of Atlantis, Eumalosa was neither the biggest, nor quite the smallest. In a shallow valley, encompassing both the city-state and its countryside, the domain of Squelos was shaped like a skewed rectangle, extending, as did all the kingdoms of Atlantis, from the hills near the outer cliffs of the island down to the innermost of the semi-circular canals. Here were its docks and quays, the primary fish market, and the seven galleys, along with a handful of small craft, that made up the navy of Squelos. When summoned by the high council the modest navy of Eumalosa took its place as a small component of the great fleet of Atlantis.

A moderately broad avenue, paved in baked bricks, stretched from the sacrificial square by the palace, unreeling for a good distance to the east. It was technically called The Avenue of Our Most Glorious King Squelos, but was more commonly known as King's Way. Here, strode Brimm, Selinn and Snoori, weapons returned to them, dodging carts pulled by ill-tempered oxen and sedan chairs lofted by muscular servants with a tendency to spit at anyone in their way. They stayed close to one another, aware that they might have enemies here—Spund loyalists, or sacerdotal assassins—and as they went the trio of newcomers glanced with mild curiosity at the rudely built shops and inns lining the way.

Like tributaries to a river, King's Way was fed by narrow, crooked side streets thick with reed-roofed hovels and the occasional larger, stone-walled domiciles of merchants. Eventually King's Way led to the barns for the royal stock, and the barracks for soldiers and sea-warriors. Just beyond the barracks awaited the slightly more comfortable garrison of guards. There too was the musty, chilly structure, both well-house and grain storage, where Brimm and his companions had been lodged.

The air was thick on the King's Way, heavy with impending rainfall. What now should he do, Brimm wondered. Sell the ceremonial dagger of Fress, sell the stock animals, and leave this Atlantean kingdom for another? Or accept the possibly onerous duties of his new post?

What was the hurry? Brimm felt he'd proven himself enough today. And after all, why rush to duties likely characterized by headache-inducing tedium? Despite the obeisance he'd given Squelos, he had not been here long enough to feel loyalty, nor yet devotion. Indeed, the king struck him as an absurd figure. There was time enough for duty.

They continued pressing through the mid-morning crowds along the King's Way, stepping over animal droppings and away from beggars who were likely also cut-purses, until they came to a wine shop that struck Brimm as being less squalid than the others. It was beginning to rain in thick, warm drops that would soak them in moments if they remained in it.

"Let us take shelter and refreshment here," said Brimm. "There is something I need to tell you, something which cannot be discussed at the garrison."

* * * *

The wine shop was little more than an open air shed, with grimy, questionable cushions and three-legged stools scattered about. Brimm and his companions sat on cushions in a corner that smelled of old urine. A bow-legged man with a long beard tended a table on which rested two large bronze jugs, tin cups, and several corked amphorae. Shimmering fringes of rain water wavered from the edge of the thatched roof.

Snoori went to the bow-legged man, gave him a coin and poured himself another cup of wine from a pitcher. He returned to stand beside Brimm. "In their great generosity they restored our weapons to us," said Snoori, touching his javelin leaning on the back wall—the only true wall. "But we still have no shields. I *do* so desire a shield, if we're going to make war for Eumalosa. A shield. Armor. A bow and arrows. Bodyguards…"

Sitting cross-legged on a cushion, Brimm was shining his silvery piercer upon his sleeve, holding it to the light to see if it was dull, and then shining it some more. "We will have shields, Snoori, and even armor." After a pause he added thoughtfully, "Bodyguards are unlikely. But I may be able to summon something useful."

Disdaining wine, Selinn stood nearby, watching a chariot roll clunking by. "We could have used your something useful with the minotaur and his Ram Lord. It was a near thing."

Snoori groaned softly. "The minotaur—only now are my legs turning to jelly." He sank onto a stool.

Brimm nodded. "Three men squashed like bugs for the amusement of the crowd." He sighed. "One mis-step and they'd have squashed us too."

"Snoori," said Selinn, examining her own sword. "I wish to…express…" She grimaced, as if what she was to say came hard. "…my gratitude to you. You pulled me away from the Ram Lord in a most timely fashion."

Snoori looked at her with gaping surprise. "You are, ah…you're thanking me? I mean—naturally, you would."

She grunted in irritation and sheathed her sword. "Brimm, what did you mean, about there being other help?"

"In fact," said Brimm, regarding his elongated reflection on the blade. "I wish to consult…" He glanced at the wine tender, and lowered his voice, as the others leaned closer to hear. "I wish to consult the dead."

Snoori winced. "Must you? Haven't we had enough truckle with ghosts?"

"Something happened today…An occurrence making the colloquy necessary." He glanced at the diminishing rainfall, and judged that it was would soon end. "I would speak to the dead partly—about the dead. Who is better informed on the subject? And I would query them also about the living."

Both Snoori and Selinn looked uncomfortable. "Snoori is right—why stir up the dead, Brimm?" Selinn asked. "It's generally considered vulgar to awaken them."

Snoori nodded glumly. "I've heard they become annoyed. I myself dislike being awakened from a good sleep."

Brimm shrugged. "Urgus told me that the dead know the sly man's way to magical power. I am…" He hesitated, hating to admit it. "…not *fully* trained in sorcery. And the king is going to ask me to magic something."

Snoori shook his head. "This plan reeks of the grave, Brimm. An especially unclean grave."

"Does it reek so?" He gave them a rueful smile. "We have an enemy who has the same odor about her. Cleito attacked me today, when I fought Spund. Her soul, her vengeful wraith, tried to distract me at a critical moment, and nearly succeeded."

"Cleito's ghost?" Selinn looked to the water slithering in the gutter as if she thought to see a ghost there. "So, your javelin throw did indeed kill her! I was not quite convinced of it…"

Brimm nodded. "It seems she died—but she does not forgive. She has lived for centuries, accruing dark spiritual power. And now she uses that power to stalk us. She will wait for her chance and bring woe upon us." Seeing Selinn's eyes narrowing in thought he said, "If you're thinking our splitting up might improve the odds, Selinn—think twice. Cleito will blame us all—and could appear to each of us, wherever we go. Consider too, that I kept you safe from that ghost last night—my rune drove it away." He sipped the dregs of his wine, and said, "I may well need help from the dead to stop her for good and all."

"You may well stir up a hornets' nest of spirits!" Selinn retorted, shaking her head. "I have seen it happen."

Brimm gave them his brightest smile. "If I have a little help, I can keep all under control! I need two people I can trust to assist me."

Snoori groaned. "Oh, not me, please Brimm!"

"And certainly not me!" Selinn said hotly. "The Moon Goddess would hardly approve!"

"But what I learn may be of benefit to Ur. Does your goddess not favor Ur?"

Selinn snorted. "Of course. But how would Ur benefit?"

Brimm lowered his voice. "We may learn a great deal about the plans of the Ten Kings of Atlantis. Their ancestors, their dead relatives, their murdered enemies…all watch from the shadows. They can be made to speak of Atlantean plans for Ur. And judging by Breeke's remarks, yester-eve, something is planned for your people, Selinn."

Snoori grimaced. "You were just denying being a necromancer, Brimm. But now…"

Selinn took off her casque, ran fingers through hair, nervous with indecision. "Where would you carry out this…necromancy?"

"Keep your voice down! No one must know of this. As for where it will be done, we must take advice."

Brimm appraised the wine-tender, who was growling orders at a beardless young man with spiky black hair. The young fellow had just arrived, wet from the rain. He set about refilling the jugs from a tilted amphora; he wore a stained and patched brown tunic, and sandals that looked about to fall apart. "Careful, Zerzi!" the wine tender snapped. "You're splashing wine about with mad abandon!"

"I scarcely spilled a drop, grandfather," said the young man blithely.

Brimm put his sword in its scabbard, took a bright silver coin from his purse, and approached the wine tender.

"I cannot change such a coin!" scowled the gnarled old man.

"I am a stranger here…"

"Something quite evident from your outlandish accent."

"I require guidance to a place for burial. A close relative has been laid to rest near here. You can keep the coin in its entirety if you'll guide me there this evening."

The wine tender tugged his white-streaked beard and sniffed. "There is only the place where the poor are thrown into the sea, up above, on the cliffs—long miles from here—and there is the Necropolis of Eumalosa. Some call it the Labyrinth of Shades. No other burial place do I know of, nor do I care to."

"And do you know how to find this Necropolis?"

"It is west of here—somewhere." He thrust out his hand, palm up. "Now, the coin!"

Brimm drew his hand back, the coin held as an enticement just out of reach. "I wish to be guided directly to it, just after the moon rises."

"In the darkness? Not I!"

"Why, the place is fearful," said the young man. "But…" He shot an arm out, snatching the coin from Brimm. "I will brave the soul-lickers, the night gaunts, and the oozing shades, and take you to the Necropolis tonight! I know it well!"

CHAPTER SIX

Brimm, Snoori and Selinn followed Zerzi through a black-shadowed maze of gray stone. Bleached by the moon, the stone barrows hunched about them, like animals gone still before the pounce. Some of the death-barrows were great blocks of squared stone, capping tombs; others were mere mounds of stone.

Such was the necropolis, the Labyrinth of Shades: the ancient cemetery of Eumalosa.

Selinn was normally a fearless woman. But there was a note of foreboding in her voice as she asked, "Brimm—why must we explore this place at night?"

"First, because Urgus prescribes it. He says the spirits who linger are more talkative at night, once the moon has risen, for then they are more active. And second, we must do this as clandestinely as we can. Before we are done we may be violating tombs."

"Must you admit to that aloud?" asked Zerzi, glancing back with a look of disapproval. "You don't know what might be listening."

"Lead us then and be quiet about it," hissed Selinn.

Zerzi grunted and resumed leading them through the outer barrows of the Necropolis, a mazelike arrangement of stony humps and mounds following the gradual slope of the hill up to the left. Here and there between the mounds, standing stones caught the moonlight, seeming to lean toward them for a better look as the party passed.

"How is it you know this city of graves so well, Zerzi?" Brimm asked.

"I used to meet my love here—but it was during the day," Zerzi said, sighing. "Ilda and I needed to see one another where we felt safe from the eyes of the living…And the dead sleep during the day."

"What became of her?" asked Selinn.

"Exiled! They won't tell me where. Perhaps to Thrace. She is the daughter of a wealthy man. He sent her away, because of me. I ache to see her again—there's little hope I ever shall."

They came to a place where pathways between the tombs intersected; here, bigger dolmens hulked, throwing deeper shadows.

"Labyrinth of Shades indeed," Brimm said, softly, looking uncertainly about.

"Which way now, boy?" Snoori asked.

Zerzi hesitated. "For your purposes, the center of the necropolis—this path." He pointed.

"Perhaps we should have a torch after all," Brimm said. "We could go back for one."

"No," Zerzi said. "The light would be seen—the village is below us."

He struck off on the path to the southwest, and they followed at a short distance.

Then Zerzi came to an abrupt halt, so that Brimm almost bumped into him. Zerzi was staring into the darkness, off to the left. Brimm paused and squinted that way—and saw nothing but obscurely shifting shadow.

"What is it?" Brimm asked.

"I heard a voice from there!" Zerzi pointed. "Calling me!"

"I heard nothing."

The four peered nervously into the darkness. Brimm thought of Filkin's Instant Torchlight—but was reluctant to use it, for the same reason they had no conventional torches: there was still the danger of being seen and taken for tomb robbers.

"Ilda!" hissed Zerzi.

A shape, pale and dark at once, coalesced ahead of them on the crooked path between the tombs. Brimm made out a woman's form, lithe, small, wrapped in a tunic. Her face showed palely when she came smoothly into the moonlight. It was an oval face, with almond eyes gazing at Zerzi in quiet, unblinking adoration.

Zerzi started toward her. "You're here!" They stopped just two paces apart, gazing at one another in wonder. "You ran away from them!"

"I have been hiding here," she said, her voice so soft Brimm could scarcely hear her.

"Why didn't you tell me?"

"I called to you," she said, her voice a soft stream of melancholy, "but you did not come."

"How could I hear you? I was in service, pouring wine for boors and fools, away in the village—and thinking you forever gone from Atlantis!"

Zerzi reached for Ilda, but she slipped back just out of his reach. "You mustn't touch me. I am unclean now."

"You! Nothing could make you unclean! If someone has misused you, I will kill them myself, and thus right the wrong!"

"No one has embraced me but you, Zerzi! No one ever will."

It occurred to Brimm that when she spoke, her lips did not move. And he became conscious of a distinct tingle at the top of his head. "Oh no," Brimm said. "Zerzi—she is dead."

"Dead! She is no ghost! I see her bosom heave with breath! Her eyes are bright with life!"

"You see the breath of death," Ilda said sadly. "We breathe the ether. My eyes show the shine of death—it is what wandering souls use to light their way." She gave out a moan of anguish. "I tried to escape them, Zerzi, when they took me to the ship. I rushed to the rail, and threw myself into the sea. I swam to the shore—but they rowed back, and were waiting for me, and my own father struck me with his war club. Perhaps he did not mean to kill me. And he did not! They brought me here, thinking me dead, and wound these cloths about me, and anointed my body and sealed me away. I woke in the tomb...I could not move!"

"No!"

"Yes, Zerzi! I cried out to you, I called to you...In your dreams I came to you..."

"I thought them merely nightmares!" Zerzi cried, falling to his knees, pressing fists to his eyes.

"And so, death claimed me, and this place with it. At night I wander, but cannot leave the bounds of the Labyrinth of Shades. I long for the sleep of the Great Peace, but it is not to be mine..."

Zerzi sobbed into his hands. "I failed you—and you cannot even rest!"

"Perhaps I can find a way to release you, Ilda," Brimm said. "If you will do something for us."

Slowly, she turned her head to gaze at Brimm, as if she'd only just seen him.

"You are the magician," she said. "The one called Brimm the Savant."

"Who spoke of me to you?" he asked, chilled.

"Cleito. She called you a monster."

"Indeed?"

"But her own soul shows itself, when she is not careful, and I have seen what she is: a devourer of men who are sacrificed to her."

"Then do not let Cleito sway you, Ilda! But lead me to the lords of this place—for every necropolis has its king, its lords and ladies. Speak for me, and I will find a way to release you!"

"We shall see." She turned from Brimm and reached out a slender wisp of a hand toward Zerzi—and then drew it back when he made to take clasp it. "No! After this night, you must let me go into the Great Peace. And do not grieve, Zerzi, because in death I have seen the transience of life; I have looked upon the dreams that we call our hopes, and listened to the sirens that we call our aspirations. All is vanity, the echo of Narcissus. Life is like a fire that grows from coals that turn to ash even as the fire grows higher; its finish is in the ashes. Do not cling to ash. Seek out instead a light that does not fade."

She turned away, and glided between the stones, toward the center of the necropolis. Brimm followed, and—sobbing—so did Zerzi. The others came more reluctantly along behind.

Up the hillside they went, the dead girl drifting effortlessly, the humans toiling along behind her. At last they came to a flat place at the summit. Here was a big tomb, a great sprawling tomb with four towering standing-stones about it, and carvings embellishing its lower edges. A royal sigil was carved over a door sealed with stone. A royal family lay here, Brimm supposed; perhaps many generations were interred here. Brimm, Zerzi, Selinn and Snoori stopped short, as one shared impulse, within a stride of the moon-cast shadows around the tomb. They all felt it unseemly to go closer—they felt a warning in the air.

Ilda stood before the great shell-shaped tomb, and raised her arms, but did not speak in any voice audible to Brimm. Yet he felt, rather than heard, the invocatory whispering in her heart. Long, tremulous moments passed, as the whispering faded.

Then, luminous figures of green and gray blue stepped forth from the shadows under the stony roof of the tomb. There was a dozen, at least; but one in the center caught Brimm's gaze and held it. Not merely the specter's crown drew the eye, but his innate nobility. The ghost of a stocky, bearded man flowered at them; he had a furrowed forehead, under the golden wreath, and deeply set eyes, a firm, almost grim mouth; his raiment was a robe of spider threads woven with the blue part of moonlight. For this was one of the first lords of Atlantis, and one of the first true kings of mankind.

"Who calls Eumalos?" the king's voice echoed. He sounded angry.

But the royal ghost knew the answer when he looked upon Ilda. "It is you! Only your kindred blood could bring me out tonight. I chose to commune with the Great Peace. But you have disturbed me."

"Lord, I beg your forgiveness," said Ilda. "I too yearn for the Great Peace, and this sorcerer says he will bring it to me, if I open the gateway to the Lord of this city of night. You, great Lord, can enter the Great Peace, and emerge from it as he pleases. I am trapped here. I am your cousin, your kindred, and beg you to hear this man."

"Let him step forth and speak then," rumbled Eumalos. "But if he speaks of the secret without commanding it, then he is a liar, and a thief, and I will curse him into the belly of a malodorous demon!"

Brimm felt sickly, hearing that. *Still,* he told himself, *I do command the secret, from time to time, a little.* He stepped a little closer, and spoke up, though his voice quavered. "Lord Eumalos, King of Eumalosa, oh divine, glorious—"

"Cease this unctuous toadying!" thundered Eumalos. "What do you want?"

Brimm blinked, cleared his throat, licked his lips and called out, "My Lord—a blight is loose upon the land. The creature once known as Cleito has turned her ill-will upon Atlantis! She once fed upon warriors seduced to her temple, and now she roams at will—"

"Do you suppose me unaware of her?" Eumalos roared, with such force that Brimm stepped back and the tombs rattled and cracked. "The odious creature floats about hissing and demanding we worship her! She keeps just out of my reach—but if she once comes close enough I'll send her to the world men call Saturn! There awaits someone who will gorge on her soul."

"My Lord—I honor your sentiments! She is my adversary!"

"She is everyone's adversary! What of it? More important is the fate of Atlantis—something she hisses and sniffs about! Can I not see it? The shadows converge! And is it not my own blood kin, Squelos, who brings it upon us?" The wraith of the ancient king began to stalk back and forth, as he must have in life when he was in a fit of fury, shaking his fist and declaiming. "He and Glaban, who fancies himself Sovereign of Asesseon! His mighty ancestor Aseos would be shamed should he waken and hear of this! Glaban flirts with the Three Angers and would destroy Atlantis for his own sake! The fires of Ares and the wracking of Volcanus will consume this land if he has his way! He is mad! And what does Squelos do? He wastes his time planning to conquer Ur, and kneels to Glaban and begs a portion of his spoils! What spoils will there be for the fool Squelos if Atlantis is sundered and sunken into the sea? Squelos, my own blood—I wish I had strangled my offspring to stop his bloodline!"

Gad, that's rather harsh, thought Brimm. But aloud he said, "I understand, my Lord Eumalos! How can I set your mind at rest?"

"How? Why, stop his unholy alliance with King Glaban, and prevent them from using Cleito from rousing the demons of the deep world! What else?"

"Ah…what else indeed. If I'm empowered to do it, I shall do it, my Lord. But I need to know more—can you tell me—"

"Be silent!" The words rang in their minds even as they shook the stones of the necropolis. "I can bear this world no longer! As for you—" Brimm *felt* the eyes of Eumalos upon him. "Because you have touched on two matters of concern to me, I will give you two particular gifts: an uncertain lantern which may shed shadow as well as light, and a stone from the icy heart of Jupiter! It is called the Cold Heart. The stone will give you three things: power, temptation and restlessness!" The dead king laughed—a most unpleasant sound. Then Eumalos pointed a bony finger at Brimm. "The Cold Heart is hidden under the couch of a queen: the wife of the buffoon—I will not be obscure. When I say the buffoon, I mean King Squelos. When you hold the stone up to the gleam of Jupiter in the night sky, the Uncertain Glamor will make itself known. The Glamor is a person, and will speak. He will offer you protection from Cleito…for a time."

Snoori cleared his throat and whispered, "Brimm—could you ask him to repeat that? I'm not sure I…I mean, did you grasp what—"

"Shut up, Snoori!" Brimm hissed out of the side of his mouth.

"Now!" boomed Eumalos. "I return to the Great Peace with my loyal retinue—and this misplaced child, known as Ilda, may go with me, and there find the solace that was stolen from her…"

Eumalos clapped his hands together, and an iridescent shimmer flared out from their contact. The shimmer fluttered, but remained, and swirled about him, lifting Eumalos and his entourage in the air—moaning, Ilda rose with them, the spirits twining like strands in a rope.

Zerzi stumbled after her, calling her name—and leapt, catching at her ankle. He touched her spiritual corpus—and at the touch a furious light rippled down through him, separating his flesh from his bone, like well cooked meat under a sharp knife.

He fell asunder. His spirit was exposed in the process, rising, ascending eagerly, to twine with Ilda…

Then came a low thud, followed by a high-pitched tone, the shriek of space splitting apart; darkness enfolded Brimm and his company, as if the column of light had entered into a doorway that led only to blackness…

The light was engulfed, and vanished utterly.

* * * *

For a stunned time, the three who remained stood in shocked silence;

Brimm trying to take it all in. Snoori and Selinn were staring in horror at the sodden, bone-scattered remains of Zerzi.

"Brimm," Snoori said. "Can we go? May we *please* go now?"

Brimm nodded. "But there is something I must do first, and alone—I feel responsible for…for bringing him here." After covering Zerzi's remains with a makeshift mound of rocks fallen from the old tomb, Brimm turned away, and started down the hill. "Where do you go, Brimm?" Snoori asked, hurrying to catch up. "We have no guide in this labyrinth!"

"It is only called a labyrinth figuratively. I can see the lights of the village. We will head that way."

"And if we encounter tomb ghouls or—worse—the thirsting dead?"

"Then I shall try what spells I know. Those failing, we shall see which of us can run faster."

He sighed, as Selinn skidded down the hill to his side.

"What will you do now?" she asked.

Brimm did not answer directly. "I am not sure what I will say to Zerzi's father. He will probably demand payment."

They wended their way down the hill and through the maze of dolmens and tombs. They passed standing stones and scowling gargoyles and noisome barrows. They encountered no tomb ghouls, none of the Thirsting Dead, and in time made their weary way to their quarters—but they stopped just outside the rude wooden door, hearing dismaying sounds from within: moaning, evil chuckling, and weeping.

"The devourers of the necropolis await us here!" Snoori exclaimed, taking a step back. "They lay in wait to catch us by surprise in our own sleeping chamber!"

"If so, they smell of a barnyard," said Selinn, as she boldly threw the door open.

A cow, several sheep, and two goats cropped on the hay that had made up their sleeping pallets in the squalid stone chamber—more squalid now, with the animal droppings. The animals looked at them in surprise and commenced a series of bestial complaints. What had seemed a moan was a moo; what had seemed a sob was the bleating of sheep; what seemed an evil chuckle was the call of a goat.

But there was indeed laughter—it was coming from behind Brimm. They turned to see a tubby little man with long graying yellow hair, red cheeks and tattered toga, with a wineskin hoisted on a shoulder. The little man drank, he corked the wineskin, laughing, and waved a grimy hand. "So, you have your gift from the king! He did not give us a place to stable these beasts hence you must sleep beside them, ha-ha!"

"Who would you be?" Brimm asked coldly.

"I am Binchus, steward of the barracks and the outbuildings thereof!"

"And this outrage—these beasts stabled in our quarters…Whose idea was it?"

"Ah! The killing of their captain did not sit well with his lieutenants—Vilnip and Kelk, by name. They thought stabling the beasts here would be amusing—that you would receive a message thereby, and that, ah…"

"That *what?*"

"That you are not to imagine that Vilnip and Kelk will be ordered about by…vagabonds!"

"Interesting," said Selinn. "We shall see."

"It is all most amusing!" laughed Binchus.

"And where are you quartered, then, Binchus?" Brimm demanded.

"Why, I?" His breast swelled with pride. "I have the Steward's chambers, it adjoins the barracks, of course!"

"Do you know what posting the king gave to me?" Brimm asked, fixing his gaze on Binchus's red-rimmed eyes.

"I heard something—Captain of the guards?" Binchus scratched his head, and shook his wineskin to see if there was anything more in it. "The king makes such arbitrary decisions at times."

Brimm drew his piercer, and stabbed—the wine skin. The remaining wine spewed upon the sputtering Binchus.

Brimm shook the blade free and then pressed its point to the steward's quivering jowls. "As Captain of the guards I outrank you!"

"That—that has never been clearly established!"

"This point…" He pressed the blade ever so slightly, so that a little blood ran along the blade. "…establishes it!"

"That's right!" Snoori called out, laughing. "You've made your point!"

"I, Brimm the Savant, am your superior officer, Binchus! And as such I and my lieutenants here will establish ourselves in the steward's quarters! If you are displeased—take it up with the king!"

"But where will *I* sleep?" Binchus whined.

Snoori grinned, reached out, and thrust Binchus into the makeshift stable. Selinn shut the door on his protests.

The animals mooed and bleated with protests of their own.

SEVEN

Brimm woke from a dream in which he heard Eumalos speaking to him, again, repeating his instructions.

The stone, Brimm thought, as he sat up on his cot. The Cold Heart of Jupiter.

"I will give you two particular gifts: an uncertain lantern which may shed shadow as well as light, and a stone from the icy heart of Jupiter! It

is called the Cold Heart. The stone will give you power, temptation and restlessness! It is hidden under the couch of a queen: she who admits to being wife of the buffoon. I will not be obscure. When I say the buffoon, I mean Squelos. When you hold the stone up to the north star, the Uncertain Lantern will make itself known; it will speak, and will offer you protection from Cleito...for a time."

Clearly this was no ordinary dream. Already King Eumalos had grown impatient; had dug his spurs into Brimm through the medium of the dream world.

"Very well, King Eumalos," he murmured to the shadows. "I believe I understand at least some of what is asked of me. But it puts me at dreadful risk. The queen..." He closed his eyes and shook his head.

"Who are you speaking to?" Selinn asked, through a yawn. She sat up, and struck flints to light a taper. Once, twice, and with the third time it was lit. Her face glowed in the dimness. Brimm thought it looked, in that moment, like the face of a particularly fine marble statue he'd once seen of the goddess Diana.

"You do that so adeptly," he said wonderingly. "I always fumble at it and burn my nose with sparks."

"You have been spoiled by magic." She stood up, just out of the lamp-light, and began to dress. "I was given a herd of my father's horses to watch over; I was required to stay with them, in the grassy canyons, on cold and moonless nights, through mating and foaling, for a year. Food was brought to me once a month, and if I ran out I had to hunt rabbits and wild goats. I was usually alone, but for a hound, and had to make fire or have none..."

Brimm nodded, trying not to be overly impressed. Snoori gave out a great snore then, from the next room, and Selinn laughed softly.

She does laugh, sometimes, he thought.

Then her expression became serious. "Just as you said, Eumalos spoke of Ur—Squelos plans to conquer it. And here I am in the service of Squelos! Against my own people!"

"Still—you left Ur behind. Were you sent here by command of king or goddess? Or did you flee to Atlantis? I ask only that the knowledge might enable me to help you."

She narrowed her eyes as if about to give out a rebuke. Then she sighed, and relaxed. "Yes, I suppose, you being a magician, there's little I can conceal from you..."

If only that were true, Brimm thought.

She shrugged. "My uncle, a malodorous old drunk, wished me for his third wife. I went to the Temple of the Goddess, and swore myself to her—there, he is forbidden to despoil me. But he paid the High Priestess to make me a Concubine of the Gods—and in that ceremony he would wear a mask, and take me for his own. He swore that if I did not submit to him, the gods would see that I died for my impertinence. In Ur, this means someone would poison me! The Seer of the temple saw that I must depart Ur to save myself. And to meet the destined one here."

"The destined one?"

"The man with whom I will walk until I can walk no more. Oh, I have no idea who that is. Might be that old fool who sleeps with the sheep now, for all I know."

Brimm laughed. She smiled and turned away and he felt he would get no further confidences from her.

He went to the window and threw open the shutters, letting in the dawn light. The gray-blue morning light illuminated a weedy yard, a fence of crumbling stones, with decaying sharpened stakes pointing outward from it, and beyond, a pasture, where several horses sleepily grazed. They were thickset horses with rings of fur hanging over their shanks. The sun was rising on the right, to the west, and it was just beginning to crest, in soft-red suffusion, along the rising cliffs enclosing the great island. Birds were giving out long, complicated calls from the tree line beyond the pasture. Now came a bawling cow driven by the scowling Binchus. Wielding a switch, he was driving the animals, one by one, into the pasture so he could claim his new quarters.

Brimm smiled. But when looked again at the small, crumbling wall, his smile faded and he remarked, "This barracks is poorly protected."

He turned to look at their new quarters. There were two large rooms, with sleeping couches on the wooden floor. Along a stone wall stood cabinets and hearths and shelves, and a low oaken table—there was also a great deal of debris, wine skins and half eaten fruit and abandoned fur boots littering the floor, all remnants of Binchus's time.

Things must be set in order, beginning with our quarters, before I seek out the Queen, he decided. Cleansing the home-hearth, Urgus had said, is the first step to clarity of mind.

"These quarters are befouled," Selinn remarked, noting his appraisal of the place.

"Yes. It will be cleaned—and we will not clean it. I have a couple of fellows in mind for the task. There are figs yonder, on the table, and a jug that may be water. Let us breakfast, and then we'll find Vilnip and Kelk…"

* * * *

Yawning, Snoori followed them into the common room of the barracks. The small sleeping chambers of the barracks were arranged in a semi circle around the common room. Near the right hand wall was a hearth under a blackened hole in the ceiling and within the hearth the coals of a late-night fire yet glowed. The floor of beaten earth was littered with wine flasks and clay cups. A few pikes stood against the wall and several rather ripe geese hung upside down on pegs, waiting to be shorn of feathers. On a much nicked table of raw wood lay the quarters of a small deer. A wooden post stood in the center of the room, with a couple of war hatchets stuck in it. A few stools were scattered about; sparse light slipped through slit-like windows.

Mouths agape in sleep, three men sprawled on straw pallets, one of them hugging a wineskin to him. Brimm guessed they were supposed to be keeping watch. All three snoring men were fully dressed in leathers and rough cloth, though one had taken off a single boot before falling asleep.

Brimm found an expired torch in a wall sconce, carried it to the coals, lit it anew, and walked over to the snoring guardsmen. "Ho!" he shouted, waving the flame close to their faces. "Rise or burn!"

Recoiling, gabbling in alarm, they awoke, and still did not close their mouths, gaping at him in outrage.

A fox-faced guardsman, his long brown hair lank, his overbite impressive, scrambled to his feet, then clutched and his head, demanding, "Who are you?" The guardsman looked for his pike, found a bronze sword, flourished it, snarling, "What do you here?"

A bearded man with a round face snapped, "They are thieves, come to rob us! The King's Guards! How they will howl when they boil alive in the Jaws of Poseidon!"

"I recognize this man!" said the third guard—a red-headed man with a scraggly beard and trembling, freckled hands. "I know them all!" They turned to the fox-faced man. "Vilnip—they are the ones who defeated the Minotaur and his companion! They are the ones who killed Spund!"

"I alone killed Spund," Brimm said calmly, drawing his piercer. "And so was made Captain of the Guards in his stead. Do you dispute the choice of the King?"

"I…" Vilnip dartingly licked his cracked lips. "No. Not as such."

"Then put aside your weapon. I've come to wake you to your duties."

Vilnip tossed the weapons aside, and rubbed his aching head, squinting the while at the windows. "It seems but dawn!"

"Yes. You will have a busy day, you must get started. Binchus has informed us that one Vilnip and one Kelk persuaded him to stable our stock in our quarters. Is this true?"

The round-faced man stammered. "He said *Kelk*? But it was *Vilnip* who—"

"Silence, Kelk!" Vilnip growled. He staggered over to a wooden tub of water, and dunked his head in it.

Kelk reached for his wineskin—but Selinn kicked it aside. "Wine will not help your work. Drink water—and clean our new quarters!"

"What new quarters are these?"

Snoori chuckled and twirled a mustache. "Binchus has taken our former quarters—and we have his! You will clean the steward's rooms for us!"

"But Vilnip and I are sub-captains! We are not meant for menial tasks!"

"You have been replaced as sub-captains by Selinn and Snoori," Brimm said curtly, as he put the burning torch in its sconce. "And your pay will be cut accordingly."

"What! We will denounce you to the king for this! We have served long—and you are outlanders! Mere interlopers!"

Brimm shrugged. "You have failed in your duty, squandering your night in drunkenness. I wonder what other malfeasance are you three responsible for…"

"We three!" protested the red-headed man. "I am but a gatekeeper! A little wine—but I have engaged in no malfeasance! It was they, Vilnip his crony Kelk, and their captain, Spund, who skimmed the funds for maintaining the barracks and paying the men—"

"Silence, Drubb!" shouted Vilnip, spraying water from his drenched head as he spun on the gatekeeper. "Those are lies—all lies!"

"Lies? Then what of the coins you've secreted away?"

"A poor man's savings!"

"Which poor man?" Snoori asked, snorting.

"I mean they're *my* savings!"

"Your filchings!" declared Drubb. "And you make excuses about paying the rest of us our full wage!"

"Interesting, this tale of filched coins," said Brimm. "Where are they hidden, Drubb?"

"I don't know—I heard them speak of it late at night, and heard the clink of coins—"

"Better shut your mouth before you swallow a dagger, Drubb!" hissed Kelk.

"Well, Vilnip?" asked Brimm. "Where is it?"

Vilnip averted his eyes. "There is no stolen money to be found and I will not let you steal away my savings!"

Brimm grunted and knelt on the floor, scraping a rune in the planks with his dagger. "Snoori, Selinn—bring that rascal here."

"Which rascal?" Selinn asked.

"The squint eyed one, namely Vilnip."

Snoori and Selinn frog-marched Vilnip to Brimm, who grasped the guardsman's wrist, forced the man's right hand onto the rune. *"Let the Lord of Sneaks reveal his own,"* Brimm intoned. *"Let Hisp fulfill his con-*

tract with the servant of Urgus, and show the thief's hand, and what it has stolen!"

Vilnip cried out like a man burnt and indeed his hand shone with a red light that pulsed from within. The hand twitched as with a life of its own and tugged his arm, stretching it out like a snake searching for a mouse.

"My own limbs betray me!" Vilnip sobbed.

Brimm pushed him away—and Vilnip staggered toward his own sleeping chamber to the left of the others, his arm tugging him along.

"A man pulled by his own arm, now that is a curious thing," said Snoori, bemused.

Brimm and Snoori followed and saw that other guardsmen were stepping out of their sleeping cells, scratching their groins, yawning, staring in confusion at Vilnip as he hurried to catch up with his own outstretched hand, which seemed to want to crawl through the air to its goal.

Brimm saluted these other guardsmen, maintaining a lofty mien of authority, and stepped into Vilnip's chamber. Here, Vilnip was whining as his hand bloodied its fingertips, scrabbling at a plank under a piss pot.

Brimm called out to the Lord of Sneaks: *"Enough, Hisp! Stand by until you are needed again!"*

Vilnip's hand went limp and he clutched it to him, whimpering.

Brimm turned to Snoori. "Snoori, would you be so good as to look under that plank?"

Snoori knelt, moving the pot and the plank—which came up easily—and frowned at the dirt underneath it. "I see nothing. Ah, but the dirt has been disturbed…here." He dug down with his fingers, and came up with a leather sack large enough that it had to be forced from its socket in the earth. "There's a small fortune in here! Well done, Brimm!" He turned Brimm an arch look of inquiry. "And why didn't you use this spell before, when we needed, ah, resources?"

"Because it is a spell devised by Urgus, who has a somewhat exaggerated ethical standard. The money must be returned to those to whom it belongs—or woe will follow the magician. We have enough woe following us, as it is. We cannot keep this money. It will be distributed to the other guardsmen. But first—let us call Hisp again and search the chamber of Kelk! Hereafter Vilnip and Kelk will fetch, clean, and labor in full for us and the others, until I am satisfied—if they complain to the king, this embezzlement will come to light!"

* * * *

Grumbling but compliant, Vilnip and Kelk were hard at work cleaning the former quarters of the steward for Brimm and his sub-captains, as the rest of the guardsmen sat about the common room, counting up their new "savings," chuckling with pleasure.

"How kind Vilnip and Kelk were to put this money aside for us," cackled Drubb. "And we thought they were taking half our wages to line their own pockets!"

The others laughed. Brimm smiled, and raised a glass of noon wine to them. "After they're done cleaning the steward's quarters they will start on this common room—and they will clean the straw from your beds and replace it with fresh."

"To Captain Brimm!" called Drubb, raising a hand. "May the gods protect him!"

The guardsmen whooped in approval. Brimm nodded. This was what he'd hoped for—that his new charges would offer loyalty in return for their missing gold.

Some of the men were leering at Selinn, however, and that did not bode well. He feared for the lives of the guardsmen. Brimm looked the men over—then pointed at one of the oglers, a beefy man with irregular black teeth, beetling brows, thick black hair and an expansive beard. "You! What is your name?"

"Me, captain?" the man blinked at him with drink reddened eyes, and put a dirt-blackened paw on the small war-hatchet in his belt. "I am Reenus! The best hatcheteer in the King's guards!"

"You are gawping at this soldier, to my left, with disrespect! She is my sub-captain—which makes her your superior! Yet you moon at her like a bull at a cow! If you do not treat her with respect—"

Selinn interrupted him with a touch on his arm. "Captain—if you do not object, I'll handle the matter myself!"

Brimm shrugged. "As you please."

"Oh, you can handle me, you slip of a thing!" burbled Reenus, as the others laughed.

"But can you handle *me?*" Selinn asked, looking at him coyly. "If you can take hold of me, you can have me."

"Now this is a sensible woman, at last!" Reenus crowed. "I'll peel that armor off you in a trice!" He charged toward her, his hands outstretched.

Selinn stepped aside faster than a blink, slipped past his left arm and spun like a twirling dancer so that she was behind him. Carried by his own momentum, he stumbled by. She followed him, drawing her sword, and cracked him on the back of the head with its pommel, knocking him flat on his face.

The guardsmen roared with laughter.

Snarling in inarticulate fury, Reenus got to his feet, turned and rushed her.

"He's in for it now," Brimm murmured to Snoori.

Snoori nodded—as she kicked a stool under Reenus's feet. He was immediately tripped up, and fell, smashing the stool to flinders.

Another roar of laughter from the guards. She calmly put her sword back in its scabbard. Reenus got to his knees, drew his hatchet from his belt, and threw it at her, the blade spinning with vicious force.

Brimm almost jumped to intercept it—

But Selinn caught it neatly by the handle, spinning her arm to absorb the impetus, and on the return threw it back so that its thin iron blade stuck in the floorboards just under Reenus's groin.

His mouth dropped open as he stared down at the hatchet. The men hooted and clapped.

She reached out, tugged free a hatchet from the post, and, without looking—having already marked the place in her mind—she pointed with her head to the right. "You see the goose on the left, Reenus?"

Even Reenus turned to look. Already her hatchet was spinning to its mark, cutting through the dead goose's neck. The goose's head dropped to the floor while the hatchet was left quivering in the wall.

The men gasped and looked at her with newfound respect.

She pulled the other hatchet from the post. "The next man who leers at me will find he has only this hatchet between his legs." The men stared at the hatchet, then the one she'd used on the goose. "Well?" Selinn demanded. "Who's next?"

The men glanced at one another, and then dropped their gazes to the floor. None of them spoke.

Reenus got to his feet, pulling the ax from the floor—then he tossed it at her feet. "You're the best hatcheteer here, and it must be the work of the gods—for it ain't natural, but it's so. I'll follow you, lady, wherever you choose to lead!"

One by one, the other men gave her their respect, some with a mere grudging nod, some with real humility.

"Now, Reenus," Brimm said, "find your breakfast and commence setting this room in order. After that find two others and set up a guard around this place. At this point it could be taken by a gaggle of small girls."

"Ho, there, Captain Brimm!" called someone from the door.

Brimm heard a little mockery in the use of Captain. It was Lord Breeke, in the doorway, hands on his hips. "Come outside, Captain!"

Brimm nodded. "Snoori, Selinn—see my orders are carried out!" He noticed them exchanging looks of amused pique. His sudden ascendance over them was not particularly welcome.

But Selinn nodded. "Come on, Snoori, we've nothing better to do."

Outside, Brimm joined Breeke in the brightening morning.

Lord Breeke was patting the neck of a war horse; this one, the color of rust, stood by the hunt-master's own waiting horse, both beasts shifting their hooves and snorting with impatience. "I see you have the men in hand, Brimm/ Or you suppose you do. Now, I will instruct you in riding a horse. We have two errands this morning and we shall need them."

Brimm grimaced. The creatures made him nervous. He was used to riding yaks—which were slow but dependable, and their thick fur made good handholds. "Certainly, Lord Breeke. And the errands?"

"We will take a turn around the walls of Eumalosa, so that you will see what is well and what needs righting. And then—you are to ride to meet the Queen, in the woods yonder. Apparently, she has matters of magic, or perhaps something more you may find more arduous, to take up with you..."

EIGHT

"Keep astride the horse's back, centered on its spine. Clasp it with your knees—but do not clasp it too hard." Breeke shook his head. "No no, guide it with the reins, but do not tug them like a child, Brimm!"

"Like this?"

"Better. Give it its head, let him guide you till you *must* guide him—you can steer with your knees—"

"But you said the reins—I—"

The rust colored horse gave a wriggle like a fish in a net, and Brimm was tossed willy-nilly into the air. He found himself thumping into the sun-dappled grass of the pasture.

Lord Breeke chuckled. "Perhaps a chariot would be more suitable..."

Brimm got stiffly to his feet and glanced toward the barracks, which was just the other side of the pasture. With displeasure, he saw Snoori at the fence, grinning at him and whispering behind his hand to a bemused Selinn.

Growling, Brimm stalked over to the horse, clasped it firmly by the withers and climbed back on, just as Breeke had taught him—anyway, it was an approximation of what Breeke had taught him.

"I will learn how to do this," Brimm said, gritting his teeth and glancing sidelong at Selinn.

"Because she is watching?" Breeke asked archly.

"What? Who?"

Lord Breeke laughed.

Brimm sat nervously astride the horse, and nodded toward the low wall of stone and spikes that surrounded the southerly reach of Eumalosa. "Let us turn our attention to the defenses—they are sorely lacking. The wall is crumbling, the spikes rot, and the entirety was inadequate from the start."

"It's no surprise that the guards are unguarded but the walls around the king are stout," said Lord Breeke dryly.

"If an enemy discovers they can over run the king's guard and kill them as they sleep—how well is the King protected then?"

Breeke shrugged. "Squelos is concerned more with assassins than armies. Atlantis is protected by ten armies, ten navies, and by the armor the island wears—its cliffs."

"Is there no conflict between the kingdoms of Atlantis?"

"Not the sort that is played out with steel. Arguments, words, accusations are thrown about instead. So far. Elasippos and Impheres are the two most powerful kingdoms of Atlantis, on the other side of the island. Squelos and our neighbor, King Glaban, have been in some sort of alliance to try to change the balance of power within Atlantis. He is quite secretive about it…But I don't expect a war."

"Suppose Elasippos and Impheres decide to maintain the balance of power with force of arms? Who is to stop them?"

Breeke scratched his chin and nodded. "We'll speak to Squelos of it. If you put it that way, he'll heed. Best if all fortifications are improved."

In an hour and a mite more they'd completed their ride around the small city, its outbuildings and palace walls, and then Breeke turned his horse toward a nearby woods. Already saddle sore, Brimm allowed his horse to follow—it seemed to want to follow Breeke's steed—and they entered a moss-carpeted stand of baobab, following a thread of a trail between the spectacularly wide trunks. Soon they reached a copse of whistling thorn and quiver trees, none of them big and all dramatically shaped, twisted madly or astonishingly thick at the base.

The two riders continued through pillars of light admitted between the trees, and then came upon a thin, clear brook. They turned to follow it upstream, soon reaching a place where it bounced down a hillside. Near the top of the hill, a spring gushed from a cleft under a group of palm trees.

Brimm and Lord Breeke let their horses drink from the pool at the base of the hill, and Breeke, his mouth crooked with an inner amusement, said, "She awaits, up top, near the palms. Think nothing of her eunuchs, they stand guard but will be quite disinterested. You can tie your horse up to yonder snag. Leave your sword and dagger here. Go now, climb the hill. Do not disappoint Her Glory."

Sighing, Brimm slipped down from his mount and tied it up. He stretched, wincing, and turned to Breeke, thinking that perhaps he could persuade the hunt-master to undertake this chore—but Lord Breeke's mount was already carrying him into the shadowy woods.

Do not disappoint Her Glory. So be it, Brimm thought. She's not an unattractive woman.

But it could be like dancing along the edge of a cliff. If the King found out…

Brimm unbelted his sword and dagger, draped the belt over the horse's back, and climbed the path. It was a short trudge to the top of the hill. Here he paused, and looked upon a soft crater, a depression in the hilltop covered with moss and grass, naturally embroidered with flowers on vines that stretched across the ground. Around the top of the hill stood a ring of palm trees. Maitha was reposing, up on one elbow, on a long, intricately embroidered couch, about twenty strides away. The couch was set up on a brocaded, silken carpet, fringed in golden tassels. Between Brimm and the queen waited two plump identical men. He took them to be eunuchs, and he was correct.

The shaven-headed eunuchs, apparently twins, scowled identically at him and stalked up to him at the same moment. They wore red capes and white togas, and armored belts fitted with several bladed weapons. "Weapons?" asked the one on his right.

"I left my weapons on my horse," he said.

The eunuch snorted in disbelief and they both reached out, one with a right hand the other with a left, and patted his person thoroughly, searching for hidden weapons and perhaps vials of poison.

Satisfied that he was unarmed, they waved him through to the Queen.

She was refreshing her wine glass from a silver pitcher as he walked up. On the side of the silver pitcher was the raised image of a god, possibly Osiris. The Queen of Eumalos was ornamented with a scarab amulet of lapis on a golden chain, gold bracelets, anklet rings, and a long tunic, slit up the side to her waist. Clearly, there was nothing beneath the tunic but golden-brown flesh. Her feet were bare; her toenails were covered with ground quartz, glimmering when she shifted in the dapples of sunlight.

What of the stone, hidden beneath the queen's couch? Brimm wondered. What of the Cold Heart of Jupiter. Could Eumalos have meant this couch?

Brimm knelt before her and inclined his head. "Great Queen. Your beauty is like a mingling of the rising and setting sun. It is like the sea when the moon dances on—"

"No doubt," she interrupted. "Sit down near me, on the carpet there, and calm yourself with some wine."

Brimm obeyed, crossing his legs as gracefully as he might. He took up a waiting chalice, and poured himself some wine.

He glanced about. A lovely scene marred only by the eunuchs now sitting on the rim of the hilltop, their backs to the queen, gazing out over Atlantis, and murmuring softly to one another.

"Your guardians…" Brimm said softly, nodding toward the eunuchs, "Are they twins?"

"Nilfi and Ilfi? They are, yes. They were a gift to me from my father when I was married to Squelos. They were twelve at the time of my marriage—I was only fourteen myself. They have been castrated since infancy, and well trained."

"Perhaps the queen should have more formidable warriors for her protection?"

Maitha shrugged, drank a little wine, and put the chalice on the low wooden table. "Most warriors of Eumalosa are sworn to Squelos, not to me—and prone to speaking indiscreetly. Nilfi and Ilfi are fiercely protective of me. They're quite capable of killing a man in my defense. I have seen them do it. They also taste my food."

"A wise precaution."

"Additionally, soldiers are encamped a short distance down the hillside behind me."

"No doubt they brought the carpet and couch and table here."

"And brought me in a palanquin. They will come if I call." She blew out a long breath, seeming exasperated with the need to explain. "You, sir, are beginning to bore me. I had hoped for more from a self-styled Savant."

He took note of her barbed use of *self-styled*. "Perhaps I am not so acute as usual—I am stunned by your beauty, and close proximity, great queen." He leaned slightly closer to her. "Your perfume is rose essence on a base of labdanum, with a tinge of myrtle?"

"Very good! Are your other organs as sensitive as your nose?"

"That is not for me to judge, great queen."

"Too much sensitivity is a bane; too little is unpleasingly beastly."

Taking a chance, he asked, "Is there such a thing as *'pleasingly* beastly', ma'am?"

She chuckled, and reached for a little silver fringed blue bag on the couch; he hadn't noticed it before. "There certainly is!"

She opened the bag, and for a moment he hoped she might draw the Cold Heart of Jupiter from it. Perhaps she had been forewarned by a seer. Could it be so easy?

But instead she took out a tiny bottle of some rose-colored oil.

"Your perfume?" he asked.

"No. This is…a special combination of oils and herbs used by women of my nation, to the south—we use it to anoint certain men."

"What sort of men?"

"Men who may be desirable—but who could possibly carry a dark influence within them. Any danger in them—the wrong sort of danger—will be revealed."

She held it in her hand, rolling the bottle over her fingers with a thumb, and looked at him with the gaze of a cat, as if pondering his possibilities.

"And you claim to be a sorcerer…"

He considered revealing that he was little more than an acolyte. But to rise in the world he must stay close to the world's thrones. The occupants of those thrones must consider him valuable, if they were to keep him close. He merely gave a small acquiescent bow.

"But are you *indeed* a sorcerer?" she murmured. "Consider: My husband, dear Squelos, has taken a flotilla to inspect a small island we have annexed. It's only a day's sail from here—his belly can't bear more—and he'll be back shortly. But look…" She pointed up at the clouds, visible between the palm fronds. They were moving quickly to the east. "A strong wind blows east. Can you foretell—will it keep him there awhile? Will a storm rise and hold him on the island? If so…I will be able to, ah, entertain visitors at the palace, in peace. And perhaps, the next evening, I might attend an important meeting in his stead…"

He said, "As for the weather, I foresee…" He glanced up at the clouds, hoping for certainty from there. But no certainty came to him. He remembered a simple incantation intended for just this purpose: so that mariners might know the weather. But Brimm was unsure he could remember the spell.

"Well?" the queen asked, her back stiffening.

Brimm cleared his throat. He could always pretend to predict the weather, and if he was wrong he could blame it on someone having displeased the gods. That usually worked. "A moment, your glory."

He blew into his hand, marshalling his magical energy, and used the fingers of the same hand to make an intricate pass in the air, murmuring, "Zirrish, I ask only to see what is to be—this wine, I sacrifice to thee…" He poured a little wine into his palm and cast it into the air. It vanished. "And I give my promise to sacrifice a goat to you on the morrow. So! Will a storm push to the east, this day, so that ships are bound in their harbors? I ask you with these names…" He spoke several primordial names of power.

To his surprise—he hadn't thought he'd remembered the incantation correctly—a small whirlwind, no bigger than a turban, was forming between him and the queen. As he watched, it flattened into a small whirling cloud which quickly dispersed to reveal a conjured image, as if seen by a bird high in the sky:

A flotilla of Atlantean ships bobbed in a harbor, beaten by furious wind and rain, their sails furled, their anchors attempting to hold them in place. Wind streamed the Eumalosan flag atop each ship's mainmast. The galley oars were shipped. Better to wait till the storm passed. Risking snapped oars and dead oarsmen was not thrifty.

"And there you have it, my queen!" declared Brimm. "A storm indeed, and blowing easterly!"

"They don't seem to be attempting beat against the storm with their oars."

"It's too great a storm, your glory. It will blow itself soon enough. They will wait at least a day. The storm will surely delay your beloved." Brimm snapped his fingers to dispel the image—mere theater—as under his breath he uttered the words that made it vanish like smoke on the wind.

"Ah!" the Queen cried, in mock displeasure. "Poor Squelos! The king will indeed be windbound! How sad." She glanced up at the palms bending in the rising wind, and smiled with the subtlety of a butterfly's yawn. "But as I would have more discretion than this place allows us—" She glanced over her shoulder, in the direction of the soldiers waiting on the other side of the hill, then returned her little bottle of mysterious oils to its bag. "To-night, come to the western gate, when the moon rises."

Brimm bowed, wondering if the Cold Heart was in the palace, perhaps somewhere beneath the queen's couch. Or was it here?

As the queen poured them a little more wine, talking vaguely of plans for a meeting at the Keep of Glaban, Brimm leaned back a little, casually placing a hand, as if to brace himself, on the carpet close to her couch. Urgus had taught him to sense magical devices through the palms of his hands. The Cold Heart was a powerful magical artifact. Were it buried anywhere near...

He sensed nothing special buried close by. Wait, what was that? Ah, merely the skull of a murder victim buried a good distance below, its ghost still mewling as it had done for a century and more.

So, the Cold Heart was not here. More likely it was in the palace.

He was sure Maitha was a dangerous woman, and quite possibly treacherous. But he could make no excuses. He had to find the Cold Heart of Jupiter...

* * * *

"You don't object?" Brimm asked.

Selinn was sitting across from him and Snoori at the table in the common room.

"Of course, I don't object!" she declared, apparently outraged. She stared fixedly at the window, where the setting sun was reddening the windowsill—and perhaps it was reddening her face. "Your tryst with the Queen could not concern me at all!"

Brimm nodded mechanically. "Why should it?"

"Exactly!" She sniffed, and used a dagger to toy with the sliced lamb on the platter. She jabbed it lightly several times. "Why should it."

"Just so," said Brimm.

"Precisely," she said.

Snoori looked back and forth between them in puzzlement. "You are both curiously repetitive."

"And why shouldn't we be?" Selinn demanded, glaring at him.

"Why not indeed?" Brimm said, in a low voice, reaching for his wine cup.

Snoori blinked and scratched in his beard. "If Brimm needs the magical object to increase his power, very well. It increases our well-being too, for are we not companions? If he has to sleep with the queen—"

"Enough, Snoori!" Brimm snapped, glancing at the short hall leading to the guard's sleeping barracks. Someone, it seemed to him, was hovering just out of sight, listening...And hearing too much.

Brimm used his dagger tip to scratch a rune on the table top, touched the rune with his left hand, muttered the necessary words, and with his right hand flung the bolt of light—all in the space of a long breath.

Filkin's Instant Torchlight flashed harshly at the edge of the hallway.

A familiar voice squawked in fear, and Vilnip staggered out into view, rubbing his eyes. "Sorcery!"

"And what of it?" Brimm drawled.

"Some nations burn sorcerers!"

"And some do not," Brimm said, standing. "Some make them advisors." He strode to Vilnip, caught him the collar and flung him staggering into the common room. "You are spying upon me, Vilnip!"

Vilnip blinked blearily as Brimm loomed menacingly over him. "Not at all! I was just taking a moment, there in the hall, to contemplate, ah, the cruelty of the Fates!"

"They are cruel indeed, Vilnip, for I now plan to implant in you the living fire that eats bone! It will slowly cook you from the inside, using your skeleton as fuel! It takes a full day for death to bring you release! Now, let me see...How did the spell go? Ah, yes. *Insatiable Sezzel the bone devourer, I summon thee from the cosmos of fire—*"

"Wait!" Vilnip cried. "I will tell you only that I was concerned to hear the queen mentioned! I was worried that, well, someone might take undue advantage of her, and, ah..."

"And you planned to tell whom? In exchange for what?"

"I? Tell someone? No! Never!"

"You need not restrain yourself," Selinn said. "Speak freely, Vilnip! Who would believe this ungainly fellow—" She gestured at Brimm. "—this construction of broomsticks and a dour hangdog face, would be attractive to any woman, let alone the queen?"

Snoori nodded. "She's right, you know. She's certainly correct."

Brimm gave Snoori a cold look. "You need not be so definite."

He turned to Vilnip. "Do you concur with these two?"

Vilnip nodded thoughtfully. "Now that I consider the matter, the queen is, after all, not likely to take you into her bed. I must have misheard."

Brimm rolled his eyes. "And you will not go about gabbling your misunderstandings?"

"I am discretion itself."

"I doubt it. Now—go out and clean up the horse stalls. And remember the devourer of bones when you consider speaking behind my back."

Vilnip winced but went purposefully out to the animal sheds.

When Vilnip had gone, Snoori asked, "Is there such a thing as the bone devourer?"

"Not so far as I know. But sometimes the imagination is a more powerful deterrent than real magic."

* * * *

The winds continued to blow forcefully to the east, as Brimm walked up to the high, heavily reinforced gate of the palace. Tall palm trees bent together in the wind, as if in secretive conversation, and the waning moon seemed to be racing as clouds charged past it. An electricity was in the air, and he could smell sulfur, from one of the hot springs nearby, as he hammered on the gate with the butt of his dagger. One of the eunuch twins opened, right away, as if waiting for the knock. It might have been Nilfi or Ilfi, Brimm could not tell.

"Umf," snorted the eunuch, brows knit with disapproval. "I was afraid you'd show up. So be it. Give me that knife, and all other weapons."

Brimm handed over the dagger and his sword belt.

"Come this way."

He had not gotten ten paces when four soldiers surrounded him, held him fast, and searched him for good measure. They came up with nothing, and their captain nodded at the twin, who led Brimm across a garden lined with gigantic flowers, of a like Brimm had never seen. Some had great green stalks with blossoms shaped like a flamingo's head; others formed enormous cloyingly-perfumed trumpets that dipped toward the procession as they marched by. The walls kept the wind out, and yet the gigantic growths rustled softly.

Brimm strode with his escort across shiny green-black stone flags like those he'd seen in the temple of Poseidon, and up stairs of pink granite that clung to the side of the palace. At the second bend of the stairs they came to a door guarded by a one-eyed sentry with a crossbow in hand. He scowled at Brimm, but stepped aside, and muttered, "The door to the left."

Brimm nodded, took a few steps down a narrow corridor faced in checkers of alternating pink and black marble, then saw someone else approaching: a tall man in a blue robe, his head shaved, his beard dyed blue to match. Indeed, he had blue-painted lips and fingernails and eyelids, a color sacred to Poseidon. Brimm recognized him from the battle with the minotaur: the priest of Poseidon himself.

CHAPTER NINE

The priest raised his hand in a gesture of sacerdotal pomp. "Hold! I will speak to you before you see the queen."

Brimm had already come to a stop. "There being not much room in the passageway, I have already halted. You are the priest of Poseidon." Brimm gave a small, purely ornamental bow of respect.

"And you are the one who styles himself Brimm the Savant." His expression was dispassionate but his voice sneered acidly.

"May I know your name, Lord Priest?"

"Everyone of significance already knows it. I am Mestor, nephew of Cressis, who was son of Elipsistor, who was son of Buruss, who was son of Resqender—who was the first Priest of Poseidon. His father was Slorin, who was son of Beneprion, who was son of Perrus, who was brother to King Mestor. I am named after my glorious relative, one of the ten kings of Atlantis."

He had recited all this with the ease of long practiced. "I am most impressed. You wished a word with me?"

"You are the Brimm who killed Cleito, in contradiction to the will of Poseidon?"

Ah. Brimm had been afraid this might come up with these Poseidon worshippers. "Ah yes. Most regrettable." Brimm shrugged. "You see—she was trying to eat me. And my friends." Mestor snorted. "And why should she not?" Mestor took a step closer, bringing with him a powerful scent of myrrh. His skin was shiny with it. "Cleito was intended for immortality; you are a mortal pawn of the gods, good only for their amusement and, if needed, their sustenance!"

"Technically, she was at best a demigoddess, having begun life as a mortal. Still—I was only engaging in carrying out the will of great Poseidon, and no doubt Baal, and all the other gods. They did not choose to thwart me, hence I conclude—"

"Cease! That's the second time you've used that foolish sophistry! The greater gods can be thwarted by evil gods! Who knows what foul being you serve? But the will of the great gods finds fulfillment at the moment of their choosing. In time, it will deal with you, Brimm—you who also killed the sacred Minotaur!"

"Well, I cannot take all the credit for that, not entirely. There were three of us and we were asked to try to defeat the thing—"

"Do not engage in banter, false magician!"

"Now sir, you wound me! But I shall take no offense—I must excuse myself, as the queen herself has asked me to counsel her on magical matters. That is my errand tonight."

Mestor snorted. "Magician, tread lightly here. The sea is scarcely a kraken's leap away. I could speak ten words and spit on you, and you would be washed away within the hour as the sea sought you out, to carry you to its depths, where your corpus would feed those who creep and whistle in the blackness…"

Brimm now was actually impressed—by Mestor's eloquence. But not by his threats.

"And I could expose you for a fraud, as all priests are," Brimm said. "However, I am no great magician. I served one once. Urgus himself…"

The priest raised his eyebrows—they had been shaved off, but the effect remained. "Indeed? Urgus?" Then he frowned. "It matters not. You call me a fraud! I shall have to prove you wrong!"

"Perhaps I spoke hastily—you may be a shining exception to the rule." He bowed again. "I apologize." Best not to antagonize the man. A priest, after all, could command footpads, and assassins. "And now—the queen wishes me to, ah, consult the stars on her behalf."

"Bah! What do magicians know of the ways of the stars! But go—only, I warn you, once more…tread lightly!"

"Always!"

* * * *

Brimm found the queen standing at the window, gazing out at storm-blown clouds tearing past the sharp points of the waning moon. The moonlight was just enough to outline her otherwise unadorned body within its diaphanous silk raiment. The thinly woven silk rippled in the wind from the open window; her black shoulder-length hair fluttered.

"My queen, I am at your command," said Brimm, kneeling.

She turned away from the window. "At last. How you dawdle." She strode to a mass of cushions at the center of the oval room.

"I was delayed by your own priest of Poseidon," Brimm said, standing. "He wished to convey some sort of murky warning."

"Mestor? Yes, you have gotten on the wrong side of him. But few are on the right side of him, besides obedient catamites." She patted a large pillow close to her. "Come, and sit—no, first, shed your boots over there. They look dirty. Have you bathed?"

"Yes, great queen."

"It is well. Squelos does not always remember. Nor does—but no matter."

Having removed his shoes Brimm padded over to the big silken pillow. She was sitting within arm's reach; her pert breasts and shaven pudenda drew his eyes. She was a strong woman, all demands and assertions, yet there was softness, a delicious receptivity within reach, if he dared.

"Is it true that silk comes from spiders, my lady?" he asked, as he settled on the pillow. It was all he could think to say at the moment.

"No, silk does not come from spiders. Another creature, rather like a worm, makes silk. Detestable to look upon—but it is a creature whose emission is beauty itself. I have a blind, noseless musician who is much the same. I cannot bear to look at him, but he plays sweetly. Would you care to hear him?"

"As you please."

The blind musician was summoned—a disfigured, gray haired fellow in sandals and a toga, he emerged from behind a screen painted with images of whales and kraken, to sit cross-legged on the floor at a respectful distance. He immediately began a plangent plucking of a harp. With the fingers of one hand he thumped the edge of the harp to keep time.

The queen gestured toward the low table of wine and glasses, and as he helped himself she regarded him silently. Her expression was serious, her lips pressed firmly together, her forehead a little furrowed. He tasted the wine—it was almost unbearably superb—and she said, "Tomorrow evening, I wish you to accompany me to a gathering. There will be a king from another kingdom there, and one other man. I have spoken with these men before, in the company of my husband, but they little regarded me. This time they will deal with me alone! Magic may be in play, so I need you there to advise me."

"I will be honored."

"Good. There are doings afoot that concern me. Squelos is too blind to see. But—if I am right…"

He remembered the warnings of Eumalos.

"Do you refer to Glaban, and his flirtation with the Three Angers?" Brimm asked airily, as if it were something he knew a great deal about.

She looked at him with pleased surprise. "So—you know of this already? You have consulted the spirits on the matter?"

"I have spoken with the spirit of Eumalos himself, great Queen."

Her eyes widened. "In truth?"

Brimm felt a cold gust of air from the window; a rumbling from the foundations of the palace. Somehow, he knew it to be a warning.

"I…perhaps I have spoken too freely, your glory. I do not wish to anger so powerful a soul as Eumalos."

"Just so! But…you are right. King Glaban sought Squelos's help in stirring the Three Angers. The power of Vulcanus against Poseidon—their old rivalry brought to bear on Atlantis! And the third Anger—a demigoddess."

"Your glory no doubt has a wiser counsel…"

"We will think of some way to delay Glaban until he can be…but that is for another time. We both must keep silent as possible—for now."

He gave her a slight bow. "Then how can I serve you tonight?"

"Why, keep my company, and I will see into you when we are close enough for a—meeting of the minds."

She took the little pouch he had seen at the hilltop, opened it, drew out the vial, uncorked it. "Come closer…And let me anoint you with this oil… And while we are intimate, you may call me Maitha. But only then."

She gazed on him with a smile, with a melting gaze, that undid his reluctance to let *anyone* anoint him with an unknown substance, and he came to sit close beside her. They were not touching, but he felt the warmth of her; inhaled all the scents of her.

"Unclothe yourself for me," she said, her voice low but commanding.

He did as he was bade, as gracefully as he could—and still it was awkward.

When he was unclothed, she began to spread the oil upon his shoulders, his back, his neck, the orbits of his eyes, around his lips, so that its odor—musky, spicy—pervaded his whole being, and almost immediately he felt an effect, perhaps narcotic…certainly the effect of a drug. The thumping, twanging music of the blind man seemed to take on some unspeakable significance, each tone communing with eternity.

He found he was lying down beside her, taking her in his arms, crushing her to him, seeking out her lips, her tongue. He couldn't remember lying beside her, tearing away her diaphanous garment, but it must have happened.

"Maitha!"

He was within her, enwrapped in her, almost lost in her. Yet he was always aware that she was Other; the Other, the feminine presence he was coupling with, was a person of power in herself. She merged with him sexually, yet remained definite, a palpable person.

There was a rising toward mutual orgasm. Then he found himself on an infinite plane that was pure Maitha: the color of her skin, the ambiance of her presence.

Maitha.

Brimm felt himself whipped by orgasm, so the fleshly plane underneath him rippled too. And rushing at him were two eyes, just her eyes alone, gazing upon him inquiringly, even as her body bucked in sexual release…

Maitha.

Her eyes, disembodied, gazed upon him.

"Yes. I can trust you," he heard her whisper. "At least for a time…"

Then, the enormity of his orgasm became too much. It crashed like a titanic wave on him.

To be followed by darkness.

* * * *

Brimm's head throbbed. His mouth was dry as a skin laid out to cure in hot sun.

He sat up, reached for the bronze wine pitcher, and took a great draught. He was surprised to find that it was filled with pear juice mixed with honey, rather than wine. Perhaps some herb had been stirred in, explaining the slightly acrid aftertaste.

The drink refreshed him, and the herb dimmed his discomfort. He looked about and found he was alone in her chamber, and there was little evidence of her having been there. Just a faint whiff of her scent—the mix of her perfume and her body—and the still-resonating effect of her in Brimm himself.

Maitha's diaphanous garment was gone. His own clothing was laid out neatly on the cushions. He dressed, and turned to the tray of breakfast sweetmeats, figs, sliced melon, dates, nuts of a sort he'd never before tasted, black bread, butter, a small butter knife. He felt addled, his mind a place of vast distances. His own thoughts traveled far to reach him. Eating might restore him to his senses.

After breakfasting, he felt stronger, more acute, though his head still throbbed. What drug had she given him? It was powerful, and the power of her personality had mingled with the drug.

He remembered the disembodied eyes; dark, lustrous, gazing into his inner being, reading him. Seeing his strengths and deficiencies.

Surely, he had misjudged her! She had brought with her the esoteric arts of the land of pyramids and the great lion with the visage of a man— the secrets of the continent sometimes called Ifri, or Ifri-qa. With Squelos near, she played the part of a decadent, detached, empty-headed royal. But in truth she was far from that.

He felt a bizarre mixture of ecstasy and shame sweep through him. Was he now Maitha's slave?

Brimm found himself envisioning Selinn. Suddenly she seemed a kind of living refuge and he longed to be with her.

But the refuge would not take him in. She would turn him away to wander the living desert, where the great disembodied eyes of Maitha hunted him, and made him their captive…

Then he remembered the words of Eumalosa'a ghost—the Cold Heart of Jupiter was found under the couch of the queen.

Brimm got up and looked about, checking even behind the screen where the musician had waited. He was alone.

He moved to the long, wide pillow that served as the queen's couch, and pushed it aside. Under it was a silk carpet. That too he tugged aside. The floor was flagged in thin black marble. He pushed at each flagstone, felt that each was firm—except here, just beneath the place where the queen had laid her head. The flagstone was slightly loose. He tried to pry it up with his fingers, and only succeeded in breaking his fingernails. He looked around, remembered the butter knife, fetched it, and used it to pry at the edge of the stone. It moved a little.

Footsteps in the hallway. Boots.

Brimm froze, thinking that it would not look good to be caught prying at the floor of the queen's chamber.

He heard the steps coming close to the door. They paused. A gruff voice called out, "Are you still in there, Captain Brimm?"

The title confused him until he remembered that the guardsmen would know him by it.

"It is I!" Brimm called. "Am I summoned?"

"Not as such. It's just that we don't allow the queen's…her visitors… to, ah, tarry here too long."

"I am indisposed! Withdraw and I will soon be gone!"

"Very well."

The boot steps withdrew. Brimm let out a long breath and resumed prying at the stone. The butter knife bent—but at last the flagstone popped up. Beneath it a niche had been cut in a support timber. Within the niche was a small box of resinous black wood, no broader than a man's hand. He drew it out, and it opened of its own accord. Within lay a piece of something like agate, colored translucent crimson, shot through with milky streaks, a flattish oval. It seemed unremarkable to Brimm.

He reached out to the stone and felt the tingle of magic before he'd even touched it. When he picked it up a chill went through him, becoming a powerful shudder, so that his teeth chattered and his skin contracted, and he had a momentary vision of craggy peaks of ice where dirty-blue winds roared and a voice echoed angrily through frozen canyons.

Then he saw another place, from high above, as if seen from by some god in the sky.

Atlantis itself.

Angry faces rose up over the land, and roared at one another. Poseidon. Vulcanus.

Facing off, furious with one another.

Above the two angry gods appeared a third figure—scarcely more than a blob of ectoplasm at first.

Then—it was Cleito.

Cleito expanded from a blob of ectoplasm to become a dark, translucent spirit floating above Poseidon and Vulcanus—a woman above, octopal below. She reached out with her ethereal tentacles and entwined Poseidon and Vulcanus…and at this touch they both roared.

The flaming red fist of Vulcanus struck the land…and Atlantis buckled, fissuring. Molten rock lashed out from the fissures.

A blue hand raised up over the land, Poseidon's watery fist clenched, and came down, and the sea swallowed Atlantis—steam boiled up and all was hidden…

Brimm drew his hand back, and the vision snapped shut—even as he snapped shut the lid of the box.

Trembling, unsure of what he'd seen, but afraid that perhaps he did understand, he thought, *Truly I have discovered the Cold Heart of Jupiter.*

Brimm gingerly picked up the box. Fighting the impulse to put it back under the planks, to hide it away from his sight, he tucked it into his sash. Then he set about replacing the flagstone, the carpet, the pillows. He bent the little silver knife back into shape as well as he could, and returned it to the tray. Its condition would puzzle some servant.

He found his boots, put them on, and hastened from the room. He did not wish another encounter with Mestor. And there were things he must do, in some place of safety.

Dire things.

CHAPTER TEN

"I haven't much time," Brimm said softly, as he came to stand beside Selinn at the window of the common room. "I have a rite I must perform, and soon…" He glanced around, saw that no one else was near. Snoori was taking far too much enjoyment in ordering the guardsmen in a march, back and forth, near the crumbling wall. They watched the absurd display, and might have laughed if there was not something in the air haunting them both. "After the ritual, I must attend the queen…"

Selinn sniffed, and shrugged. "Why tell me this? Why not just go, and your mistress's bidding?"

"I…why do you take that tone with me? That implicit reproach?"

"I don't know what you mean," she said. Her tone was lofty—but her eyes, glancing at him and looking quickly away, showed hurt and confusion.

Brimm licked his lips, and took the plunge. "I have always felt a bond with you. From the moment we met I felt that you and I…that we belong together, in some way. Whether as friends—or something more."

He broke off, feeling foolish. But then he saw that she'd turned away from him.

"Don't be absurd," she said, her voice thick. "I…am a princess of Ur. You are a barbarian of the north with a few magical passes to hand. We…I could not…"

"You forgot to mention that I'm not the most handsome of men. I am not a demigod fighting on the battlefield, all muscles and fierceness…"

She turned to him, her eyes glistening, a rueful smile flitting about her mouth. "It is true that you are not those things. But—you are a warrior. You have more than your share of fierceness. That I have seen. And you have something else—you have the beginning of wisdom. Like me, you have one foot in this world, one in the hidden world. But—I am a priestess of the moon goddess." She sighed. "In truth I should return now to Ur, and to the temple. I should call upon the King to decide my fate. I have asked myself, what keeps me here? Is it this gangly man with his dancing sword and his foolish smirk? Ridiculous!"

"And yet…" He reached out to touch her hand, which rested on the window sill. "The mind has reasons for one course, the heart has reasons for quite another—so said Urgus."

She frowned but she did not remove his hand. "You still smell of her perfume, her oils."

"Not mere perfume. It was a drug. It has worn off, yet last night I lost all control, all constraint."

"And you surrendered to her gladly!"

He shrugged. "I am only a man. But—Selinn—"

"Only a man, indeed!" She withdrew her hand and turned away, murmuring to herself, "My foolish dreams take hold of me, at times…"

"Heed me, Selinn!" Brimm implored her. "The drug released my spirit, and my soul rose to another place. There her mind looked into mine. Then this morning I had a vision. I beheld terrible things—a grave danger to Atlantis."

"Yes, yes, most interesting." She waved a hand dismissively. "I must prepare to return to Ur, and to the temple. To throw myself on the mercy of the king…"

"You cannot return now, even if you should want to," Brimm said. He placed his hands on her shoulders. She stiffened at his touch. He leant near and whispered, "I fear someone will overhear. Listen, now. The kingdom of Atlantis may be doomed. Great powers are coming to bear. You heard Eumalos, as well as I."

"Then it is all the more certainly a time to leave!" She shook loose and turned to face him.

"My destiny is tangled with this land—I feel it the way a tree feels its roots. I hope to avert what may be coming, and, in time, to discover what Squelos' armies plan for Ur! Surely that is of interest to you. You can leave here if you choose—but, Selinn, by the time you take ship, it will be too late. Cleito is scheming to destroy us all, this very night! I have seen what will happen. I need your help to avert the darkness sweeping over Atlantis…"

* * * *

It was early evening when Brimm arrived at the hilltop. He stepped through the screen of palms and looked at the land beyond. Some of the planets and stars were risen not far above the wine-purple horizon. The wind had blown the clouds asunder, but more raced in from the west.

The hilltop, half encircled by palms, seemed ideal for what Brimm had in mind. Here Brimm had first met in private, more or less, with Queen Maitha. Now, her servants and carpets, her table and pillows were gone. To one side was the place where the spring emerged to father the waterfall and the stream. Below it was the forest, and beyond it Northwestern horizon, and Jupiter ascending in the sky.

"When you hold the stone up to the gleam of Jupiter in the sky, the Uncertain Glamor will make itself known. The Glamor is a person, and will speak. He will offer you protection from Cleito…for a time."

There was no one to be seen. Snoori was watching their back trail, Selinn was just over the rim of the hill, sitting beside the waterfall, her weapon at ready, to watch Brimm's back. Perhaps in fact he didn't need her here. But he wanted to keep her close, afraid that she might impulsively leave the island. She might die, attempting it, if he were not there to help.

He drew the box from his sash, opened it, plucked out the stone and—shuddering from the touch—held it up so that it over the big star that was Jupiter.

Nothing happened.

Wait, he told himself. Be patient.

His fingers were going unpleasantly numb.

Was Jupiter a star? he wondered, trying to distract himself from his growing discomfort at touching the Cold Heart. Urgus had said each of the planets was a world, and Jupiter a great globe—for Urgus had explained what few on the Earth knew, that this world too was a globe in space, circling the sun. "But the other planets of this solar system, so I have been told, contain no corporeal life. Yet in some planets there are disembodied creatures, god-like beings, who can scarcely be told from a tornado. They are living, thinking storms…and Jupiter himself is the most powerful of these…" The planets at times emanated an influence, Urgus believed, generated by these gods; sometimes benevolent, sometimes baleful, sometimes both mingled.

Now there was a crackle around the Cold Heart, a sparkling which became a myriad of tiny lightning bolts—and Brimm felt a searing pain in his hand. He could not hold onto the stone and his twitching fingers let it fall to the turf. There it began to glow, emanating a sickly red light shaped like an urn. The urn of light was projected by the Cold Heart, and in its midst was a man's face. He had a mustache curled on the ends, improbably large brown eyes, upslanted eyebrows, a swatch of fiery hair, and the ears of a wolf.

"Have you come to release me?" said a voice in his mind—as the face's lips moved. "Did Eumalos send you to set me free, at last?"

"Eumalos has declared you will do my bidding! As for going free— that is at least partly contingent on your obedience to me. I am a magus, and your master. You may know me as Brimm the Savant."

The creature rolled its eyes and sighed. "Another magus; another savant."

"Been lending you out a great deal, has he?" Brimm asked, as he rubbed feeling back into his hand.

"Not for a century or two. Or perhaps it's three. What is it you require of me?"

"You are the Uncertain Glamor?"

"I am known as *Certain* Glamor, sir! But—it's true Eumalos calls me Uncertain." He gave once more his prolonged, dismal sighing. "It's painful to be so confined, and so impugned. What do you want of me? There's not a great deal I can do, so confined. I may advise you, Brimm the Savant. And perhaps do a little more."

"I am told you can restrain Cleito."

"That hideous creature? Hardly, unless I get her in here with me."

"So Eumalos misled me!"

"I said *hardly*—I didn't say not at all. I can restrain her…barely. A trifle. Somewhat. For a short time."

"How short?"

"A span of seconds, perhaps twenty, perhaps twenty-five. Then, if you do your part I may be able to do more with her."

"And how can twenty seconds be of use?"

"Choose your seconds! Suppose a great armored war chariot is rushing by—a thrust into the spokes of its wheel, at just the right moment, with just the right tool, will upset the vehicle and destroy its rider! But you have to act with precision! I remember an instance—"

"Enough! I would now have you illuminate the meaning of a vision I have been given…"

They spoke a little more, for as long as it takes wax to drip down the side of a moderately large candle.

And then Uncertain's visage returned to the Cold Heart. He vanished, and the red light vanished.

Only shadows, rushing wind, and the call of crickets remained to counsel Brimm.

* * * *

"I saw a red light; I thought I heard a voice, but I couldn't be sure," said Selinn, as they walked along the stream. "Did you succeed in your purpose?"

"I have learned what I need to do—now I must do it. I am doubtful of success."

"You sound gloomy. In fact, you give me chills."

"Then that is something, anyway, that we share."

"Brimm!" called Snoori, striding up, his face alight with pleasure. "I was beginning to think I would be alone but for dark spirits in this wood. Do you know, I'm sure I heard a night bird call me by name, and some sort of sloth was grumbling at me."

"He envied your mustaches," said Selinn.

"No doubt! Where do we go now?"

Brimm patted his sash. "We have an invitation. As I was leaving the palace, one of the queen's eunuchs brought me an order to meet the queen at the Keep of Glaban. It is not a palace—but a small fortress on the border of this land and his own. I am permitted to bring a retinue and I have chosen the two of you, if you are willing. I may bring two others. It is a journey of perhaps an hour on horseback. We must be alert. An acolyte of the priest of Poseidon was walking by, as the order was given, and perhaps heard something. I do not trust the priest, and I'm afraid we may be followed by someone with evil intent…"

Brimm climbed up on his horse and led the way in the thickening darkness, threading the trail to the guardsmen's barracks at the edge of Eumalos.

Here he found Drubb and Reenus sharing a wineskin in the common room. "You two are growing fat here, with no duty to attend to," Brimm told them. "You will come as part of my guard as I undertake a confidential mission for the queen. Requisition two chariots. In each chariot one of you will face backwards, holding on to a strap, and watch the back trail…"

* * * *

The moon was in its sickle phase, providing only sparse light. But the windstorm had moved on, and the sky was immaculately clear so that the clusters and rivulets of stars, like strewn gems on black cloth, were fulminating in glory.

The starlight was enough to illuminate the stone road to the border with Asesseon. Brimm led the way on his horse; behind him came the two chariots. The poorly cut road was uneven, sloping from its right side down on its left, as it paralleled the high rim of Atlantis.

"In Ur," said Selinn, as she drove the chariot horse, "the road would be etched into the hill, and flattened out."

"Some places in Atlantis it is that way," said Drubb, as he held hard onto the rollicking chariot to keep from risking his life should he offend Selinn. "But here, the Squelos chooses his own way of doing things: Quickly and cheaply."

In consequence of the slope, Snoori was sometimes tilted onto Reenus when his grip on the leather strap weakened. Reenus would irritably shove him back into place. "On the way back," declared Snoori, "I shall sit astride on the chariot horse."

"You may not live so long. If you crush me again I'll hatchet you. We're in the rear of the procession and I will say it was all a mishap..."

They stopped midway to the keep, at Snoori's insistence—he had brought along bread, cheese, dried fish, a skin of beer. Brimm was reluctant to stop—he had been commanded to reach the keep an hour before midnight. And it seemed to him, too, that if the company stopped they would be more vulnerable to attack.

As they let the horses rest and sat about the road in a circle, Brimm was glad of the meal—but his gaze constantly swept the dark places beyond the roadside. To either side were thinly wooded slopes, one up and the other down. Above were outcroppings of ancient volcanic rock. There was cover, out there, for anything wanting to attack them.

"We must finish and go on, quickly," Brimm said.

Snoori took a pull on the beer, wiped his mouth, and said, "Are there beasts to fear in these wild places between kingdoms? Bears, or wolves perhaps? I have heard of great cat called a lion—they're said to be like our mountain cats, but larger."

"Once lions roamed here," said Drubb. "They had great tusks. But they were all killed by hunting parties. Wild dogs are said to roam to the south. And of course, there are the giant rats."

"The *what?*"

"There are still some enormous rats in this land," said Reenus, nodding gravely. "They live in tunnels in the hills—they are each as big as a man, equipped with teeth long as your fingers, like curving daggers, and they roam in packs of three and four. Their sport is tearing men to pieces, when they catch them alone at night."

"Indeed, Brimm," Snoori said, peering into the shadows under the trees and outcroppings. "Perhaps we should hurry on our way...."

Selinn chuckled. "I suspect these two are telling tales to make your skin creep, Snoori."

"Then they have succeeded." Snoori's eyes widened as he stared into the shadows near an outcropping up the hill. "There—something as big as a man...and moving stealthily!"

Brimm stood, drawing his piercer in the same motion, and squinted into the dimness—he saw nothing at first, then looking down the hillside, glimpsed a quick, stealthy motion. "Up, everyone! They're on both sides!"

They had no sooner gotten to their feet than the shadows charged them.

It was men who rushed them, however. Some looked to be mercenaries, others were men Brimm recognized. Kelk was among them, coming from upslope, and Mestor's acolyte was there too: a bald man in a leather toga; he had a cleft lip, and wide, angry eyes. He charged Brimm with a spear ending in a curved blade. "Heretic monster!" he snarled, driving the blade at Brimm's throat.

Brimm sidestepped, grabbed the spear by its haft, pulled hard so the acolyte crashed facedown onto the road. Instantly, Brimm drove the piercer through the man's leather toga and into his heart.

Selinn was there, suddenly, using her sword to slice through the wrist of a big man, coming from down-slope to swing a spiked war hammer at Brimm's head. Selinn struck true: the hammer flew askew, missing, taking the gripping hand with it, and Brimm finished the mercenary with a slash to his throat.

He turned to face Kelk—but Kelk fell dead at his feet, Reenus's hatchet deep in the back of his skull. "Always was a worthless skulker of a man!" growled Reenus.

Snoori shouted a curse, and Brimm saw the Hyperborean was using his pike to keep two more mercenaries at bay, men with black hair and an Asian cast to their faces—Snoori jabbed furiously at one then the other, backing away—and losing ground.

Brimm rushed to his aid from the flank, slashed deep into the forearm of one of Snoori's adversaries, twisting the blade so the man squealed in pain and staggered back. Selinn was running to deal with the horses, which were rearing, terrified. Frightened, the horses could be as dangerous as these armed footpads.

Brimm blocked the sword of one of the mercenaries besetting Snoori—the force of the man's blow made Brimm's wrist sting—and then Grubb was there, having circled behind them. He swung a war ax hard, right and left, and both men tumbled to the ground, twitching, pouring blood.

Panting, Brimm and his companions looked around for more enemies—and found none. Snoori had a few minor wounds, and Selinn had some bruises, but they were all otherwise intact and their horses had been stayed from stampeding.

"I feel a fool," Snoori said. "We should not have stopped."

"I think we got them all," Brimm said. He extended sensory energies in the night, searching for enemies. Nothing but some small animal, crouching in a den. "There are no others about. Let us bandage you as we might and move along. Here—I have some salve in the saddle bag…"

Selinn kicked the acolyte's body petulantly. "This one ran straight as an arrow right at you."

"He is Mestor's acolyte. Had he used arrows instead he might well have gotten me. But Snoori saw them and gave us our chance."

"It's clear who your enemy is," Selinn remarked, as she calmly cut the throat of a mercenary who was showing signs of life. "Mestor."

"Yes. And Mestor will try again…"

CHAPTER ELEVEN

Even driving the horses hard, they reached Glaban's Keep at the border with only minutes to spare.

One of the queen's eunuchs was waiting impatiently for them by the outer gate. "Come!" he hissed. "You keep a king and a queen waiting! You should be beaten for it, but there is no time."

King Glaban's warriors reluctantly moved aside for the motley company, as the chariots trundled through the gate. Brimm walked, leading the horse, his rump aching. He had enough of horseback for awhile.

The gate of thick logs had hardly swung shut, and Brimm had just taken in the towers, lodge and stables ranged around the courtyard, when a ripple ran through the world, a palpable wave shuddering through the firmament, making the horses tremble and stare around wildly, their ears perked. Then the earth shook so that the company swayed, clutching at one another to keep from falling. The stone courtyard cracked; dust trickled down from the eaves of a two-story wooden lodge on the right. Birds squawked from a nearby woods, and flew in confused spirals over the trees.

Brimm wondered: Am I too late?

Then the shaking eased, and abated. The night quieted, and the guardsmen and warriors looked nervously at one another.

"Just a normal shaking, for Atlantis," said Drubb, though his voice betrayed doubt. "Nothing…unusual."

Still they waited, as Brimm didn't want to enter a tower which might at any moment be tumbled down. The horses were snorting, hooves anxiously clattering on the stones of the courtyard. Selinn went to quiet them.

Another minute. Two…

The birds flew into the darkness. The horses quieted. Silence reigned.

"Nothing more," Brimm muttered, relaxing. "At least for now."

Perhaps Cleito has already begun…

"Enough," snapped the eunuch. "Put away the horses and we will go to the tower."

In a trice the horses were stabled and Brimm was led by the eunuch to the low door at the base of a squared-off stone tower. Selinn tried to accompany him—but the eunuch hissed at her, in a manner that reminded Brimm of Urgus's pet cobra. "Back! Only the sorcerer may come!"

"Wait here, Selinn," Brimm said. "Watch for assassins."

"They may be waiting for you up those stairs."

"I doubt it. But we shall see."

Brimm reached out, cupped her shoulder with his hand. She hesitated—then reached up and put her hand on his.

He turned away, and walked to the door of the tower.

* * * *

"First," said King Glaban with glum urbanity, "we experience a quaking of the land. Then your wizard enters. Is this a coincidence?"

The queen shrugged. "There have always been quakings in Atlantis."

Brimm had taken a place standing respectfully behind the queen, who sat on a cushioned stool at one end of a long rectangular mahogany table… Maitha wore a blue gown, and held something in her lap—a brass bottle of some kind. On the center finger of her right hand was a large golden ring with an image of Poseidon's Kraken pressed into it. She hadn't worn it when he'd seen her before.

Glaban sat at the other end of the table. King Glaban had thick wavy black hair reaching his shoulders, and a carefully trimmed beard accenting the deeply chiseled hollows of his face. His eyebrows were shaved, replaced with red lines; his eyes were an odd golden-green, like a raptor's.

Beyond the table was an open window which admitted an evening breeze. The breeze fluttered the flames on two small oil lamps set on the table, and the fire of torches set in wall sconces.

Standing behind Glaban was a man who might be a priest, or a magician. He had long matted hair and beard, stained red with clay, and he wore a cloak of rough black wool that was much in contrast to Glaban's silken black and golden toga. His eyes were hidden under craggy, red-dyed brows. On his forearms were red tattoos, runes, and crossed hammers, a symbol of Vulcanus, god of metalworkers as well as volcanoes—god of fire in all its forms. Brimm guessed the man was a *flamen* of Vulcanus, a high priest of the volcanic mysteries.

Glaban made no move to introduce the flamen, and the man did not speak for himself. Still, the flamen radiated a grim confidence. In his right hand he gripped a wooden staff that was taller than he; on its tip was an unlit hemispherical oil lamp of bronze, stamped with hieroglyphics.

"There is no doubt," came the rumbling voice of the flamen, "that the earth-shaking is an omen. Something is coming. Someone has invited them. She is near."

Brimm was impressed. "I agree with the honored flamen, your majesties. Cleito is behind this. But she does not operate alone."

"It may be as you say," said King Glaban, tapping the table with his fingers. His gold rings clinked softly. "But the quake we felt may also be an omen of coming success. Queen Maitha—is your man trustworthy?" She nodded. "I have used the arts of my people and looked into his mind. He can be trusted."

The flamen looked solemnly at Brimm. "He is trustworthy."

"Then," said Glaban, "I will ask you, Maitha, are you prepared to take the step your husband dared not take? He sometimes said perhaps yes, he sometimes said perhaps not. You are here in his place. I would have a definite answer from you."

"That is why I am here," she said. "I say, *yes*—let us use the dark spirit to free the power of the gods, and with their combined fury, destroy our enemies."

Brimm felt icy fingers clap hold of his spine at that.

Glaban smiled—a cold smile showing uneven teeth. "And your part in the matter, Maitha?"

"Mestor swears that Poseidon awaits the summoning. We are ready."

"My Queen," Brimm said, hearing a strange choked hoarseness in his own voice. "Perhaps we could talk in private—and you could apprise me of what to expect. I may be of more help if I know…"

She waved a hand dismissively. "You are here in case I need you, and for that alone. Until then, be silent and observe…"

"Forgive me, your glory—I have reservations that the forces you would unleash can be controlled. I have seen certain visions—"

"Maitha!" King Glaban snapped. "Are you going to let this mewling upstart deter us? Bid him be silent and let us proceed! The stars and planets are ideally aligned! We must not delay!"

She turned King Glaban a fierce look. "Are you commanding me, Glaban?" Without waiting for his answer, she turned to Brimm. "It's a simple matter—the ten Kingdoms are controlled by a council of kings. But if we destroy the kingdoms of Elasippos and Impheres, we will have the power to dominate all the others! Eumalosa and Glaban's Asesseon have a secret pact to share power should the others fall. Now, that is more than enough.

Observe and stand ready should I need you."

Clearly she had given Brimm this explanation only to teach Glaban not to bully her.

"But my Queen—how can you be sure these forces you will release will destroy only those two lands?"

"They are on the other side of Atlantis."

"Fire and water, earthquake and rock-fall—they understand no frontiers, your glory! All of Atlantis is interconnected!"

"True," said the flamen, chuckling. "And Vulcanus will enjoy this to its utmost!"

"Cleito cannot be trusted," Brimm insisted. "She is but a spirit now. If Atlantis is destroyed it does her no harm!"

"Also true!" cackled the flamen.

"Come now—the stars are aligned!" thundered King Glaban. "Let us begin—or we lose our chance!"

Queen Maitha frowned, then took a deep breath, and nodded. She stood, raised the brass bottle, and intoned words in a language Brimm did not recognize—then she poured the contents of the bottle onto the table.

Brimm felt magical energies rising around them…

What could he do? Run? To where? He could not bring himself to attack Maitha. There was only one course…

The contents of the bottle appeared to be water. But it was water with a mind. It splashed onto the table then pooled, and seemed to runnel purposefully this way and that, as if seeking something. Then, impossibly, it rose up into a small living fountain.

The flamen was stalking around the other side of the table—here he took his place halfway between the king of Asesseon and the queen of Eumalosa. He banged his staff twice on the floor. The lamp atop the staff burst into flame.

The flamen extended the staff, touching the flame to the water…

In response, two small figures swirled up into being on the table. One was Poseidon, complete with trident, formed in ice. The other was Vulcanus, complete with a smith's hammer, formed in fire.

They were miniature, on the plane of the table, but somehow, they resonated with hidden dimensions of enormity.

The two gods glared at one another: warriors about to do battle.

The flamen intoned a series of phrases, in the same unknown language used by Maitha…and the figure of Vulcanus stalked forward, raising its hammer. He struck—but some barrier separated him from Poseidon. Who also strike with his trident—an invisible barrier stopped the trident from reaching Vulcanus.

"Ha haaaaa!" cackled the flamen, his eyes alight with glee. "The wall

between will soon come down!"

It occurred to Brimm, then, that the flamen wanted Vulcanus fully released; that he would revel in the destruction of Atlantis.

"My queen," Brimm breathed. "He and Cleito will kill us all!"

"Silence!" hissed Maitha.

Then Cleito herself appeared, almost life size, over the center of the table. She was transparent, ghostly, partly octopal—but it was her. She looked directly at Brimm.

Now I will kill you, Brimm, she said, without speaking a word. He could see the message in her leering face.

Cleito reached down to the invisible barrier...

She was going to destroy the barrier between fire and water. The two opposing forces would rush together, in actual physical fact, somewhere deep beneath Atlantis. An explosion would result...and Atlantis would be engulfed in hellfire, rent by earthquake and drowned by the sea.

Already the tower was beginning to shiver, then to shimmy, as the cold of Poseidon and the heat of Vulcanus tried to rush together, each eager for the explosion of rage...

"What is happening?" Maitha asked. "Why is this tower shaking? These forces should affect only our enemies, far from here! Brimm! Tell me!"

"My queen—Cleito and the flamen want the entirety of Atlantis to be destroyed!"

"It's what Vulcanus would want!" the flamen crowed, his mouth opened to show a tongue of flame. "And it's wonderful, it's beautiful!"

The air pressure in the room seemed to increase; electricity spat at the window. From somewhere came a ghostly laughter.

Choose your moment, Uncertain Glamor had told him.

I cannot wait—everyone in Atlantis is about to die.

Cleito was opening the doorway—he could see the translucent wall now, and it was cracking open.

The room shook and the ceiling spilt dust.

"What is happening?" Glaban shouted. "Flamen—these energies are not to arise here!"

The flamen laughed. Queen Maitha screamed.

Brimm reached into his sash, found the Cold Heart of Jupiter and clasped it into his hand, immediately grimacing from the burning cold. His hand ached at the touch.

Then he spoke the words, calling out to Eumalos—he felt his own natural energy-sheath, the field of life-shine about his own body, and he invested it with power. He stretched it out...and encompassed Cleito with it.

She seemed unable to resist—Uncertain was holding her fast.

Cleito threw back her head and shrieked. The ear-piercing scream made the queen back away from the table, covering her ears. The walls shook—from the quake or Cleito's shriek?

Brimm drew the spectre closer, held up the gleaming, lightning-troubled stone, the Cold Heart of Jupiter...and Cleito's spirit was sucked into it.

Then Brimm saw to his horror that the small figures of Vulcanus and Poseidon were growing...and struggling with one another as they grew, thrashing, clashing their weapons together, Poseidon's frozen triune clashing with Vulcanus's glowing-red hammer. With every blow the world shook, and the thunderous vibration came not from these swelling, ethereal figures, but from below, from caverns somewhere under Atlantis itself. The floor rollicked, and Brimm had to clutch the edge of the table to keep from falling.

"Go!" came the voice of Uncertain, from within the Cold Heart of Jupiter. *"Run, Brimm! I have prevented Cleito from fully achieving her purpose! Even now I pursue her through the cold confines of my horrible little world! But a reverberation spreads out, and hell will follow! Go quickly!"*

"Brimm!" cried Queen Maitha, as she struggled to stand, while the floor's bucking threatened to fling her against the wall.

Brimm tucked away the Cold Heart and caught her upper arm—now was no time for royal niceties—and drew her to him. Scooping her up in his arms he staggered to the door. He staggered not under her weight, but by the shimmying of the cracking floor. He was thrown toward the open door by the shifting of the tower, now beginning to lean. The flamen was dancing about, howling with glee. He seemed impervious to the tilt, and swung his staff as he danced so that the flaming tip roared. King Glaban was trying to rush past Brimm and Maitha, but Brimm shouldered him aside and carried his charge down the skewed, rippling stairway—a stairway gone mad—straining every nerve and muscle to keep the queen from falling. They teetered, and he nearly pitched headlong more than once. But at last they reached the ground and ducked out through the low door even as the tower fell behind them.

Rushing away from the tower, Brimm heard Glaban shrieking with fear and agony as the great stones came unstuck and fell atop him.

Brimm had a blurred, shifting glimpse of Selinn and Snoori trying to get to him, as they ran across the shaking courtyard, where gaping cracks spread like black lightning and red flames gushed up spouting gobbets of molten rock.

He lost his balance and fell, the queen atop him. Maitha jumped to her feet and, to his surprise, helped him to stand on the quaking earth. Drubb was there, staggering toward the gate, which had fallen apart with the quaking. In the background Reenus was shouting incoherently, waving his arms—and then the ground opened up, flames licked out like a chameleon's tongue wrapping around prey, drew Reenus screaming into the cracked earth.

Selinn was shouting something but Brimm couldn't hear it over the roar of the falling lodge. He took the queen's arm and guided her toward the gate, the two of them dancing crookedly in the chaotic music of the earthquake.

As they passed out of the keep, the ground seemed firmer, the shaking less. Gasping, they hurried on, at last coming to a meadow perhaps a hundred strides from the gate. At the edge of the meadow a dozen trees had fallen and much of the road had slipped down the hillside. Snoori and Selinn were already there, holding onto the newly exposed root of a fallen tree, and the twin eunuchs both sat weeping on the ground nearby him, hugging one another. Selinn threw herself on the ground, panting, as the shaking subsided.

The queen shook Brimm's grip off, and walked unsteadily to a tree stump, where she sat, cursing in the language of Ifri.

Brimm sat wearily on the ground, and looked at the keep. The scene was curtained in billowing dust. As he watched, aware of his heart pounding, the dust settled—but smoke rose up, flames rose high, and more black smoke…and then the earth opened, like a giant's hands unfolding, and the entire keep fell in, greeted by a geysering of fire and smoke. Lava burbled up, flowing black and red to fill the cap and stream down the hillside…

There was a hellish ringing in Brimm's ears, so it took him a moment to hear Selinn shouting at him. "We must go! The burning stone may not stop here!"

"It will stop here," came Uncertain's voice from the stone. Only Brimm heard the creature speak. *"Nor will the kingdoms of Elasippos and Impheres be much affected. Glaban is dead. His son will take his place. The Queen's plans are thwarted. Lord Eumalos should be pleased with me. But will he say so? I doubt it."* And he gave out his long, histrionic sigh.

Brimm got wearily to his feet, and turned his back on the keep. He trudged off toward Eumalosa. Snoori, Selinn, and the twins went with him.

After a minute Maitha followed them, her head bowed.

* * * *

They found some of the horses, still trembling, at a stream some way to the north. Brimm gave the queen his mount, and the others, except for Snoori, shared the mounts who remained. The chariots had gone down with the keep. Nilfi and Ilfi shared a muscular black horse that had once belonged to Glaban; Selinn and Brimm shared an unsaddled chariot horse.

Snoori chose to walk.

As they made their way toward Eumalosa, Brimm spoke in low tones, telling the others all that had happened. He asked them not to speak of it to anyone till he could confer with Lord Breeke.

Brimm might another time have delighted in this moment of closeness with Selinn, as her arms clasped him atop the horse. But he was too stunned, too shaken by what had happened. And he was troubled by questions. Was it truly over? Were Poseidon and Vulcanus satisfied, as Uncertain claimed? Had it really been them—or had he seen some sort of illusion, a materialization of the collision of icy water and molten rock under Atlantis?

And—was it all really an omen, as he feared, a foreshadowing of what would happen, some day, to all Atlantis?

The made their way slowly to the town, arriving soon after dawn. Eumalosa buzzed with talk about the earthquake, and the pillar of smoke that marked the end of the Keep of Glaban. There was rejoicing as Maitha rode down the road of the king.

Her husband had just arrived. What would she tell Squelos?

But Brimm knew her for a clever woman, and supposed she would weave a story that Squelos could accept.

* * * *

Brimm and his companions ate, and rested, and then Brimm met with Breeke in the hunt-master's quarters. Over a cup of beer Breeke told him that the volcanic outbreak had indeed ceased. His runners confirmed that the lava field was already cooling. "These things happen from time to time in Atlantis," Breeke said, wiping ale froth from his mouth.

"Perhaps not like this. I feel there are things you should know..." Brimm gave him an honest account of what had happened—he trusted Breeke.

The hunt-master nodded. "Thank you for saving our queen from her own folly."

"Then you believe me?"

"I do. I keep an eye on the queen's doings—and her dabblings. And I have seen strange things in my time. She is too much influenced by Mestor, who surely had a hand in all this. But do not speak of this to anyone else. And do not permit your companions to tell anyone."

"I understand. But—what of Mestor?"

"On your ride back, the Queen heard your friend Snoori speaking of the ambush along the road. And of the acolyte leading it. She confronted Mestor, who said it was none of his doing. The acolyte, said Mestor, had always been a bit mad. Mestor claims he had discharged him. The acolyte was attempting to get back into the good graces of the priesthood—and using poor judgment."

"Mestor is lying."

"Quite probably. But we will try to keep him from interfering with you, after this. Now—you have duties to attend to."

Brimm attended to his duties, thinking ruefully that no one else was likely to ever know that Brimm the Savant had saved Atlantis from destruction.

Or perhaps Atlantis's salvation was more the work of the spirit of King Eumalos, and his servant Uncertain.

Still, Brimm thought, as he lay down on his pallet in his quarters that night, Urgus would know what had happened. The master magician had friends among the elementals, who spied on the great affairs of the world. They would tell Urgus all. The master would know that Brimm had done the work of a magician, acting as intermediary between the world of men and the hidden world, to good effect.

Yes, Urgus would know. And for once, Urgus just might be impressed with Brimm the Savant.

Or perhaps not.

Brimm was weary, as he stretched out on the pallet, but also strangely energized. He could not sleep. He tossed and turned restlessly. He thought he heard a whispering from the Cold Heart of Jupiter. Uncertain, trying to get his attention.

I can make you greater than Urgus, if you will listen to me. We can conquer Atlantis, Brimm. You have triumphed tonight—but no one knows! I can see to it that you triumph again and again, and the world will know of each victory! But first, you must...

Brimm sat up, removed his sash, set the Cold Heart of Jupiter in its box, and thrust the small box into a larger box. This he put into a cabinet, a good distance from his pallet.

Eumalos had warned him that he would be made restless, tempted by Uncertain. Now, the whispering seemed distant, almost inaudible.

I can see to it that you triumph again and again...

Brimm lay down once more—and then a light moved toward him in the dark room.

He reached for a dagger—

And saw the light was cast by an oil lamp in Selinn's hand. She was carrying a small bottle in the other hand.

She sat down by him, placed the lamp on the floor, and then opened the little bronze bottle. She poured oil on her hands and began to rub it on his face, and chest, singing softly to herself. There was no drug in the oil—it was mere frankincense. It was Selinn's touch that drugged him, the intoxicant of her womanhood...

Soon, weariness forgotten, he drew her to him, and she came willingly. That night he triumphed again, and again, as did Selinn. And those were the only triumphs that mattered.

✗

www.ingramcontent.com/pod-product-compliance
Lightning Source LLC
Chambersburg PA
CBHW050820180626
46814CB00004B/1374